ZOÉ

T. A. Ford

ISBN: 1-4196-9147-3
ISBN-13: 9781419691478

ACKNOWLEDGEMENTS

Zoé would have never made it out of the confines of my online blog without the help and support of many people. First and foremost, thank you to my copy-editor and writing friend Erica Langdon, without whom this book simply would not be. The sleepless nights, tireless days, and titillating debates on pirate-speak, have forever bonded us. Thank you so much for your editing, grammatical corrections, and your historical consultation. I look forward to a lasting partnership with you for many stories to come.

A special thanks to Lois Troutman, who also provided historical facts and research that opened my eyes to a world where Zoé's story had to be told.

Special thanks to my mother. It was your faith in me and our shared love of reading that has brought me thus far. To my friends and family, let me say that your support, patience, and encouragement make me proud to present this tale to you. I love and thank you all.

To my muses Renee Elise Goldsberry and Michael Easton, meet Zoé Bouchard and Gianelli La Roque, inspired by you. Heartfelt thanks to all my cranky reviewers, loyal readers, and talented authors at Divasnluv. Through you, I found the courage to enter the world of publishing. I dedicate this book to you and *Jovanners* everywhere!

ZOÉ

"Is it true what they say? The château has over 130 rooms, all made of gold?"

Zoé's eyes lifted from her book of poetry. It had served as a welcome distraction from the sourness in her stomach. A look of tired sadness passed over her features, but she concealed it with a patient smile.

"Where did you hear such gossip?" she whispered, preferring not to stir Madame, and once again become the focus of her never-ending criticism. If this trip proved successful, she'd lose the shield of love her stepsister provided, and be forced to endure under Madame's bitterness.

"I heard the servants whispering of it this morning. Do you think it's true?"

"Rooms paneled in gold?" Zoé dropped her eyes and shrugged. Though Marianne's life was the charmed one, Zoé, too, had heard the whispers. It was possible the Count lived in a palace filled with treasures. Her long lashes lifted again to her sister's smiling face as she accepted the deeper truth. It was Marianne's life to be presented to such a suitor; it was hers to remain in the background, alone.

"Château La Roque. There it is!" Marianne gasped when she spied it out of the window. *Madame* choked, coughing on her guttural snore, and awakened with a start. Zoé, now intrigued, moved forward to peer out of the carriage window. The château, perched high on a snow-speckled incline, dominated the horizon. It loomed in the distance like a mythical castle of labyrinthine secrets. Vines of ivy, tough enough to have survived winter's frost, twisted along its stone walls, while thick tendrils of milk-white mist swirled around its octagonal towers.

The prolonged anticipation was almost unbearable. What awaited them all behind the aged, exclusive walls had been whispered about between she and Marianne for weeks. *The same as always*, a warning voice spoke in her mind. Pretension, respectability, and exclusion, packaged with tolerant pleasantries and veiled acceptance awaited her, certain to remind her of her place.

Zoé sank back into the shadows with a sigh. *It was so.* If their father's wishes were fulfilled, she'd lose Marianne, the only other person besides her father who loved her. And she would lose her to the master of that estate — Le Comte Julien de La Roque.

And who was he really? Would he love her sheltered, dear sweet sister as much as she did? Or would he be the man the maidens whispered about? A Casanova who collected women's virtue for sport and gave no thought to heartache? He was said to be more handsome than any man in Narbonne. Tales of his amorous exploits traveled as fast as the wind along the Aude River.

As the carriage turned up the road to the château, Zoé sat perfectly still. Her thin fingers were locked tensely in her lap. She wondered if her worries were purely the result of selfishness.

Their father had told many stories of La Roque's military successes and dismissed rumors about the Count's ways with women, but Zoé could not, for she believed that every rumor concealed a hidden truth. She could only pray that in his quest to see Marianne married, their father would not destroy his youngest daughter.

The carriage stopped. Madame Bouchard gave Zoé and Marianne a stern look, which they returned with obedient nods. The opening of the door invited the pale late-afternoon sunshine to pour in, and a handsome young footman appeared to assist.

Zoé held her place. For once, she was grateful to be the last attended to. Finally, it was her turn.

"*Mademoiselle,*" said the footman.

She extended a slender hand, and emerged, head bowed. Her bonnet shielded her face from view and her cape gave little hint to the exotic beauty that stopped many a Frenchman in his tracks. The footman bowed his head in greeting, as was proper when welcoming a family of such prominence. Zoé sensed him lift his head to peer under her bonnet.

Her eyes, a tawny shade of brown, captured his and held him to the spot. Recovering, he looked away with a deep blush. Zoé dropped her eyes. Of course, he expected a fair maiden with skin of cream, and eyes the color of rain. Feeling his gaze return, she looked up and caught his self-imposed superiority, and uninvited hint of lust. When she first became aware of how her charms affected men, she'd taken such reactions as compliments. Now, they made her uneasy. She'd learned long ago that certain men felt free to take liberties simply because she was *une femme de couleur.*

"*Merci,*" she replied, removing her hand from his.

The black mares at the front of the carriage kicked their hooves with a snort, adding a little distraction to the scene.

"*Baggages, garçon!*" the horseman yelled to the footman.

The icy breeze stroked her face and the silver ribbons of her bonnet fluttered, carrying them from beneath her chin. She tried not to read any unwelcoming portent in the chilly greeting and held her head high as she faced the unknown.

Well, it was not necessarily the unknown. Her fate was already set, thanks to the African blood coursing through her veins, blood she cherished because it was the only tie to her long lost *maman* and a culture foreign to her.

Zoé rarely felt this kind of envy, but as Marianne's giggles drifted to her, she couldn't help but feel a sense of sadness and compare their fates. Marianne would go on to live in a grand manner, but Zoé had little chance of marrying a man of Comte La Roque's stature. Such men would always view her just as that footman did.

She made her way across the pebbled path to the château. The soft folds of her cape rippled with each step. She had to take care. The last of the morning frost had left the path slick and treacherous.

Another sign, she thought, and then scolded herself for being so superstitious.

Suddenly a feeling of being watched struck her. She looked up, just in time to catch the fluid movement of a curtain falling back into place. Squinting against the sun, she wondered whether her eyes weren't tricked by unseen shadows.

"*Pardon, mademoiselle.*"

Two footmen heaving trunks between them angled up the path. She stepped aside to allow them passage. The young man who'd helped her down from the carriage brushed past her, and then tossed her a backward glance. She averted her gaze.

"Zoé! Come, *chérie!*"

It was Marianne, standing before the massive arched doorway that marked the château's main entrance. Zoé quickened her pace. She didn't want to draw the ire of Madame Bouchard. As Zoé neared her white half-sister, she once more felt a surge of love for the sixteen-year-old. Marianne was so young, and so lovely. How could she not?

The girls looked like mirror images of each other with matching creamy-white cashmere capes. Marianne's bonnet shielded her golden locks from view but it couldn't hide the merriment in her emerald-green eyes. The sisters were equal in beauty as well. If not for skin tone, they could have passed for twins. For Zoé, it was proof that she, like Marianne, was a proud daughter of Bertrand Bouchard. Some might consider her to be just his bastard child from his African mistress, but no one in Narbonne dared say it to her face.

"Why do you dawdle so?" scolded Madame.

Zoé was disappointed to realize that her stepmother was already irritated with her. The carriage ride had been pleasant enough, especially while Madame slept. But now that the time was approaching when Madame would have to introduce her stepdaughter to strangers, her stepmother's hostility was quite evident.

Zoé had heard that Madame was once quite beautiful. Perhaps this was true, but it was hard to imagine. Madame was short and portly, with flaming red hair. She covered her thick, flaccid features with heavy white powder, and darkened her cheeks and lips with rouge the color of blood. She had a distinct mole above the right curve of her lips and venomous green eyes, that in their own chilling way, were indeed quite beautiful. But for Zoé, Madame's outer beauty, or lack of it, didn't matter. What mattered was the inner ugliness of which she was capable.

A stately gentleman appeared and the staff, who had gathered to the front of the château to greet the guests, parted to allow his approach. Zoé felt his gaze pass over them and stop on her. The flash of surprise in his eyes told her that he had not been informed that a mulatto woman would be within their company. But from the way his eyes shifted between the mulâtresse and Marianne, he surmised that she was indeed a Bouchard.

He addressed Madame, who batted her lashes at him.

"*Bonjour*, Madame Bouchard," he said. "Welcome to Château La Roque."

"*Bonjour*," she replied.

ZOÉ

"I am Gérard. *Mon seigneur* has instructed me to see to your needs," he said with a respectful nod.

"Indeed." Madame replied, with an upward toss of her chin.

"This way."

With an elegant bow, he stepped back and ushered them further into the main hall. Zoé was aware of the maidservants staring at her and the amused glances they exchanged. She felt Marianne slip her hand into hers and gave her a warm smile.

The château was as grand on the inside as it was on the outside. In Zoé's opinion, one could tell a lot about a person by the way they decorated their home. Her family's home held a touch of femininity; it was to be expected under Madame's governance. Comte La Roque, and those who had preceded him, had taken great measure to ensure his home was equal to the prominence of the La Roque name. Zoé gazed about in open admiration. Her eyes followed the length of the walls, which were adorned with paintings of La Roque's ancestry. She leaned back to gaze at the hand-painted, golden domed ceiling that depicted artistry beyond her dreams. A mahogany stairwell curved along one wall, leading to the upper areas of the château.

Zoé absorbed every detail and was reassured. Yes, Marianne would have a grand life as the lady of this house.

Upstairs in his chambers, Julien La Roque stepped back from the window. He took one last look at himself in the tall mirror in his bedroom. His dark hair, glistening like polished wood, tapered neatly to his collar. Instead of the platinum wigs he donned when conducting business, he preferred a single gentleman's bow to restrain his mane. He stroked his trimmed mustache and goatee, which connected to long sideburns outlining his jaw.

At six-feet-two, broad-shouldered and brimming with vitality, La Roque enjoyed the kind of physical presence that allowed him to dominate a room the moment he entered it. Some said it wasn't his height, but his hypnotic, crystalline blue eyes that were the most compelling of his features. His eyes were indeed so clear and blue that his last bedmate remarked that they reminded her of moonlight. And his handsomeness did not end there. With a squared chin, a slightly up-turned celestial nose, and thick silky brows, his strong features held an unmistakable sensuality.

LaRoque's quick wit and unassuming manner had given him a clear advantage both in politics and the bedroom. However, his philandering had also drawn criticism from those he respected. Finally, to silence the wagging tongues, he decided to entertain young women of appropriate social status and give the appearance of seeking a bride. Once the tongues were silenced, he would abandon the quest and enjoy women in ways to which he was most accustomed.

Speaking of...

His thoughts turned to the young demoiselles whose arrival he'd watched through his window. There was no need to keep them waiting.

He shot his cuff, adjusting the ruffles that extended from under his sleeve. His eyes caught his manservant's reflection in the mirror and he turned.

"They've arrived?"

"They await you in the salon," Gérard bowed.

La Roque allowed himself a smile of satisfaction. How quickly matters advanced. He'd met Bertrand Bouchard only weeks prior and listened to him pitch the virtues of his daughter, Marianne. La Roque had only extended the invitation after hearing of the land in Marianne's dowry. Acquiring it would further his business interests along the coast.

"*Trés bien*, Gérard. I will join them now."

He strode from the chamber and descended the steps to the foyer. Crossing the long hall he found himself more than curious. He thought he'd seen a *mulâtresse* with them. This would prove interesting.

The sound of girlish laughter floated out into the hall. Stopping just outside of the entranceway and stealing a peek, he spied two of the loveliest young creatures he had ever seen, sharing his *chaise longue* and giggling.

There was the attractive woman-child with hair as golden as sunshine, pinned up on either side of her head by jeweled barrettes. The rest of her hair hung in ringlets that cascaded past her shoulders. Soft ivory shoulders beckoned him. Her throat appeared warm and shapely above her low-cut bodice. She was ripe, and he felt compelled to know her.

A slow, secretive smile formed on his lips. He envisioned the ways he would possess her. Then Gérard announced him, bringing him out of his wicked thoughts. He watched a moment longer as she readied herself for their introduction, then stepped under the arch of the entrance way.

But then he took note of her companion, her face previously concealed from his view. All thoughts of the first young woman fled. This *mulâtresse – quelle belle femme!* Her hair, dark as ebony, pinned up from her face, fell in long, graceful waves to the center of her back. Her smooth skin glowed with pale golden overtones; and the high, exotic cheekbones that set off her delicate features captivated him. He couldn't take his eyes off her full mouth. A soft pink shine glossed her lips, making them appear to be dew-kissed. Not since his travels to more foreign regions, as an attaché serving a General in Napoléon's army, had he seen such a beauty. She dropped her eyes under his steady gaze.

Her ladylike manner radiated youth and innocence. He had to know more.

Madame Bouchard stepped forward, drawing his attention. Until that moment, he hadn't noticed her. His mind made an instant and admittedly unfair comparison. She wasn't a bad-looking woman. She might even have been attractive once, but being in the same room as her lovely daughters put her in a ghastly light. He took in the heavy white face powder, the large streaks of rouge from cheekbone to ear, and the severe black and gray dress. More than anything else, however, he noted the look in her eyes: determination and a hint of desperation. Good. The balance of power was most definitely in his favor.

"*Bienvenue à Château La Roque, Madame,*" he said.

"*Mon seigneur* Comte La Roque, it's a great honor to finally meet you," she said, batting her lashes and extending a gloved hand.

La Roque approached. He kissed her hand, but shifted his eyes once again to the dark beauty.

"The pleasure is mine. And whom do we have here?"

"May I present my daughter, Mademoiselle Marianne Frances Bouchard," she said, directing him to the pretty blonde. Marianne dropped a low curtsey.

La Roque kissed her gloved hand, too. Her bashful smile as she looked into his face was endearing. Such purity was hard to find, he thought, with the appreciation of a connoisseur.

Flustered from the brief contact, Marianne dropped her hand.

"*Enchanté*," said La Roque in his deep, smoky voice.

"*Mon seigneur*," she replied, with another bob of her head.

Madame Bouchard cleared her throat. "Her companion, Zoé Camille Bouchard."

Zoé, standing behind Marianne with her eyes cast downward, stepped forward and offered a slight curtsey. La Roque kissed her hand as well.

"*Enchanté, mademoiselle.*"

Not as easily captivated as Marianne, Zoé looked him in the eye, but corrected herself before Madame saw her brashness. "*Mon seigneur.*"

La Roque noticed the way she gracefully made her presence known and unknown. There was wisdom in her poise that her sister didn't possess. She mocked him and his position with a stolen look. How refreshing and different from most of the women he met.

Madame Bouchard cleared her throat again, and by that small sound alone, La Roque understood the situation. Zoé must be the husband's child, the product of *une petite liaison*. Madame had evidently agreed to raise Zoé as her own, but the girl was to be Marianne's companion, nothing more. This meeting was to pair Marianne with a proper husband, not Zoé.

"Comte La Roque, Marianne has been anxiously anticipating this meeting. Haven't you, *ma chère?*"

"*Oui, Maman. Mon seigneur,* I've been told of your many exploits and I hear that you are quite the sportsman."

La Roque nodded. "You like sports, Mademoiselle?"

"Oh, I love croquet and riding," she said. "Nothing as adventurous as you, of course."

"Excellent," he replied with little interest.

Madame Bouchard smiled. "With your leave, *mon seigneur,* we will stay for a week to give you the opportunity to become acquainted with my Marianne. With the proper escort, of course. My husband shall join us near the end of our visit."

La Roque cast his eyes at Zoé. "Of course, you are more than welcome to stay for as long as you wish. Gérard will prepare your accommodations." He gave the valet a nod and Gérard hastened off to inform the housemaid.

La Roque steered the discussion toward their journey, and was solicitous enough to include Marianne as well. In this way, they passed a couple of minutes in light and pleasant conversation. He gave attention when Madame and Marianne spoke, but his gaze always returned to Zoé, who watched, but said nothing.

A tall, thin handmaiden entered the room. La Roque welcomed her.

"Ah, Geneviève, will you please show my guests to their quarters?"

She curtsied. "*Bien sûr, mon seigneur.*" She turned to Madame. "This way, *s'il vous plaît.*"

La Roque explained that he would see them shortly at supper and escorted them out of the room. He stood in the doorway, his gaze following them. He saw Marianne grab Zoé's hand, saw her whisper something and Zoé reply. He thought he heard the words "handsome" and "bore." His eyes grew openly amused.

My, my, my. These two cherries would be fun to pluck.

When they were only a few steps out the door, Marianne grabbed Zoé's hand and said in a loud whisper, "He's handsome."

Zoé rolled her eyes. "He's a bore, if you ask me."

"Well, no one asked you!" Madame Bouchard snapped.

Zoé cast her eyes downward. "Is it so inconceivable that I would have an opinion?" She then lifted her eyes and leveled them on Madame. "That I'd be entitled to it?"

She heard Marianne sigh. She knew her sister hated it when they quarreled, a common occurrence as the days progressed.

Madame raised a finger. "I warn you. I tire of your insolence."

Before Zoé could respond, Marianne took her hand and pulled her away. At the foot of the stairs, the sisters let go of each other and grabbed their skirts to ascend the winding staircase. Midway up, that familiar sense of being observed stilled her. She glanced over her shoulder. La Roque stood still at the entrance to his salon, watching them.

Watching her.

Though he smiled at her, his eyes impaled her. There was something lazily seductive in his look, and though she didn't understand it, she felt it.

Marianne now stood at the top of the stairs and looked back down at her sister with irritation. "Zoé? *Viens!*"

Zoé's eyes cut upward to her impatient sister. When she looked back once more LaRoque was gone. She went quickly up the steps to join the others, forcing all thoughts of him from her mind.

The chambermaid led them down an enormous hallway to their individual rooms as coachmen brought up their luggage. Her room, not paneled in gold, was grand and fit for a queen. Hand carved out of cherry, the bed sat one *metre* off the ground with doubly thick goosefeather-stuffed mattresses. Walking over to the left side of the room, she admired the large fireplace and the crackling fire that burned within it. Touching the intricately carved mantle, she imagined her sister living there and nodded approvingly.

Except perhaps for the wandering eye of Comte La Roque himself, this place made for a perfect life for her sister.

❧

A short while later, Zoé and Marianne descended the stairs and headed for the drawing room. Their late arrival didn't afford them the proper introduction she was sure Madame had wanted. Of course that would be her fault too. She was not surprised to see additional dinner guests who'd been invited for the evening. Zoé shied away from the conversation. Welcoming the solitude, her eyes swept the collection of authors lining the bookshelves. Oh how heavenly it would be to sample just one of the many delicious tomes.

From behind her, supper was announced.

The guests were shown to the dining room. La Roque strolled out, speaking with acquaintances old and new. Madame and another stately woman both tried to gain his attention but were politely escorted to their seats. Smiling, indulging the polite chatter, he lifted his gaze to the girls as they approached the table. Marianne reached for Zoé's hand, squeezing it and whispering through clenched teeth.

"He watches."

Zoé returned the squeeze. "Don't be afraid. Don't give him that power, chère, especially if he is to be your husband."

Zoé was seated. Her dining companion, a darkly tanned man with jet-black curly locks, spoke to her in Italian and she shook her head, indicating she didn't understand.

"I say — what is your name?" he asked with slow measure.

"*Pardonnez-moi*," La Roque's voice boomed, silencing the table. "I thought all my guests had been properly introduced.

Mademoiselle Zoé Bouchard, may I present Monsieur Dominic Giodarni."

Zoé looked over, surprised he'd even heard the question from his position at the head of the table. She didn't feel malice or sense any mockery. His gentlemanly nod to her actually gave her something more: his intended interest. She felt Madame's eyes on her, and didn't know how to proceed.

The unwanted attention made her nervous, and she wished it to stop. Smiling through the greeting, she averted her eyes. She knew that his subtle flirtation would have to end. Father protected her from the unfairness of her birth and the prejudices placed upon her because of her skin, but he couldn't shield her from something like this.

A heaviness centered in her chest. A wealthy man like Comte La Roque would never take her as his bride. That would be too scandalous. He merely wanted what most men of his stature wanted from her: a taste of forbidden fruit.

Supper progressed, as did the table conversation. Zoé listened. Most of the men at the table deferred to La Roque, calling for his opinion on local *partisan* developments that threatened their wealth and stature under King Charles. He gave witty answers that prompted laughter over topics she didn't understand. She was relieved that his lustful glances had ceased and hopeful that Marianne could find a union with a man this well regarded.

Once supper was over, all were invited into the drawing room to share brandy and discuss more politics. Madame Bouchard bragged about her "other daughter," telling the guests what a songbird her Zoé was.

"Zoé, finally you can be of some use. Play for us," she said.

She stiffened, momentarily abashed, but thankful for the color of her skin. It concealed the flush of embarrassment in her cheeks. Madame had a knack for turning something rewarding into something uncomfortable. Yes, she loved to play, but when called upon to perform at these gatherings, put on display like a caged bird, it was a hurtful reminder that Madame acknowledged her only when it served her purpose.

Marianne squeezed Zoé's right hand, giving her a smile of reassurance, and Zoé felt ice spreading through her stomach. He was watching. His blue eyes pierced the distance between them. But when she looked into Marianne's eyes, her sister's affection soothed her anxiety. They never spoke openly about the way Madame treated Zoé, but Marianne, in her own sweet way, was always there to comfort Zoé and give quiet support.

"Why don't you sing and I shall play?" Zoé whispered to her sister, who she knew preferred the privilege.

Marianne nodded and Zoé took a seat at the harp. Looking up, she saw La Roque smoking his pipe by the fire with a smile of appreciation as he observed her. She drew her fingers across thin taut strings and a ripple of harmonious notes filled the air. Marianne began to sing.

"My Marianne has been singing from the cradle. You are in for a greater treat," Madame stage-whispered haughtily to her nearest neighbor.

Zoé heard the veiled insult. Where her sister's voice was whimsical and light, she'd been told by her father that her own voice carried her mother's soul. Relaxing, she played and escaped in music as she did with poetry. Smiling proudly and watching her sister, she caught his watchful stare from the corner of her eye. She was careful to ignore it. She could feel his magnetism that made him so self-confident, and feared it. He was growing bolder by the minute.

Thankfully, the song ended.

Everyone applauded and Marianne curtsied. Zoé would no longer be held under his watchful gaze. For that, she let go a soft sigh of relief.

La Roque removed his pipe. "Now the question remains, is her sister's voice as lovely?"

She froze.

"Oh, Zoé sings beautifully!" Marianne replied.

"I should very much like to hear for myself." he said, and the beginning of a smile tipped the corners of his mouth.

Madame shot Zoé a look that demanded she oblige.

"Very well," Zoé said. She went to the pianoforte and took a seat, spreading her skirt across the tufted bench. She lifted the lid to the ivories and began to play. She sang a song her mother taught her, closing her eyes and immersing herself in the music. In her mother's song she found a bottomless peace.

It was her heartsong that she offered, and part of her reveled in his open admiration. She nearly stumbled through the words when he gave her an oblique nod and a small, conspiratorial smile. Her gaze turned toward Marianne. Her sister looked unhappy. One of the guests, a woman who'd been introduced as a duchess, leaned over and whispered something in Marianne's ear. Marianne simply nodded, and took a sip from her wine glass.

When the song ended, everyone gave generous applause. Zoé gave a modest curtsey and took her place next to her sister. Up close, she could see that Marianne wasn't merely unhappy, but furious.

"Did I offend you?" Zoé asked.

"You're doing it again," Marianne said.

"Doing what?"

Marianne tipped her head toward La Roque. Zoé followed Marianne's gaze and understood. She was somewhat angry at herself for having possibly encouraged him.

"I'm sorry. Really."

Marianne shrugged, looking into her goblet. "Like you said, he's a bore, anyway. I don't want a man who has eyes for my sister." She was silent a moment, and then looked up. "We must never let anyone come between us. Promise me that neither of us shall entertain his advances."

Zoé noted the sadness in Marianne's eyes. "But you know that he will never want anything of substance with me."

"Why not, Zoé? Don't you know how many suitors Father has turned away for you?"

"They weren't suitors," Zoé said bitterly. Marianne was so naïve. Those men wanted her as a mistress, not a wife. Father would never allow that and for that at least, Zoé was grateful. She regarded Marianne. "I promise you that nothing shall come of Comte La Roque and any intentions he may have toward me."

"Good."

Zoé knew that if she agreed to Marianne's promise, her sister would not keep the same. Marianne liked the monsieur, and if he chose her, she would readily become his bride. It was just as well, for Zoé. His advances would never lead to anything more than what she saw in his eyes.

ZOÉ

Shortly after midnight, Zoé stirred. The persistent need to relieve herself caused her eyes to flutter before she fully awoke. It was strange waking in another bed. Her head fell over to the right, and she waited for her eyes to adjust. Once aware, she decided to venture to the private closet that she knew was down the hall. She rose, stretching out of her sleep. Loose tendrils of her hair fell to her face as she climbed from the bed. The thin floor-length gown she wore provided little warmth. So she donned her dressing robe and slippers, then retrieved the candelabrum from the nightstand and lit three pointed candles.

Zoé slipped into the hall and stepped cautiously through the darkness. Earlier, she and her sister had discovered that the toilette was on the adjoining wing. It was next to a library that had called to her in her sleep. Books were the one single place where she truly felt free.

Cupping the flames with her left hand, she ventured forward. The flickering candles cast a warm yellow glow over her face as she walked, her heavy velveteen robe flowing behind her. Her eyes swept the paintings along the corridor. Landscapes hung on both walls, interspersed with portraits. Though her home was lavish in Narbonne, its modesty was glaring compared to the château's unyielding charm.

Concerned about dawdling, and possibly stumbling upon Madame who slept more during the day than night, she quickly made her way. Within minutes she was again in the hall headed for her room. Then she stopped. The light pouring out of the library door, which was ajar, caught her eye. In her haste, she'd passed the door just minutes before, not noticing. Zoé stood in the drafty hall weighing her options. She could return to her room as expected, or steal a moment to find a jewel to pass the night away.

Thinking no more of it, she entered, stopping to put the candelabrum on the end table near the door. All in all, it was not an unpleasant room. However, it was not as immaculate as the others. She surmised this was not a library, but the office of La Roque. It was a bit cluttered: books were piled on chairs and on the floor, and his desk was covered with papers.

She knew it was wrong of her to enter his personal chamber, but when her eyes fell upon the hundreds of books lining the floor-to-ceiling shelves, she abandoned all thoughts of leaving. Drawn to the collection, she tilted her head curiously. How odd to find authors such as Théophile Gautier, Alphonse de Lamartine, and translations by Gérard de Nerval in his private collection. Why would the Comte own such a diverse assembly of work? Maybe, like Father, he didn't know of the lurid, exotic tales that lay between the pages. But when she thought of the blue heat within the Comte's gaze, she imagined that he must know. Fully.

She stepped in closer to select a book, but her hip connected with the desk, knocking one to the floor. When she looked down she saw none other than Victor Hugo's *Nouvelles Odes et Poésies Diverses*, published just a few years ago and a rare find. Hugo himself had received a royal pension from King Louis after writing the anthology.

Zoé's spirits soared. It was like a dream realized to have the pages at her feet. She lowered slowly and picked up the treasure, dusting it off with her delicate hands. Her fingers stroked the olive-green leather. The binding was finished with raised floral gold embroidery. The book was as beautiful as she imagined Victor Hugo's words would be inside.

Zoé's heart fluttered wildly beneath her breasts. Her mouth curved into an unconscious smile, and she rose.

La Roque appeared in the doorway, looking at her curiously. She stood before the fireplace reading something he could not see. Zoé had no idea he watched her. She turned the page and began to recite in French the first passage, savoring each word.

"Well, look what the night brings," he said.

Zoé whirled around with a jolt; the book fell from her hands. "Pardon, *mon seigneur*, I am so sorry, I didn't mean to –"

La Roque stepped forward. His eyes dropped to the book splayed on the floor, then lifted to Zoé's.

She bowed her head. Her heart pounded, and her face grew hot with humiliation. La Roque knelt and picked up the book, turning it over to read the imprint on the spine. "Ah, Victor Hugo?"

How shameful of her to be caught in one of his private rooms. Madame would be furious and certain to tell Father. Avoiding his eyes, she tried to think of an appropriate explanation. "I passed the room... and the books... *mon seigneur*, I was wrong to enter."

La Roque touched her chin with the tip of his index finger, lifting her face to look into her eyes. "I'm an admirer of Hugo as well."

She blinked at him curiously, locked in his gaze. He handed her the book. "Would you like to read it?"

"I couldn't."

"I'd be offended, *Mademoiselle* Bouchard, if you didn't."

"It is a rare piece."

La Roque chuckled softly. "I have others. In fact, I have one personally signed by Hugo. In my chamber."

"Signed?"

"He's a friend." La Roque held the book out for her to accept. Zoé sucked in a breath and reached for it, the tips of their fingers meeting in the exchange.

"*Merci*," she said, trying to avoid the tanned plane of his chest, exposed by his open blouse.

La Roque looked back at the shelves. Zoé followed his gaze, admiring the collection once more.

"My mother loved to read. As do I, thanks to her."

She studied his profile from the corner of her eye. Underneath his classically handsome features she found a hint of sadness. His voice carried the same tone her father's did when he spoke in private of her long-dead mother.

La Roque continued to stare at his mother's books. "The times I can remember her at her happiest was in this room with these books. I suppose it's why I chose this room for my personal use." He stepped forward and Zoé watched him. "It was she who taught me to read. To appreciate things of beauty."

With the slight turn of his head, he leveled his eyes on her again, making a deep blush cover her cheeks. "What's more beautiful than a poet's words? I say it is the reader who understands those words."

She pressed the book to her chest. "My mother taught me to read as well, before she died. I have her favorite book of poems."

"Then you must let me show you my private *pièce*. Victor himself left a sonnet that only you can appreciate, *Mademoiselle*."

"I could not."

"It is just in the chamber beyond this one."

"No, no, thank you. It's very late and I am tired," she said, trying to step around him. La Roque blocked her passage. She held on to the book but bravely raised her head to look into his face.

His gaze dipped to her breasts and below, and she was reminded that the flickering light of the fireplace revealed more than she intended due to her open robe. Pulling it shut she stepped back.

"I daresay I have never met an actual angel." His soft voice urged her to believe him. "What if I said please?" he asked with a theatrical pout.

She smiled, but shook her head again. "Pardon, but I must return to my room."

"*Mademoiselle...*"

"*Oui, mon seigneur?*"

She dropped her eyes again. Her fear now getting the best of her, she was afraid to look at him, afraid of what she might see in his eyes — afraid, too, of what he might see in hers.

"I think that you are the most captivating woman I've ever seen."

Her heartbeat quickened. He put two fingers under her chin and forced her to look at him once more. Her eyes met his. An openly sensual light passed between them. She knew she was in danger, but she didn't know how to respond. On several occasions during their travels, she had encountered gentlemen who made unwanted advances. Not once had those men or their offers affected her. But La Roque was different. He understood her love of poems because he shared it, too. She sensed he shared in her feelings of loss as well.

"What is it that you want, *mon seigneur?*"

"We scarcely know one another, but I feel somehow we do. I want to know if that's true."

He touched her long curly hair and twirled a lock in between his fingers. She drew back and the silken curl slipped from his hand. His words confused and captivated her.

"If your wish is to know me, then you should speak with Madame."

She took a step to pass him, and he took a step to block her.

"You are a *lady,* aren't you?" he asked.

"Please. Let me go, *mon seigneur.*" After a moment, she added, *"Je vous mendie."* I'm begging you.

"Victor Hugo's words from his pen, just in the other room—" he looked back at the door then to her "— it shall only take a moment. No one shall be the wiser."

Her eyes searched his. Dare she trust him? She swallowed. When would she ever be able to see the fresh writings of a poet so grand? If Father found out, he would kill her, and Madame… She had no idea what Madame would do, but the thought of flouting her stepmother's precious rules and regulations emboldened her. She felt more confident under his desires, and decided she could handle herself very well.

She swallowed hard, lifted her chin, and boldly met his gaze. "*Bien.* Just for a moment."

La Roque ushered her into his chamber through an adjoining suite, where an ebbing yellow glow from the flames of wall-mounted candles tossed shadows around the furnishings. She paused just past the threshold to his boudoir, taken aback by the opulence of it all. It was a lush mixture of gold and silver, brocade and velvet, with *trompe l'oeil* overhead and priceless carpeting beneath. It was also chilly, however, the fire in the fireplace having gone out. She gave a little shiver.

"Come," he said, and started toward two closed doors on the far side of the room.

"Where?"

He gave her a little smile, and then took her by the elbow.

"You'll find it warmer in here," he said and threw open the doors to his inner chamber.

She hoped his comment referred to the temperature of the room and not to any intentions toward her.

This room was warmer. A fire crackled in the fireplace, radiating a seductive welcome. The dancing flames cast the room with a soft orange glow.

She couldn't help but notice the canopied bed. It was large and high, fit for a king. Carvings of braided swirls curling upward decorated its four thick posts. Heavy drapes hung from the canopy of the bed and were tied around each post. Atop the thick mattress was a matching crimson quilted counterpane; large pillows were tossed about.

Zoé moved through the masculine room with an outer show of confidence. She turned with a start when the door closed behind her. "The Victor Hugo, *mon seigneur?*"

La Roque's gaze roved and appraised her lazily. He was disturbing to her in every way, for one moment she understood him, then the next she feared him. When his jeweled eyes lifted back to her face he gave her a nod and looked beyond her. Zoé turned to find a book turned downward with reading glasses on top. Lowering the one she held on to, she approached.

It was a first edition with simple binding. She picked it up and laid the *Nouvelles Odes* on the table in its place. From behind her she heard his soft yet determined approach. She ignored the heat she felt when he towered over her. He reached around her and took the book from her hands, brushing her fingers, and turning the page. She was now in the center of his arms with him peering over her shoulder.

"Here——" he said, stopping on the handwritten passage. "Here he speaks."

Zoé dropped her eyes to the pages, enthralled. La Roque smiled slyly at the fresh amazement he saw on her face, from the corner of his eye.

"Be like the bird that, passing on her flight awhile on boughs too slight, feels them give way beneath her, and yet sings, knowing that she hath wings," La Roque read aloud.

"Beautiful," she whispered, wanting to touch the pages.

"Indeed." His voice was deep and sensual, sending a ripple of awareness through her. She was in his lair, on his turf, and she'd come willingly. The book closed, and she cleared her throat. She tightened her robe and folded her arms in front of her to push his arms open. He stepped back politely. Now forced to turn, she did so while taking a step back. Zoé eyed the door. He stood between her and the only possible avenue of escape. La Roque walked away with the book in his hand. She watched as he went to his bar, which lay concealed behind a wooden cabinet.

"I liked the song you sang tonight. What's it called?"

"L'Hymne à l'Amour," she said picking up the book he'd given her, and preparing to take her leave.

La Roque filled two snifters with brandy. "Do you have any other hidden talents? She shook her head no. He walked over to her and handed her a drink, which she blushed and accepted, despite her inner warning voice. "None that I care to share with you tonight."

He laughed and raised his glass.

She also raised hers and sipped the smooth liquid. It was strong, much stronger than anything she'd ever had before, but she took a good swallow and tried not to grimace at how it burned going down. Seconds later, she was astounded to feel a spreading sensation of internal warmth.

"Would this be your first time, *mademoiselle?*"

Shocked at his boldness, she could only utter one word: *"Quoi?"* What?

"Your first time... drinking brandy, I mean."

Relieved, she wondered if he were playing with her. "*Oui*," she said. "It's my... my first time."

"Then I am honored." He gave a little bow and continued. "It is very important, of course, that your first time be a memorable occasion."

Now, she was certain that he was mocking her.

He gestured for her to sit on the banquette next to the fireplace. She glanced at it. Ah, she knew this game. He would sit next to her, try to pressure her. She eased down on the seat, perched on its edge, prepared to spring up should he make advances.

With an amused smile, he took a seat in the brocaded armchair across from her. He observed her tranquilly.

"You are very beautiful, you know, especially here, in the light of the fire. It makes your skin glow."

He spoke in a friendly, neutral tone, as though his words were simply those of someone making an observation. She offered no reply.

He continued. "You are not afraid, I hope, that I would try to take advantage of you, in any way?"

She couldn't bring herself to look at him. All evening she met his gaze, openly challenging him, but now it was only when she focused her eyes on the flames that she found the courage to speak.

"Why did you invite me here?" she whispered.

"En vérité?" In truth?

"Yes, please. *En vérité.*" She forced herself to look at him.

"Because ever since you arrived, I have been dying to know how your lips would taste, what the touch of your skin would feel like."

She was appalled to feel an inner surge of answering desire. She lifted her chin. "I'm sorry to disappoint you, but I'm not in the habit of responding in such a manner to strangers."

"But we are far from strangers, *mademoiselle*. You are a guest in my home, in my chamber, by the fire, sharing a brandy with me."

She didn't know how to respond. He was right, and yet so very wrong. This was not how it looked. But propriety was about appearance. Measured so, this was indeed a very improper situation. She had accepted a forbidden invitation. What had she been thinking? It wasn't only the prospect of seeing the Victor Hugo that convinced her to enter. It was the glimpse at his soul. He shared something with her, something she understood. That kinship drew her like a moth to his flame.

She drank the rest of her brandy too quickly, and felt it rush to her head. She just wanted to escape before things got too far out of hand.

Seeing her gulp down the dark liquid, he chuckled. "I hope I don't make you nervous."

"I am sorry if I gave you the wrong impression, but I shall not be swayed from my principles."

She got to her feet and he did, too.

"You know, I admire you," he said, "for your courage in resisting me. But we both know your lot in life."

Despite the warmth of the fire, she felt a chill. "Do you intend to force me? Is that your kind of courage?"

"I could. No one would question me on the matter."

She started to retort.

"But," he added, "I rather enjoy the chase."

He set his snifter on the little table next to his chair and went to her. She fell back a step, unsure of what to expect. She braced herself for a rough touch, but all he did was remove her brandy glass and place it on the fireplace mantle.

"Since you've been bold enough to enter my room, you could at least grant a man his parting wish." He took her hand. "One taste, one small taste, and I promise to bid you goodnight."

Zoé looked down at his hand touching hers. How did she get here? Her heart pounded and she breathed in deeply, exhaling slowly. She had never kissed or been kissed by a man on the mouth. She only exchanged polite pecks on the cheek with her father in greeting.

"I'm very curious about what's under this robe," he said.

Before she could object, he untied the sash and her robe fell open. With a gasp, she pulled the robe shut, but too late. From the blazing blue heat of his gaze, she knew that he saw her dark nipples peeking through the delicate fabric of her virginal white gown, and perceived the contours of her body underneath.

"I must go," she said.

"No, don't."

She tried to step around him. As before, he blocked her.

"Haven't you ever desired something so badly that you would do anything just to have it?" he asked, moving her hair from her shoulder to her back.

"No."

"Let me kiss you, and you shall."

"I don't—"

"Let me show you the pleasures you hide from."

Looking into his eyes, then his face, taking him in and urged on by the effects of the brandy, she touched the silky hair that fell around his shoulders. The brandy, the flames, his presence and his desire: it was all so very intoxicating. Her heart raced as she felt his hand slide down her hip.

And now she was truly afraid – not just of his desire, but her own. He ignited an inner ember she was barely aware of. He turned a spark into a flame. She was deeply aware of her own longing. For one intense moment, she wished they weren't bound by principles and etiquette. Then she caught herself and knew she was in grave danger.

She drew her hand back, feeling betrayed and trapped by her own weakness, a weakness unleashed by the brandy, and seduced by the idea that this man of privilege, of noble birth and lineage, this man who could have any woman he wanted, actually wanted her.

He smiled at her confusion and pulled her into his arms. "You bewitch me," he whispered and gently bit down on her lower lip.

"*Mon seigneur*, we can't." She willed herself to be strong, to see him for who he was, to not give in to his advances. There was still time to escape.

He slid his hand around her delicate throat, lifting her chin with his thumb, causing her hair to fall down her back. Closing her eyelids, she felt the warmth of his breath as he brought his face close to hers. Never had a man touched her so intimately. His hold was firm yet tender, direct yet deceptive, inviting yet frightening.

Her body responded with a mind of its own. She moved forward into his embrace, becoming entangled in his web of deceit. She felt his hand at the back of her waist and was surprised at his strength as he pressed her still closer, crushing her breasts against his chest. Beneath the brandy on his breath, she could smell his desire, and feel the stirrings of something strong and demanding against her thighs. Her fingers slipped from the front of her robe. He parted the folds and eased his hand inside.

This was all so unreal. It must be happening to someone else. She lost all sense of reason and fearful restraint. She sighed, her eyelids heavy with passion, deaf to the warnings screaming in her mind. A price was to be paid for the kind of crime she was about to commit, and it was high, very high, but at that moment, she didn't care.

His mouth brushed against hers, and then increased its pressure. His tongue licked her lips before demanding entrance. Instinctively she obeyed, allowing him inside. Her eyes widened at his taste, but then slid closed again as his tongue probed and took control.

This man threatened it all: her virtue, her sensibility, everything, as he dominated their kiss, forcing her to follow his lead. Tasting the brandy on his lips and smelling the spicy aroma from his pipe, Zoé lost all sense of etiquette and breeding. She put her arms around his neck and began to kiss him back.

His kiss became something she didn't understand, going deeper and further than she intended. She held on tightly for fear of slipping away. He placed a hand on her hip and pressed her against him. The powerful pressure against her thigh alarmed her without her fully understanding why.

She pushed herself away, but he pulled her back. Before she fully realized what was happening, he'd slipped the robe from her shoulders. It lay in a heap at her feet and the only material between her and him was a thin layer of silk. Stunned, she fought harder and broke free.

"We must stop this! I can't!" she cried. Part of her wanted to experience every inch of what he promised to bring, the other remained terrified by her circumstances.

"You can and you shall," he said, snatching her back to him. He lightly cupped one breast and gave it a light, exploratory squeeze.

"*Non!*" She wrenched herself away and grabbed up her robe.

He caught her by the arm. "I'm sorry, but something has taken hold of me. It's so strong, I can't... I can't let you leave. You must feel it, too."

"*Je vous en prie.* Please, let me go."

"Relax. What do you feel? Tell me."

"I don't know. This isn't proper and you—"

"No one's here. It's just you and me. What happens to us now will shape our lives. Can't you feel it? Don't you want it?"

She turned him no answer. She would lose this battle and she knew it. No matter what she did, she would lose. If she managed to escape, she would lose. And if she didn't...

He fingered the ribbons holding together the neckline of her gown, and then gave them a little tug. The flaps of her gown slid open, revealing her breasts to him. For a moment, he simply gazed at them, and then, to her surprise, he took hold of her right breast, lowered his mouth to it and gently suckled. The touch of his lips sent a jolt of heat through her, one that penetrated her loins. Without realizing it, she gave a little groan, and the hands that had pounded at his chest in resistance now gripped him. He released her breast and regarded it with affection.

"There, you see how she peeks out at me? She wants me."

Zoé looked down to see how erect her nipple had become.

"Whereas in my past dalliances I needn't ask, tonight I will. May I have you?" he asked in a husky whisper.

"Quoi?" she said, surprised and confused. After all this, was he really asking her permission? Did he think her foolish enough to believe that it mattered?

"You heard me, mademoiselle. I want to hear you say it. You have a voice when you are with me. Forget what's expected and tell me your wishes. May I have you?"

She struggled with an answer. For looking into his eyes, he didn't appear insincere. On the contrary, his wild sapphire eyes mirrored a secret longing that she too felt inside. To be heard and seen for who they were, not what they were. Was it crazy to believe that a man of his position had such desires? Maybe. But he was so compelling, his magnetism so potent, she'd believe anything.

"Come now," he said. "It's not that hard to speak for yourself, is it?"

Looking away into the fire, she thought about her lot in life. She wasn't Marianne. He wouldn't have dared be this brazen with Marianne. But he wanted her, and that made her feel special. She had little control over her life and saw that someday Madame would pass her off to some foreign suitor. Several unappealing men had already made sizeable offers for her. Her father had turned them all down, but one day Madame would win out. No matter how much he resisted, it would happen.

At least, this *monsieur* was appealing. And he was giving her a choice.

She recalled her promise to Marianne, recalled too that Marianne had forced it just so she could have him all to herself. No, she was not compelled to honor such a promise. For once, she could make a decision based on her own needs and not what was expected of her.

Her gaze, clouded by the effects of the brandy, returned to La Roque.

"Comte La Roque—"

He kissed her again, this time gently. "Gianelli," he whispered. "You shall call me Gianelli." Zoé's nose wrinkled at the request, uncertain of the origin of the pet-name. But he only shared that same secretive smile, the one that spoke to her heart and not her mind. "And after tonight, I shall call you Zoé."

It was in this simple statement that Zoé found hope that her life was really about to change, and in his kiss that she put her faith. Returning his passion this time, she felt more in control of the kiss.

She felt his hands travel to the sides of her nightgown and gather up the thin fabric with his fingers. She held her breath as he raised the gown above her hips and drew it over her head. He stepped back to look at her body and she felt tempted to cover herself with her hands. Instead, she stood there bravely, her breathing shallow and wondering what to do next, as he took in every swell and curve.

He lifted the hem of his shirt and pulled it over his head, revealing a muscular chest and tanned, sculpted shoulders. A long, dark spiral of hair wound down the center of his chest to fan out just above the line of his low-slung pajama bottoms.

She was intrigued. She'd seen shirtless men before but never as beautiful as him. She and Marianne were extremely sheltered. In private, they would giggle over what they thought certain men would look like unclothed.

La Roque dropped his pants and Zoé's eyes lowered with interest. Registering what she was seeing, her body's most intimate spots warmed with desire. She felt her stomach tighten as she lifted her gaze back to his face.

He grabbed her face and kissed her hard, their naked bodies bathed in the orange-yellow glow from the fireplace. He swept her up and carried her to his bed. She held on to him, her arms looped around his neck, kissing his face and eyelids, pained by a strange surge of affection that terrified her.

He laid her lovingly on the dark spread and gazed down at her, at how her hair fanned out across the pillows. Looking up at him, she saw awe at her beauty reflected in his eyes.

Zoé closed her eyes as he kissed her. She moaned as his tongue left her mouth to glide down her neck to her left breast. He circled her dark nipple for just a moment before the warmth of his mouth engulfed it, suckling. She gasped as a bolt of desire jolted her, causing her to moan in a voice she'd never heard before.

He massaged her other breast, then worked his way toward her stomach before going even lower. Drunk with passion, she looked down at the top of his head as he slid his finger into her. She gripped the sheets, never having been touched this way by a man before.

"Zoé," his voice dropped in volume, but not passion.

He began to work his finger, giving her more pleasure than she'd ever known before. What few doubts she might have still entertained disappeared in the waves of pleasure radiating from her loins. He was in deep now.

Really deep.

He put his face between her legs. She felt the tiny bristling hairs of his beard brush against her inner thighs and inhaled sharply. When his tongue started its exploration, she arched her back, crying out in ecstasy as he took her left leg and threw it over his shoulder to give him further access to her treasures.

She tugged at the sheets, her breath coming quickly, while unfamiliar currents of pleasure rippled through her. She inched upward, crazy for relief from the way he made love to her with his tongue, but he held her hips in place as he kept going. His tongue penetrated her, and she shivered. His tongue traveled back upward, flicking at her. She froze, gripping the sheets tightly, unsure of his touch and his tongue and the continual currents that made her hips shake. His eyes lifted as hers opened and met his. She relaxed under his gaze, working her hips to the rhythm of his tongue out of sheer instinct.

Blood rushed to her face, making her blush. As he sucked her, swallowing her juices, her body vibrated and the waves of pleasure mounted. Finally, she could hold it in no longer and gave vent to an explosive release with a cry. He quickly lifted up and brought his mouth to hers to silence her. She could taste herself on his tongue. It was exhilarating. She felt lightheaded.

His face wet with her passion, he pulled her further under him and slid her legs apart with his knees. She wasn't expecting what came next. He parted her lower lips, positioned himself against her and gave a strong thrust. Zoé squeezed her eyes shut. She winced at the sharp pain that cut through her pelvis. As he thrust again, she felt as though she was being ripped apart. All sense of pleasure was gone. She desperately wanted him to stop. In a panic, she struggled beneath him. She pushed and clawed at his shoulders, shaking her head. The pain was too much, and she wanted it to end.

Instead of releasing her, he grabbed both of her wrists and held them above her head, pinning her down. Rotating his hips, he watched her toss her head from side to side.

"Look at me," he said.

At first, she didn't realize that he was speaking. Between the brandy and the pain, she was frightened and confused.

"Please, no more," she whimpered, tears welling in her eyes.

He kissed her on the tip of her nose. "Open your eyes," he whispered, slowing the rotation of his hips, but still pressing deeper and deeper.

She finally opened her eyes and gazed at him through her tears. He ran his tongue across her lips, and nibbled on them. As his long, silky hair brushed against her cheek, he smiled down at her.

"It's all right," he said in his deep, husky voice. "You are safe with me. Relax. Feel it, Zoé. Give in to it."

She took a deep, shuddering breath and swallowed.

"You trust me, now?" he asked.

She gave a nod. He let go of her wrists and placed her arms around his neck. Then he began again.

As he rammed his need in and out of her, she bit her lip so hard that she thought it would bleed, but she held on tight. At one point, she dug her nails into his soft skin, and he didn't flinch. Turning his hips, he gave a mighty thrust. She felt something give way inside her, felt him slide in deep. The aching lessened, and as he rested his face in the curve of her neck, she felt what it meant to be truly desired.

His desires.

Now smiling and holding him to her, she opened herself to him. As he moaned with pleasure, she felt desired in ways she hadn't known existed. Finally, she joined him in the lovers' duet. Churning her hips, she matched his rhythmic dance, feeling the urgency of his love thrusts lessen. She began to enjoy how their bodies melded into one. No longer pained by his intrusion, she felt herself adjust and envelop his width. She was now a partner in their loving and gave as much as she took.

She sucked in her breath as he lifted her hips and pounded his hardness into her. As his pace quickened, the throbbing pain returned in waves. When he exploded inside of her, she knew that something monumental had transpired between them.

Feeling him collapse on top of her, she sighed under his weight. He raised his head and looked into her eyes.

"It is the beginning of our passion," he said.

She smiled. "I felt it deeply, too, *mon seigneur*—Gianelli."

He smiled back at her. "Would you like to stay with me?"

"What did you say?"

"Stay with me. If I speak to Madame Bouchard and ask for you, would you like to stay?"

Zoé felt her eyes well up with tears. "As your mistress?" she asked, hoping that this was indeed not the case.

He kissed her and released her from his intimate embrace. She winced at the pain. He then rolled over on his side, not bothering to look at her.

"What's wrong with that?" he asked.

She gave him an angry look and pushed herself up onto her elbows, her once tamed locks now wild around her head.

"Would you ask Marianne to be your mistress?" she snapped.

He chuckled with dark amusement. "I wouldn't ask Marianne anything. I don't want her. I want you."

Zoé sat up now, glaring at him. The smirk on his face, as he lay there next to her, naked, said it all. The seduction now over, the harsh reality of her circumstances hammered her with an unforgiving force, each blow relaying the painful truth that La Roque would never see her as anything more than a conquest.

Without another word, she got up and retrieved her clothes.

"Zoé," he said, watching her. "I'm not looking for a wife. My offer is not about your class or conception. It's the only offer I would make to any woman."

Zoé dressed in silence. Primary among the emotions rushing through her was a deep sense of shame. She flushed miserably, trying to salvage some of her dignity. She spoke as much to comfort herself as to impress him.

"Gianelli, I thank you for..." She looked at him on the bed, naked, still observing her. "For whatever this was, because as you said, the choice was mine. But I will never be anyone's mistress."

She retrieved her candelabrum, gave him one last cold nod and walked toward the door.

"Zoé!" he called after her.

She paused in the doorway, but refused to turn around, forcing him to speak to her back.

"Reconsider," he said. "You're different now and I want you. My proposal may not be the one you hoped for but it is sincere."

She spun around and exploded in anger. "Want me, *mon seigneur? You want me?* Well, you've had your taste. Savor it. Remember it, for it shall be your last!"

With that, she strode from his chambers, her back stiff and her eyes blinking hard to hold back the tears.

2

"Zoé? Zoé, wake up."

Marianne gently shook her sister's shoulders, but Zoé continued to sleep. Marianne hurried to the window and pushed the draperies aside, allowing sunlight to pour into the room. Zoé turned over with a moan. Her spiral locks fell over her face, shading her from the bright light.

"Up, up, up!" she said. She kissed Zoé on the cheek, and then shook her again.

"What is it?" Zoé mumbled, rubbing her eyes. Still groggy from her late night, she shuddered as she felt a painful throbbing in her head, proof that the night before had not been a dream. She opened her eyes, winced at the bright light and squinted at her sister's face, hovering over her own.

The sight of Marianne's smile ushered in a greater sense of regret of the night's events. In the daylight, yesterday's bold deeds seemed so very foolish. She would pay dearly if anyone ever learned what she'd done.

"It's dawn," Marianne said. "I spoke to *Maman*. I have wonderful news!"

Zoé sat up slowly. "News? What news?"

"La Roque. He told her first thing this morning that he wants to discuss terms with Father. I think he wants to marry me!"

She paled at the enormity of the news, then averted her eyes, lest they reveal her hurt. Marianne's eyes gleamed like polished jade and her cheeks were flushed with joy. Her happiness was genuine and carefree, the complete opposite of Zoé's own private heartache.

"Marry you? Are you sure?"

"I'm positive! *Maman* is very excited. She woke me up to tell me. Father is to come immediately. Do you think he fell in love with me when he heard me sing?"

Zoé laid down on her pillow and stared at the ceiling. It was confirmed. What a fool she had been. She'd given away the most precious part of her to a man who was to be her sister's husband. She had nothing to offer any suitor. When it was discovered that she was no longer a virgin, she would be cast aside. Why hadn't she considered all of this before? Why hadn't she held fast to her principles? Tears welled in her eyes.

"Oh, Zoé," Marianne said softly, touching her sister's hand. "I know what I said before, about not listening to any proposals from him, but I do like him."

Zoé forced a smile. "It is wonderful news, *Chérie*. I am happy for you."

"Come! Get out of bed. We must dress and join everyone for breakfast!" She snatched the covers back and then, looking down, paused with a frown.

Zoé followed Marianne's gaze and was surprised as well. Her white gown was soiled. Small drops of dried blood stained the material between her legs.

"What happened? Didn't it start on last week?" Marianne asked. The two girls' cycles were like clockwork, always starting at around the same time.

Zoé snatched the covers back. "I don't know why it came back on. How strange!"

Marianne touched Zoé's forehead. "Are you feverish? Do you feel faint?"

"No, no, I'm well." Despite her heartbreak, Zoé had to smile. Marianne was such a little nurse. "Honestly, I am well. Now, excuse me while I get dressed."

Marianne gave her another look of concern, and then shrugged. "*Bien*, but please hurry. I want you to come and help me with my curls. I need to look my very best for him. He will be in awe of my beauty," she giggled.

"I shall," Zoé promised. "Now hurry. Go!"

She watched her sister leave. As soon as the door closed, Zoé got up. She pulled back the covers. There was another circular stain on the mattress. She stared at it. Panic like she'd never known welled in her throat.

If Madame saw this, she would know the truth instantly. Zoé snatched the sheets off the bed and tossed them to the floor. She took off her stained gown and dropped it to the floor as well. Trying to control her anxiety, she took another gown from her trunk and dressed hurriedly. She was in trouble. She felt faint and knew it was just her nerves. Next was the armoire. She found another set of sheets and quickly remade the bed. Panting, she bundled the stained sheets and gown into a ball, and looked about. Her trunks. She could hide everything there to dispose of later. She started toward them, but heard a knock at the door. Instead, she shoved the soiled linens under the bed, just as the door opened and Madame entered.

"Zoé! What are you doing on the floor?" Madame gasped.

Zoé got up from her knees, offering an innocent smile. "*Bonne matin, Madame.* I was looking for my slippers."

"Well they're right there," she pointed, "at the foot of your bed." Madame walked over and placed the back of her hand against Zoé's forehead, which was now beaded with sweat. "Marianne told me you weren't feeling well."

Zoé gritted her teeth. If only Marianne didn't always run and tell everything. "*Non*. I was a bit faint this morning, but I am better now."

Madame sat down on the bed and patted the spot next to her. "Sit with me *ma chère*. We have certain affairs to discuss."

Zoé obeyed, icy fear twisting around her heart.

"I know you and I have had our disappointments in the past. You do know that I've raised you since you were six years old, and I think of you as I do Marianne."

Zoé stared, knowing that was false. Madame was a substitute mother to her, but she was in no way considered her daughter. Her father's torrid love affair with her mother was still whispered about on the streets of Narbonne. Madame was married into the Bouchard family after having been placed into Father's life by Zoé's cruel paternal *grand-mère*. Villagers often spoke of it being done to ensure that her son, who stood to inherit a great fortune, did not take his African mistress as his wife.

After she'd given birth to their bastard *capresse* child, Zoé's mother, Capucine, was forced to serve the woman who stole her lover. The suffering she endured under Madame's reign ensured that Zoé would hate her forever. Her mother eventually died of a broken heart. Father promised Capucine that Zoé would be raised as his daughter, and he kept that promise.

"*Oui*," Zoé said, her head bowed, as the painful memory for her dead mother churned within her, like an old wound on a rainy day.

Madame smiled at her and moved her thick black curls away from her face. "We are sending for your Father. He should be here within two days. Comte La Roque is ready to discuss the terms of his betrothal to Marianne. I want you to be very encouraging to Marianne. She is your sister, after all."

Disconcerted, Zoé crossed her arms and pointedly looked away. Why was Madame asking her to support Marianne? What did it matter to her what she thought? She met Madame's cooling stare and realized that her stepmother was hiding something. The best way to handle Madame was with obedience, but they both knew that Zoé would not allow herself to be controlled.

The door opened and a chambermaid entered, carrying two large pitchers of steamy water.

Madame gave Zoé one last reminder to get dressed. "Breakfast shall be served soon."

Zoé watched her go and felt a sense of relief. Her bottom lip, however, acknowledged her anger and disappointment. She was hurt by La Roque's seduction, and her devastation deepened at the knowledge that he wanted her sister over her. But the most painful was her own lack of control, for she wanted him even more.

"Your bath is ready, *mademoiselle*," said the maid.

Zoé fixed her gaze on the ceiling and took a deep breath to still her racing heart as she got up. She went to the basin and looked into the oval antique mirror hanging over it. She suspected that Madame and Marianne saw something in her, but didn't know what it was. She was forever changed now. In the midst of her panic she stopped to smile at her image. She grabbed her long curly locks, pinned them up, and turned her face from side to side. She was indeed different and it was her secret. Hers, and Gianelli's.

La Roque entered his drawing room and looked up. Before him stood his college friend, Flynn Sheridan, gazing thoughtfully into the fireplace. They had attended the Sorbonne together, and then later fought side by side in what had come to be called the War of 1812. Sheridan was compelled to fight by family obligation and honor; La Roque lied about his age and joined for the camaraderie and adventure, and not least, because the fighting brought him well beyond the control of his overbearing father.

The sulfuric smell of gunpowder and cannon blast echoed in his mind as La Roque recalled the fight to free the Americas of British tyranny. Though neither side officially won, the war did serve to make men of them both.

"Well look what the trade winds blew in!"

Sheridan turned around, smiling. "Bloody hell, if it isn't the Count himself!"

The two men gave each other a fraternal hug. It had been two years since they'd seen one another.

"Your letters didn't speak of a visit? How long is your stay? How was your voyage?" La Roque spoke with barely contained excitement, patting Sheridan on the shoulder.

"In a word, horrid. Many weeks at sea are enough to drive any man crazy. I'm starved for a hot bath and an even warmer woman."

Sheridan tossed his top hat to the couch and pulled off his gloves. Equal in height and build to La Roque, Sheridan's brownish-blonde hair was cut short at the nape, leaving a head of curly locks and long sideburns. His eyes were dark and deeply set. Some saw in them an expression of wisdom that he used to his advantage. But others, colleagues and friends alike, saw the hardness and cruelty endemic to those who dealt in the slave trade and reveled in human suffering.

Sheridan gripped La Roque by the shoulders and gave him a good once over. "You look good, old man. You haven't changed since we last crossed paths."

Gérard entered with a silver tray and coffee service. La Roque stepped over to the immense fireplace and leaned against its stone mantle. "You didn't answer, how long will you be visiting this time? Or dare I venture to guess, you're just passing through?"

"I am thinking of staying for a sort. A competent fellow is overseeing my plantation and, as I said earlier, I'm in need of, shall we say, French company? Someone unlike those virtuous Southern belles, who long to lead me to the altar and rob me of bachelorhood, would serve me well."

La Roque laughed. Like him, Sheridan was a notorious playboy. Their exploits in England years ago would have caused both their mothers to faint.

"Please, stay as long as you like. Tell me, whatever became of that land purchase you last wrote of?"

"Andrew Jackson, that's what!" Sheridan's contemptuous tone was unmistakable. His jaw muscles clenched and his eyes were hooded under a scowling golden brow. La Roque detected the flame of his friend's unmistakable temper simmering within that gaze.

"We put him in office to release Carolina from the burden of those unjust tariffs after the war. Jackson and his administration refuse to hear our concerns. Now we have Adams, who thinks the South can easily be ignored."

La Roque raised an eyebrow in amusement. "Well, we both know you won't be ignored."

Sheridan smirked. "Things are changing friend; we will nullify and reclaim the glory of the Carolinas. John Adams, and his Congress, will have to deal with South Carolina on her own terms!"

Sheridan made himself comfortable in one of the richly brocaded armchairs that furnished the room and accepted a cup of coffee from Gérard.

"Therefore, I do have some business dealings I'd like to talk to you about," Sheridan said.

"I'll wager you do," La Roque said. "But first we'll have breakfast. I have guests."

"I didn't mean to intrude."

"No intrusion," La Roque said with a wave of his hand. "No intrusion. You've always been welcome to treat this as your home. You know that."

Sheridan gave him a nod of gratitude.

"And these guests, do I know them?"

"I don't think so."

"That's interesting. Exactly what type of guests are they?"

"The kind you are most fond of," replied La Roque, amused.

Sheridan laughed. "I just love France!"

"I know you do." La Roque laughed, an oddly primitive warning sounding in his brain. Yes, he was glad to see Sheridan, but he also knew he'd have to keep an eye on him with the two lovelies in the house.

Zoé walked into Marianne's room, caught between love and resentment. Each morning, she had to tend to herself and deal with her corset on her own, but Marianne had to be dressed.

If I didn't love her so much, Zoé thought, I wouldn't be so accommodating.

Marianne sat before her vanity. Seeing her sister's reflection, she turned around.

"Oh, how I like your hair, Zoé!"

Zoé had pinned her locks up on the right side of her head, leaving some curls to cascade around her face. She wore another glossy calamanco, emerald-green gown that hugged her waist and pushed her breasts upward. The center back of the corset showcased the braided stitched-down pleats that connected with puffed fabric at her lower waistline. The gown swelled slightly from her hips before flowing to the floor. Emerald jeweled teardrops dangled from her ears. A matching pendant adorned her throat, with the green jewel resting at the crease of her breasts. She was a striking woman, and she knew it. She wanted La Roque to see it, too. To see what he had rejected.

"Can you help me, please?" Marianne asked.

She turned around, showing her back. Zoé grabbed up of the strings of Marianne's corset. The girl took hold of the bedpost and blew out a deep breath. As Zoé pulled the lacing tighter, her sister whimpered at the pressure. She tried to be gentle and alleviate some of the pain. Zoé helped Marianne into her gown and fastened it. Marianne glanced at herself in the mirror and was reminded of her sleep-tousled hair. She turned to Zoé.

"Please arrange my hair like yours! I want it exactly like yours!"

"*Bien*," Zoé smiled. "I'll make it even better than mine."

At the vanity, she picked up one of their iron rods and ran it over the flame of a candle. Working quickly, she tightened

Marianne's curls and then neatly tamed her sister's hair into a roll, tucked it and pinned it to her head, allowing her locks to fall down one side of her face.

Marianne was delighted. "It's exquisite!"

"Just like you!" Zoé said.

Marianne giggled. She took her rouge from her vanity case and applied it with helpful tips from Zoé. Once done, Marianne puckered her lips at the sight of her own perfection before slipping on her shoes. Her dress, similar to Zoé's, was a pale yellow, which complimented her ivory skin and golden locks. They were the exact image of each other in breeding and poise. Marianne grabbed Zoé's hand and pulled her through the door, proceeding to the morning room.

Marianne was anxious to see her future husband. But Zoé felt a knot forming in her stomach at the very thought. How could she have been so foolish? And now, how could she manage to keep it a secret?

She let Marianne lead her to the dining room with a deepening sense of dread. The sound of a stranger's voice reached them as they came down the stairs. His French was fluent but accented. From what she could gather, he was engaging in a robust accounting of his exploits and travels. Specifically, he was complaining about slave rebellions, saying that they had been "springing up more and more since the uprising of the abolitionists." Northern abolitionists were infiltrating respectable Southern homes and helping Negroes escape. Andrew Jackson's second election to the Presidency promised to bring about prosperity for Southern gentlemen, but the stranger held out little hope that Adams' Presidency would do what Jackson's had failed to do.

With a chill, Zoé realized that the man lived in the States — and that he was a slave trader.

Gérard stood at the threshold of the dining room. The sisters paused for him to announce them formally.

Zoé's sense of unease sharpened. Without having seen him, she already knew that the stranger, whoever he was, was no friend to people like her, people of a darker hue. Was this the kind of person that La Roque welcomed into his home? Again, she scolded herself for ever having dared hope, even for a split second that—

"Zoé?" Marianne gazed at her sister with concern. "*Viens.* We must enter."

Zoé took a deep breath, forced a smile and stepped inside behind Marianne.

She felt the stranger's gaze. She saw his eyes rake over her, shift calculatingly to Marianne, and then shift back to her.

His interest was obvious in the way he lowered his cup, the way his eyes momentarily widened and the way his mouth went slack. He reminded her of a hungry dog.

She glanced at La Roque and saw that he was staring at her, too, but with a slight smile. She felt a flash of anger. How dare he smile at her, after he'd seduced her the night before?

Madame was smiling at them nervously, waiting for them to be seated. Gérard led the two girls to empty places next to each other at the dining table.

"*Mesdemoiselles*, I trust that your night was a pleasant one," said La Roque, looking at Marianne first, then Zoé.

"I have had better nights," Zoé said with a direct look.

Madame's gaze shifted between Zoé and La Roque, and her eyes narrowed. Zoé wished she had not spoken.

"I slept very well, *merci*," Marianne said with a bright smile.

La Roque gave her a polite nod. By then, his attention was on Sheridan, whose gaze had never left Zoé. La Roque cleared his throat rather loudly and Sheridan blinked, as though he'd been released from a spell.

"Mademoiselle Marianne Bouchard and Mademoiselle Zoé Bouchard , may I present my old schoolmate, Flynn Sheridan," La Roque said, gesturing across the table toward his guest. "He's visiting from America."

Zoé's anger intensified. So it was true. This guest was a man who made his money from human suffering. And La Roque had close ties to him. She despised slave traders.

She felt Sheridan's hot gaze sweep her again. No doubt it wasn't just lust on his mind—but lust and money. She met his look with a glare.

Marianne gave him a dimpled smile. "It is a pleasure, *monsieur*."

Madame looked at Zoé, who forced a smile but gave only a nod.

"I must say, *mesdemoiselles*, that the pleasure is all mine," he said with a confident charm.

La Roque nodded to Gérard and the staff brought in breakfast. As Zoé ate, listening to the conversation at the table, she was ever aware of Sheridan's unwanted stares. He kept flashing her that perfect smile, but his eyes reflected less than honorable intentions. She could not wait for the meal to end.

Meanwhile, she watched Marianne flirt with La Roque. Marianne's interest was evident as she seemed amused at even the slightest conversation. For her part, Madame reminded them of all of Marianne's exceptional qualities. La Roque was amused as well, and for a while, even Sheridan's attention shifted to the younger girl. Zoé was grateful.

When breakfast was over, La Roque invited everyone to the conservatory to see the exotic plants he had imported from all over the world. To Zoé, it sounded like the plants bloomed only for his amusement. Marianne giggled with excitement, but Zoé asked to be excused. La Roque's face reflected his disappointment. He tried to object, but Madame intervened.

"Zoé hasn't been feeling well today, *mon seigneur*. I think it best that she lies down."

Zoé rose, offering a polite curtsey to her host, and turned to leave. Before she could take two steps, Sheridan also stood and excused himself as well. He expressed a need to unpack and rest after the exhausting voyage, but Zoé was aware of the look he gave her. *Mon Dieu*, he wouldn't follow her or try anything with everyone in the château, or would he? Should she stay back and wait with the others? But she'd already excused herself and the fact was she couldn't afford to stay. She had to get back to her room and dispose of those soiled linens. If the maids found them, they would tell her stepmother.

She caught La Roque looking at her and, for a hope-filled moment, thought she read not lust, but concern. He glanced at Sheridan, then back at her, and opened his mouth to say something, but Marianne reached for his arm.

"Please show me the flowers," she said. "I'm dying to see them."

He smiled at her and Zoé saw Madame's small look of triumph. Without another word, Zoé left the room, her head held high and her heart aching. Her fate was sealed. La Roque now had eyes only for her sister. Obviously, what she herself had given him the night before meant nothing. How could she have made such a terrible mistake in judgment?

In the cold light of that moment, she saw that she had not only betrayed herself, but Marianne, and risked what little security she had in the Bouchard household. The only chance she had left was to protect her secret.

She sensed footsteps behind her. It was Sheridan. Unease gripped her. She looked straight ahead, refusing to slow down or acknowledge him. The sound of the footsteps disappeared as she passed through the grand entryway and turned toward for the stairs. She didn't dare glance back. If Sheridan was still following her, then he might take it as an opportunity to speak. She had just reached the bottom of the stairs when she heard him call out to her. She pretended not to have heard him and put her foot on the first step.

"*Mademoiselle!*"

It was no use. The voice came from just behind her. She turned around and said, "*Oui, monsieur?*" Her voice was cold and polite and her tone crisp. But he was so certain of his charm that her hostility had little or no effect on him.

"I was hoping for a moment," he said.

"I am sorry, *monsieur*, but I feel faint this morning. I would like to retire."

Without waiting for him to respond, she started up the stairs. He grabbed her by the elbow and yanked her back down.

"I said I want a moment," he said, "and I won't take no for an answer."

Zoé wrenched herself away and bared her teeth. "I am not some Negress on your plantation. Your wants are of no interest to me!"

He laughed at her. "You are feisty, aren't you?" He brushed his fingertips against her long dark curls. "And oh, so beautiful."

Zoé grabbed the front of her dress and fled up the stairs. All she wanted to do was put as much distance as possible between them. Three-quarters of the way up, she paused to catch her breath, aware that she heard no footsteps behind her. She chanced a glance and saw that he had not even attempted to follow her. He was still standing at the foot of the stairs, smirking at her, looking amused and confident. She felt a surge of both relief and anger. She hated his expression and she hated what she thought it meant. Yes, she'd gotten away, but only for now. She was glad he wasn't going to chase her. Why should he bother? Men like him always believed they could have whatever they wanted, whenever they wanted it.

But he was wrong, she told herself. When it came to her, he was very wrong.

Her thoughts returned to the linens in her room, of both the hurt they stood for and the danger they posed. She ran up the remaining stairs and rushed down the hall to her room. She hurried in and knelt at the side of the bed, the ends of her corset stays pressing uncomfortably against her upper thighs. She reached under the heavy bed skirt but didn't feel the sheets. So she lifted the skirt, bent down and peered under the bed.

There was nothing there.

Fighting a rising panic, she got to her feet and brushed off her skirt. What was the maid's name? Sweet, merciful God, what was it? She couldn't remember.

She sat on the bed, buried her face in her hands and wept. She couldn't hold it any longer. She had made a horrible mistake. The pain of being used and then rejected was bad enough, but now she faced the prospect of losing everything. If Father found out what she'd done, he would be more than upset. He might well ship her away.

"She weeps?"

Sheridan stood in her doorway. Fear chilled her. She got to her feet and wiped away her tears.

"What are you doing here? What do you want?"

He entered and closed the door behind him. "You owe me an apology," he said.

"I owe you nothing. Leave this room!"

That patronizing smirk reappeared. "Now is that any way to speak to a gentleman? I just want to be your friend."

"I don't need friends, *monsieur*. Now, please go, or I shall scream."

He shook his head. "Tsk, tsk, tsk. That's what's wrong with this country. It has spoiled you niggers into thinking that you matter. The truth is that you're nothing but a dressed-up darkie playing at being a lady. So let's not forget your place."

Zoé's hurt and fear dissolved in a rush of fury. She'd met men like him before. Men who were determined to intimidate her—break her—and she'd decided never to let them get away with it. She regarded him with contempt.

"You're wrong, *monsieur*. I know my place. It's you who don't know yours. You aren't in America—far from it—and you have no power over me. Indeed, my father will have you charged if you dare lay one hand on me."

A dark flush rose from his collar to suffuse his face. Probably, no woman, black or white, had ever spoken to him that way. His hands tightened into fists, but he looked unsure. She could see he wanted her, wanted her badly, but he didn't know where to start: to take her first and then beat her, or beat her and then take her. Either way, he meant to crush her. Men like him, weak men, were drawn to her strength of spirit, but not because they appreciated it. They were fascinated but fearful of it. They needed to dominate and destroy it. His next words were no surprise.

"My, my," he licked his lips. "You're a confused girl. But I like it. Yes, I like such fire and wit."

"I have no interest in your likes or dislikes! Get out!"

Instead of leaving, he approached her. She stood firm. Their faces were only inches apart.

"You smell of honey," he said. "And your skin… it's so smooth."

He gazed down at the gently swelling curves of her breasts, watching as they rose and fell, and then raised his gaze to meet hers. He searched her face and seemed to realize something.

"It isn't just dramatics, is it? You would rather die than let me have you?"

She stared at him.

"Where are you from?" he asked. "Where were you born?"

Furious, she said nothing.

He chuckled and touched one of the rich, dark curls that fell across her shoulder. For a moment, they stood there, she holding her breath, he enjoying the silky feel of the tendril as it curled around his finger.

"Your hair," he said, "it's very soft. Then again, I bet you're soft all over, aren't you?"

He reached to cup one breast. She folded her arms across her chest, blocking him. The smirk on his face revealed his amusement at her resolve. Leaning closer, he nuzzled her cheek. She pulled away with a shudder.

"Are you cold?" he whispered. "Of course you are, because you don't know heat. I shall show you."

She glared at him, lowered arms and clenched her small hands into fists. He smiled at her as though she were merely a stubborn child and let go of her hair.

"I shall speak to your mistress," he said. "I'm certain that she and I could come to terms—"

"You shall be disappointed, *monsieur*. You will find no price on me."

"I—"

The door swung open and Sheridan turned around, apparently ready to scold some unfortunate servant for having interrupted him at his fun. He was shocked to see La Roque.

The count looked from one to the other. "What goes on here?" He looked at Zoé.

"I was just getting to know your houseguest. She's lovely."

He gave her one last glance and stepped away from her. Zoé stared straight ahead, as determined to hide her relief as she had been to mask her fear.

La Roque's eyes were dark with suspicion and his smile forced. "The ladies are in the conservatory. I suggest you join them."

Sheridan gave La Roque a nod, then turned on his heel and walked out. La Roque watched him go before turning back to Zoé.

"Are you well?"

She blinked back a tear and glared at him. "Why should it be of interest to you?"

"What do you mean?"

"You know what it means."

He shifted his stance uncomfortably. She turned away from him but could feel his presence as he approached her.

"You rejected me," he said. "What was I supposed to do?"

She turned around angrily, but before she could speak, he pulled her into his arms and kissed her. She loved the taste of him and returned his amorous caresses. Then she remembered. She pushed him away and spoke to him, shaking with anger.

"Last night, you take me to your bed and this morning you propose to my sister. How dare you!"

He winced. "But I'm not marrying your sister, Zoé, not unless you come along as the prize."

Zoé dropped her hand from her mouth, stunned. "What?"

"I have summoned your father *for you*. I want *you*."

"My father would never agree to such an arrangement." She was disgusted.

He didn't answer, just studied her. She thought she saw a hint of sadness in his eyes, a trace of world-weariness. His voice was indeed tired when he spoke, but it was a tiredness that came from the soul.

"Everyone has a price," he said, "even your father."

His words chilled her. Moments before he had embraced her and now he displayed the coldness of his friend, Monsieur Sheridan. La Roque had already taken something he did not appreciate but could never return. Now he threatened to strip her of what she held most dear: her trust in her father and belief in his love. Her father was her refuge, the source of her strength. His was a reassuring voice in a world that said her only value was as a mistress for lustful, insatiable men. And now La Roque wanted her to doubt him.

"I shall never let you near me again! Never!"

He paused in the doorway and smiled. "You may have no choice," he said with a conspiratorial wink before walking away.

Zoé rubbed her forehead and closed her eyes. What had she gotten herself into? How would she get out of it?

The sheets! Sheridan's intrusion had driven them from her mind. Worse, it had cost her time. She'd have to find that maid and quick! Once her father arrived, she would leave with him, but first she had to make sure that no one knew what had happened between her and La Roque.

In the conservatory, Madame Bouchard was enjoying the witty exchange between her daughter and Flynn Sheridan. She disliked and distrusted him on instinct, but she was proud of the way Marianne held her own against him. From the corner of her eye, she saw a young chambermaid enter and wondered what she was up to. She was surprised when the girl made her way across the room and sidled up next to her.

"*Madame,* may I speak with you?"

The older woman raised an eyebrow. In her household, servants did not speak unless they'd been spoken to. It surprised her to learn that it might be different in a household as illustrious as La Roque's.

"Oui? Qu'est-ce qui se passe?" Yes, what is it?"

"May I show you?"

Madame Bouchard's expression of surprise deepened into puzzlement. *"Bien.* But make it quick."

Geneviève led Madame out to the hall. There the maid went to a wicker laundry basket and withdrew a soiled white nightgown.

"I am sorry, but I found this gown and some soiled linen in your daughter's room."

Madame Bouchard took the linens and fingered them. She read the stains as though she were reading a book. Their meaning was clear. Her face flushed with anger. "Which daughter?" Both Marianne and Zoé had gowns like this one.

"La Mûlatresse."

Madame felt a wave of relief followed closely by a rush of anger. "Who knows of this?"

"No one."

"Bien. Take these to my room. Do not wash them." Madame Bouchard gave the chambermaid a suspicious look. This slip of a girl had betrayed the master of her house. Why?

"What's your name?" she asked.

"Geneviève."

"And you've been with *le Comte* for how long?"

"Two years."

"He's been a good master?"

Geneviève looked at her with surprise. "*Bien sûr, madame.*"

"And this is how you repay him?"

A blush turned the girl's cheeks a bright pink. She averted her eyes.

Madame considered her. She could imagine any number of reasons why the girl might have risked such a ploy. Perhaps it was jealousy, or maybe the hope of gaining favor with the future mistress of the manor. Madame decided that, for the moment at least, the reason didn't matter. What did matter was the girl's sense of discretion.

Like magic, two coins appeared in Madame's hand. She handed the linens back to Geneviève and in the same smooth motion slipped the coins into the maid's palm.

The girl's face lit up. "*Oh, merci!*" She started to tuck the money away, but Madame gripped her by her wrist.

"You shall keep this to yourself," she whispered. "Or else. Do you understand?"

ZOÉ

Geneviève swallowed hard. "*Naturellement.* You may trust in me."

Madame smiled grimly and let her go. Geneviève gave a grateful curtsey and the coins disappeared into the deep folds of her skirt.

Madame Bouchard dismissed the girl with a nod, her thoughts already elsewhere. This was a disaster. If—

La Roque came down the hall. She was instantly suspicious. Had he been upstairs with Zoé? Another assignation? Anger and indignation got in the way of her good sense. She confronted him.

"*Mon seigneur,* may I have a word?"

Looking puzzled, he agreed and indicated the open entrance to the drawing room.

Once inside, he closed the door behind them. She turned on him, so furious that she could barely get out her words.

"My daughter, Zoé... Did you—I mean, have you...?"

La Roque narrowed his eyes. "Have I *what?*"

The intense blue flames of his eyes unsettled her. She cleared her throat, drew herself up and began again.

"This morning, you said you wanted to see my husband with regard to my daughter. I believed that you were speaking of Marianne, but now I must wonder. Just what are your intentions?"

80

La Roque rubbed his trimmed beard. "With all due respect, my intentions will be explained to your husband soon enough."

So it was true. He had bedded Zoé and now he wanted to take that bastard child over her precious Marianne.

"You couldn't possibly hope to have a future with her," Madame blurted out. "She's a *mûlatresse*!"

She took bitter pleasure in his stunned expression, but if she thought he would back down, she was mistaken. He recovered quickly.

"But she is your daughter, too. Is she not just a companion? Are you now saying that she is someone less? Does your husband share that sentiment?"

Madame blinked, flustered. "She has no dowry. When her father hears of what she has done, she'll be lucky if he doesn't ship her off to America."

La Roque's anger was cold and swift. "*Attendez.* What did or did not happen between your *daughter* and me is a matter for discussion with your husband and not you."

"But—"

"I strongly suggest that you forget this conversation until then."

"I—"

"If you choose to pursue this matter and admonish her in any way, then I shall have to share with your husband how intrusive you were in his affairs. *Comprenez?*"

She was silent.

His jaw clenched. "I repeat. Do you understand?"

Her face revealed her humiliation. "*Oui.*"

He strode to the door, opened it and stood aside. She marched past him, her head held high, her back stiff. He followed. They headed back to the conservatory, with him a step behind her, tense and silent.

Seething, she thought of Zoé. No doubt the girl had planned this all along. As for La Roque—she glanced at his handsome profile. He had just proven that despite his wealth, culture and finesse, he was like any other man: foolish when it came to dark flesh.

Madame scolded herself. She should have anticipated the possibility of such a development. Thank goodness for that treacherous little maid. She'd make sure Marianne fired her. It was dangerous to have someone so disloyal in the household. But that was the future. It was the present that counted, and, for now, matters looked grim.

This, however, was not the end of it. No, she promised herself. This battle wasn't lost. Not yet, not by a long shot.

Zoé made her way to the lower west wing of the estate where the washing and cooking was done. The *femme de charge* over the staff saw her come through the door and approached.

"Yes, *mademoiselle*. May I be of assistance?" she asked.

The woman's tone was sharp and irritated. It was inappropriate when speaking to someone of her social standing. If Zoé had been in her normal state of mind, she would've said something cutting to put the woman in her place, but she was upset and had no energy for a verbal duel.

"I was looking for the chambermaid who cleaned my room."

The mistress's gaze was knowing. "Why? Is there something wrong?"

Zoé saw the other maids smirking and snickering at her. She flushed, realizing what that meant. She couldn't very well ask for the sheets now. Looking over to the right, she saw a pile of linen being prepared for the wash. With a sigh, she said, "No, everything is well," and turned to leave.

Once outside the quarters, she closed the door and leaned against it. If the sheets were about to be washed, then nothing more could come of it. She was panicking for nothing. She headed down the dark corridor and climbed the stairs, holding on to her long skirt. There was nothing to fear. She had to stop being so paranoid. Soon Father would come, and she could leave this place and her secret indiscretion behind.

Wandering the halls, she happened upon the conservatory. Entering, she saw Marianne smiling at something Monsieur Sheridan had said. Madame caught Zoé looking in and locked eyes with her. Zoé recoiled, for the look her stepmother had given her was murderous. She swallowed and offered a weak smile, hoping that Madame's anger was just from her disappearing act.

"Glad that you could join us," La Roque said, coming up behind her.

Zoé jumped and turned to see him standing close. It unnerved her further to realize how his presence intimidated her and provoked memories of his illicit touch. She flashed a half-smile.

"I'm feeling better," she said and moved away, toward Madame. Marianne saw her and excused herself from Sheridan, who cut his eyes at Zoé.

"Sister, we must ask Father to let us visit America soon," Marianne said. "Monsieur Sheridan has been telling me some of the most interesting tales."

Zoé felt Sheridan's gaze, but ignored it and focused on Marianne. "I don't want to go to America," she said, drawing Marianne away.

"Are you still sick?" Marianne asked.

"No," Zoé said with a flash of annoyance. "Would you quit saying that I'm sick!"

"I'm sorry. I didn't mean to upset you."

Zoé regretted her sharp tone. "Non, ma petite. *C'est moi qui dois m'excuser.* You've done nothing wrong."

Marianne squeezed her hand as their mother approached. Madame's stern expression reawakened Zoé's fear. With arms folded across her heavy bosom, Madame fixed her with a stony glare.

"Well, someone looks better."

"Yes, I am feeling better."

"Of course you are."

Zoé thought it better to remain silent. She didn't understand Madame's sudden cynicism and feared that the wrong response—perhaps, any response at this point—might further inflame her stepmother's anger.

La Roque joined them, his hands clasped behind his back. "Would you like to go for a ride? I think Mademoiselle Marianne said she did so for sport."

Marianne clapped her hands. "*Oui,* we both would love to!"

Zoé said nothing. She kept glancing at Madame, wondering.

"Very well," La Roque said. "Monsieur Sheridan and I would like to take you two for a ride, along with you Madame of course. But I fear you may be too exhausted to join us? Am I right?"

"*Naturellement,*" Madame said with a smile. "The girls would love to see your land. And again you are very perceptive; I think I shall retire to a nap." She turned to them both. "Make sure to be back at a decent hour."

Zoé and Marianne nodded. Madame looked at Zoé.

"When you return, Zoé, I would like a word with you."

"*Oui, Madame,*" Zoé curtsied.

La Roque gave Madame a pointed look. She responded with a polite curtsey, and then walked out. La Roque glanced at Zoé, and then turned to Sheridan.

"Looks like we're set to be their guides," said La Roque. "You ride with Marianne, and I shall take Zoé."

Marianne spoke up. "*Mon seigneur,* I am sure my sister prefers to ride with *Monsieur* Sheridan. Wouldn't you, Zoé?" She gave Zoé a hopeful look.

"Nonsense," said La Roque. "I say how we ride. Shall we?"

Marianne stuck out her lower lip, but she accepted Sheridan's elbow, wrapped her arm around his and allowed him to lead her out. Zoé watched them leave, then turned on La Roque. She kept her voice to a whisper and spoke through clenched teeth.

"Why are you doing this?"

"Because I want to... and because you wish the same."

"I want you to stop."

La Roque's response was to take her by the arm and escort her out to the stables. She tried to wrench her arm free, but he held her fast. Finally, she gave up.

Marianne glared at her as they entered the stables. Zoé sent her an apologetic smile, at which Marianne turned up her nose and looked away.

What am I going to do? Zoé wondered. She had to stop La Roque's flirtations. Soon, Madame and Marianne would become suspicious. They'd put it together and she'd be exposed. She just couldn't stand much more of this worry. She just wasn't good at this kind of charade.

La Roque asked that the Palominos be brought out and saddled. While waiting, La Roque honored his guests with a short tour around the stable, proudly displaying his stock. The horses were magnificent specimens with lean muscles and gleaming coats. But Sheridan teased his old friend, joking that La Roque's horses were emaciated compared to his own proud stock in Carolina.

"Emaciated?" La Roque repeated. "Oh, you mean not slow and potbellied? Like horses grown fat and lazy off plantation living?"

Zoé thought she caught a flash of anger in Sheridan's eyes, but his reply showed nothing but smooth and polished humor. La Roque responded in kind and the jest continued. Zoé realized that this exchange of friendly insults was part of their friendship, a friendship that had endured for years. At the thought of their many years of brotherhood, her attention went to her sister, who had openly ignored Zoé except to glare at her every now and then. Marianne had hung behind and now stood a couple of stalls back, rubbing the nose of a friendly mare. Zoé approached her.

"Marianne," she began, "I didn't mean to——"

"Don't apologize. He was just being polite to you. We both know that he's sending for Father for *me*."

Marianne's words hurt, as they were meant to.

"*Trés bien,*" Zoé said. She would show her spoiled little sister what it meant to be desired as a woman. Glancing up, she saw that La Roque paused to give a young filly some extra attention, while Sheridan leaned indolently against an empty stall. Zoé turned from Marianne, went up to La Roque and slipped her arm around his.

"That's a lovely horse," she said.

He smiled down at her. "Not as lovely as you."

Zoé glanced back at Marianne, who stood there, pouting. Zoé enjoyed a small sense of victory, but it was fleeting. Her inner alarm bells went off as the creature posing as a gentleman walked over to Marianne and murmured something in her ear.

Marianne smiled up at him. "Keep me close," she giggled. "It's the best way to ride."

"Never fear. I shall." Sheridan slipped an arm around Marianne's waist. "I most certainly shall."

Zoé disliked the way Sheridan looked at Marianne. He was not to be trusted. She started to say something, but before she could utter a warning, the horses were brought out.

La Roque placed his gloved hands around Zoé's tiny waist. There was no hesitation or clumsiness in his touch as he stepped up on the mounting block to give her a lift. She slid smoothly into the leather saddle, seating herself sidewise and grimacing from the forbidden aches of their passionate night. He gave her another conspiratorial wink, understanding her discomfort, and then in one deft move, climbed into the saddle to sit snugly behind her. Her breath caught at the sense of his closeness. *If only...*

Her gaze fixed on her sister, perched with Sheridan. He saw Zoé's look and smirked.

Zoé whispered over her shoulder to La Roque. "Will she be safe with him?" She felt him turn to give them a quick glance.

"Of course!" he said.

"But—"

He cut her off, kicking his heels for the horse to go. Zoé rested her hands on the raised pommel as La Roque guided the animal out onto his land. She enjoyed the protective sensation of having his strong arms around her. Glancing back over her shoulder, she saw Marianne giggling, her curls blowing loosely from under her bonnet. As long as the four of them stayed together, Marianne would be safe.

"Where are we going?" she asked.

"It's a surprise," he said, his face close to hers.

Once again, the heat between them ignited. She twisted around to look into his blue eyes and felt the same thrill of illicit desire she'd experienced when she'd stood naked in his room. The citrus scent of his aftershave engulfed her. He was even more stunningly virile than she remembered.

Turning her face from his, she concentrated on the scenery. Up ahead was a forest. It looked thick and dark and impenetrable. But, for now, the sun shone on her face and a breeze teased her with La Roque's heady scent. Slowly, she relaxed back into his arms and leaned against him. Closing her eyes, she gave into memories of those precious moments of lying beneath him as he made love to her.

Her dreams merged with reality, the past with the present, as she felt his right hand move upward on her tight bodice and cup the curve of her breast. His touch was firm and persuasive. She tensed, but then realized that since they rode ahead of Marianne, his caress did not put them in danger of being exposed.

"You tempt me," he whispered through the locks of her hair. "I want so much to finish what we started."

She swallowed, inwardly renewing her pledge to resist him, but making little overt effort to avoid his touch.

She grew curious as they approached what seemed to be an old cottage. Half of the cottage looked to be destroyed by fire, but the other half stood tall.

"What is that?" she asked pointing to the structure.

"You shall see."

La Roque steered the mare toward the ruins. He maneuvered the horse around the side, and then rode through a gaping hole at the back of the cottage. Inside the frame of the cottage, the ground was covered with charred, unrecognizable debris. La Roque steered the horse away from the destruction, circling the inside perimeter, so as to not upset the animal. Zoé took in everything, amazed. The roof was missing, but a lot of the walls remained, along with scorched furnishings. Zoé noted how La Roque guided the horse through the rubble with a practiced hand. He seemed at ease in this strange place. Had he known the people who lived here? Who were they and did they survive what must have been a horrible fire?

She glanced back to check on Marianne and saw the same amazement on her sister's face. She also saw that Sheridan had placed his hand rather provocatively around Marianne's waist. She wanted that animal away from her sister.

"May we get down and explore?" she asked, hoping to free Marianne from Sheridan's grip.

"Of course," La Roque said.

He brought the horse to a halt, and Zoé turned to smile at him in thanks. The words died on her lips, however. Instead, her breath caught at the desire in his eyes. For a moment, she thought he would kiss her right there, out in the open, in front of the others.

The moment passed and he climbed down. Then he reached up for her and she slid down into his arms, allowing him to pull her close. For two seconds, their faces were only a finger's width apart and she feared that *she* might kiss him.

"*Merci*," she said and stepped away, out of his reach.

Looking over at Marianne, she saw that Sheridan had performed the same maneuver, but instead of putting distance between them, her sister had giggled and remained in his arms.

Zoé held up her skirt to avoid the rubble and walked over to her sister. "May we speak?" she said under her breath.

Sheridan raised an eyebrow.

Marianne frowned. "What is it?"

Zoé ignored Sheridan, grabbed Marianne by the arm, and drew her to one side. Sheridan walked his horse over to where La Roque stood, tying his mare down. Marianne's porcelain complexion blushed a deep pink as she glanced over at them. She snatched her arm away from Zoé.

"Why must you embarrass me so?"

"You're embarrassing yourself. If you want La Roque, you can't flirt with his friend."

Marianne glared at her. "You mean the way you flirt with him?"

"I've told you, there is nothing between us. When Papa comes, I will leave." Zoé saw that Marianne was too angry to listen to reason.

"Please," Zoé begged. "You have to be smart."

Marianne took a step back. She whispered in a rush of words. "He hasn't looked twice at me," she said bitterly. "He wants you. Monsieur Sheridan, however, knows how to appreciate a lady." With that, she walked off in a huff.

Zoé started to call after her, but then saw how the two men were watching and thought better of it. She would simply have to keep an eye on Marianne.

"What is this place?" Marianne asked, looking around.

"It belonged to a count. He built it for his mistress," La Roque said, giving Zoé a meaningful glance.

Her lips tightened and her eyes returned a warning. He either didn't understand her meaning or chose to ignore it.

"What do you think of it, Zoé? In its day, it was quite grand."

Everyone turned to her, and she blushed. Eyes on La Roque, she said, "Well, apparently the mistress didn't think much of it if she burned it down."

Marianne looked back at La Roque. "*Did* she burn it down?"

He ran his gloved hand across the burnt remains of what might've been a table.

"The count burned it down, with her in it. Their love was a forbidden one. He couldn't have married her, but he couldn't abide the idea of another man having her. While he spent many a night with his wife and family, Marcela was left to roam the cottage alone. A gamekeeper observed her loneliness, and befriended her. Let's just say that the friendship evolved into something more."

"Well, he should have burned it, if she was insolent enough to bring another man into his home," Sheridan snapped, walking around and kicking at debris.

Zoé glared at him. "If he bought it for her, it was her home, too."

Sheridan laughed. "Do you know what being a mistress is like? It's indentured servitude with a nice jeweled collar. This place was no more hers than it is yours."

Stung, Zoé was about to snap back with a ready reply when La Roque intervened.

"Enough," he said, silencing Sheridan. "You are right," he told Zoé. "It was hers, but when she agreed to be his mistress, she became his. No other man was to touch her. Do you understand?"

Zoé was aware of how the others watched them. She caught Marianne's frown and worried that they would have another scene later. So, Marianne's next words surprised her.

Marianne gave La Roque a level look. "My sister will never be any man's mistress," she said and went to stand next to Zoé.

Zoé looked at her and smiled.

La Roque spoke to Marianne, amused. "Of course not, excuse my rudeness. I just wanted you demoiselles to know the sad love story of Marcela—"

"Sounds more like a horror story to me," Zoé said.

She turned and walked away. She felt the sting of the way his tale mocked her and just wanted to escape all three of them. Walking around the corner, she took a deep breath.

Before her were the charred remnants of a portrait on the wall. It drew her. With a sidewise squint, she could make out the profile of a woman.

La Roque walked in behind her. "That's Marcela."

"I tire of your games."

He came up behind her, touching her hair. "I still desire you, Zoé."

"Well, I don't desire *you*."

"I think you do."

She turned to face him. "That's what it's all about for you—the chase. You toy with me for your own amusement, and I've let you. I find you rude, arrogant, and most unpleasant. I may not have much say in my life, but I do control my own heart. I could never give it to a man like you!"

Her words struck home. He flinched. Anger and hurt flashed in his eyes. Good. She had finally fought back. She was sick of men like him. Maybe she'd find herself an African to marry and have her black babies in peace. Then she could be valued as a person and not as a piece of meat.

She went to the charred fireplace and touched the burnt mantle. This place both saddened and angered her. It had been the site of a woman's miserable life and horrible death. Had La Roque thought he would change her mind by bringing her here?

Dusting off her hands, she said. "Now that we've seen this place, can you please take us back?"

La Roque walked over with his hands clasped behind his back. "Don't you want to know why the count gave into madness and killed Marcela?"

"Not really, no. Furthermore, you said she cheated on him. What more is there to say? Evidently his hold on her wasn't as strong as he thought."

"There's plenty to say. Her sleeping with another man wasn't the worst of it, though the mere thought of another man touching her was a catalyst."

He reached out to caress her, but she avoided the embrace. Ignoring that rejection, he continued.

"He killed her because, after all he tried to do to make her feel comfortable and loved, she never gave him her heart. That was what he desired most. " He muttered to himself, "Funny… a man wanting his mistress's heart."

"I can't blame her. You can't enslave a woman and then expect her love in return. Could you live like that? I think not."

He was thoughtful. "No, I suppose I couldn't." He looked at her. "But I don't want a slave, Zoé. I want a lover, a friend and someone to share my passions and regrets with, someone to give my heart to. You willingly gave me the most special part of you last night. I can't imagine you leaving my side to give the rest of your heart to someone else."

His eyes never left hers for an instant, and his yearning made her weak. She had to close her own to find the strength to resist him. It took an effort, but she did. Opening her eyes, she frowned at him.

"You can't be serious. You are trying to romanticize this?" She gestured at the surrounding destruction. "Don't you see what this was for her? What it did to him? How could this be what you want? You could have any woman. Why do you insist on these games?"

"I'm trying to tell you that this isn't all that I seek. I want more. You could be happy with this arrangement."

Zoé could barely contain her fury. "Contrary to what you think, *mon seigneur*, I deserve more than an 'arrangement.' I know that when you look at me, you see some well-bred *mûlatresse* whom you can put up in some tower and savor all your forbidden fantasies. I am partly to blame for that delusion. However, despite what transpired between us, I am much more than that. I am no fool. I know a man of your standing would never take me as your bride. But there is a gentleman out there somewhere who will. I will wait for him."

He took a moment to answer. When he spoke, it was with quiet determination.

"I won't let another man have you, not after touching the fire that blazes inside of you. Not after seeing your capacity to love. To know you is to want you. Is it my fault that I have fallen for your charms?"

"You have no say in the matter!"

She tried to walk past him, but he grabbed her by the arm and pulled her close to him.

"Then why did you give yourself to me?" he asked. "Do you think this dream man of yours will appreciate the fact that you are no longer intact?"

A new and ugly thought occurred to her.

"Is that why you took me to bed? To lessen my options?"

His eyes revealed uncertainty. Should he tell the truth?

"Yes," he said. "That was part of it. When I laid eyes on you, I knew I had to have you. Even now, standing near you, my blood boils. I have never had a woman bring this out in me."

Her anger was swift. "That is too bad, *mon seigneur.* Because now that we are clear on your intentions, I am more determined than ever to deny you." She brushed past him, intent on escaping the space they now shared.

"Your *Madame* knows!" he yelled, hoping to stop her from what she was determined to do.

Zoé froze. She looked back at him, terrified. "What?"

"She confronted me."

"You told her?"

"No, but she has her suspicions."

"*Mon Dieu!*" she whispered.

"I neither confirmed nor denied it. She has no proof, but you should be prepared in case she questions you."

Zoé put a hand to her heart. "This is awful. She will tell Papa, and then…"

"I shall protect you."

"No," she shook her head. "I will not be your slave."

"That's not what I meant."

He reached for her, but again she backed away.

"No!" she said and ran out into the burnt corridor. There, she saw Marianne, cornered by Monsieur Sheridan and looking frightened.

"*Chérie,*" Zoé cried. "Are you all right?"

Her heart nearly broke at the relief on Marianne's face.

"Yes," said the girl. She sidestepped Sheridan, who flashed Zoé another one of his hateful looks. Ignoring him, Zoé took Marianne's hand and led her outside. She wanted nothing more than to get away. But outside she stopped. They couldn't get back by themselves. They needed the men. They were at their mercy.

She felt dizzy. She let go of Marianne's hand and put her hands to her head.

"Zoé?" Marianne peered at her. "What's wrong? Are you ill?"

Zoé's thoughts spun. *Madame knew.* She would tell Father, and then everything would be over.

Maybe I can deny it, Zoé thought. Madame probably just suspects something, from the flirtation she's witnessed.

Breathing hard, she heard Marianne calling her name, but Zoé was too overwhelmed to respond.

Marianne grabbed Zoé's arm. "What is wrong with you?"

Zoé looked at her through tear-filled eyes. "I don't feel well," she whispered, and then turned and vomited on the ground.

Marianne stepped back, wide-eyed, as Zoé braced herself with her hand against the wall and retched. Zoé's nerves were so raw and her corset so tight that she could barely catch her breath between waves of nausea. Vaguely, she heard Marianne's terrified cries.

"Messieurs! Messieurs! Ma soeur est malade! Please help!"

Weakened, Zoé sagged against the wall. Then La Roque was there, helping her to her feet. Marianne had to release her hand and watch helpless.

"Are you all right?"

Pale, she wiped at her mouth. "Please take me back," she whispered.

La Roque picked her up and carried her to the horses. With her head resting on his broad shoulders, she felt safe. In some ways, this man was even stronger than her father. He could protect her, if he wanted to. She almost laughed at the thought. Protect her? He was more likely to harm her than any man she'd ever known.

From behind her, she heard Sheridan chuckle and ask Marianne, "Are you sure you want to go back? We can let them go and stay behind."

"My sister needs me," Marianne said.

Sheridan sighed in a manner that was loud and theatrical, and apparently heartfelt.

Hearing that, Zoé smiled. Even if she'd failed at protecting herself, she'd at least succeeded, even if only momentarily, in protecting her baby sister.

After arriving at the château, La Roque helped Zoé down from the horse. He searched her face for a chance to explain himself further, but she turned away and fled inside. Marianne chased after her sister, leaving both men to watch after them.

"So are you going to marry Marianne?" Sheridan asked.

"What?" La Roque replied, still looking after them.

"Marianne told me she was spoken for. Didn't figure you for the marrying type," Sheridan said slapping him on the back.

La Roque ignored him and left the horses to his footmen.

Sheridan followed. "Well, she's too excitable for me. Now that Negress: I think I might inquire about her. She would fit nicely in my world."

La Roque turned on him. "Don't speak of her. You are not to bother her. Are we clear?"

Sheridan frowned. "The Negress?"

"I know that in America you have no regard for *les gens de couleur*, but in my home you will show respect. If you can't, then your welcome has just ended."

Sheridan couldn't believe what he was hearing. "Are you seriously going to stand before me and defend that… that girl?"

La Roque turned back to Sheridan. "I won't tell you again. Keep away from her."

He walked away and Sheridan stared after him, enraged. The plantation owner would not be forced to respect a woman he could have bought and sold. His friend had lost his mind and that haughty Negress needed to be taught a lesson. Maybe he would approach the father and offer a handsome price for her. It would be pleasurable to own her, and it would teach his friend a lesson in manners. Smiling maliciously, he formulated his own plans for Mademoiselle Zoé.

Zoé rapped lightly on the door to Madame's room and then opened it just wide enough to peek in. She saw Madame lying on the bed with a cloth across her eyes. She took it that Madame was sleeping and started out again, but in that instant, Madame spoke.

"Enter."

Fear as cold as frost chilled Zoé down to her bones. She stepped inside, closed the door and stood beside it with her hands clasped in front of her. Madame Bouchard sat up in bed and discarded the cloth. She gave her stepdaughter a look of frank contempt, and then pointed to a wicker basket in the corner that held folded laundry.

"Look at the linen," Madame Bouchard said.

Zoé stared at the basket, her heart now in her throat. She closed her eyes, her worst nightmare confirmed. She would not be humiliated into showcasing her soiled nightclothes and sheets.

"I can explain, *Madame*."

Madame Bouchard got out of bed. She walked over to Zoé, who looked at her with pleading eyes. Before Zoé could speak, she felt a blow across her face that knocked her to the floor. Zoé held back her tears as her hair loosened from the barrettes and fell across her face.

Madame stood over her, glaring down at her. "You whore! I raised you to be a lady, and you disgrace your father and me this way!"

Zoé looked up. *"Madame,* please…"

"Please what? Please don't tell your father that you are now some man's slut? That you're damaged goods? As if the shame of your birth weren't enough… now this."

Zoé looked down at the floor. There was no fight left in her. She just wanted to go home and forget this place. She wanted to forget Julien Charles La Roque.

"Get up," Madame said.

Zoé got to her feet. Like a prisoner in the gallows, she stood with eyes cast down, tried, convicted and now waiting to be sentenced.

"I shall fix this," Madame said. "I shall do it for your father, for sweet Marianne, but not for you."

Feeling contrite, the girl could only nod. "*Oui, Madame.*" At the same time, she felt a small surge of hope, a tinge of relief. She should've realized that Madame would do anything to protect Marianne and keep this from her husband. Quite possibly, she feared that he would blame her, accuse her of not being vigilant. So Madame had good reason to clean this up. But how would she do it? How could she or anyone else 'fix' this?

It was as if Madame had read Zoé's thoughts.

"You will tell Comte La Roque that you will be his mistress—"

Zoé's head jerked up. She gasped. "*Mais, non!*"

"You shall say you will serve him, but only if he marries Marianne. And you shall tell your father that you can't bear to be without your sister, that you want to remain with her." Madame regarded Zoé with blistering fury. "This will be your fate. And it's better than you deserve."

For Zoé, this was worse than anything she could have imagined. It was not only humiliating, but also perverse, and disgusting.

"But I don't have to stay here! He wants Marianne. I mean nothing to him. I just want to return home with Papa!"

Madame laughed. "He doesn't want Marianne. The man is lusting for *you*. The only way that Marianne can have the life she deserves is through your sacrifice."

Zoé burst into tears. "I don't want to be his mistress. *Je vous en prie—*"

"Silence! You should have thought of that before you opened your legs! Do this or I will tell your father the truth, and force him to accept the offer made by Monsieur Sheridan."

Zoé was horrified. She hadn't even known that Sheridan had spoken to Madame. Now, she knew that the threat to ship her off to America was real. Things had spiraled out of control so quickly. It was unbelievable.

Madame was smug, but she had overplayed her hand. That last threat pushed Zoé past her breaking point and she retaliated, feeling she had nothing left to lose.

"What if I tell Marianne of your little plan? What then?"

Madame put her face close to Zoé's. "Go ahead. I will deny every word of it and Marianne will believe me. Better still, she will hate you, for she'll know that you betrayed her and that you tried to steal her future and make it your own."

Madame was right. Marianne would hate her, and perhaps Papa, too. What would he do if forced to choose between her and his white, legitimate daughter? How could she be sure that he would take her side?

There was no way to get out of this and nowhere to turn. She felt the walls closing in on her. With a cry of anguish, she fled her stepmother's room. With Madame's mocking laughter falling on her heels, Zoé ran to her room, her hair disheveled, tears coursing down her face, her skirts billowing behind her.

Once inside her room, she slammed the door and threw her body against it. She slid down to the floor, overcome with regret and despair. If only she could take back what she had done. Closing her eyes, she wished for her mother, for her own dead *maman*, to tell her what to do.

Zoé buried her face in her hands. The life that she had hoped for would never be, and she could blame no one but herself. She had been a fool to believe that she'd ever find a suitor.

She was to be La Roque's whore and that was that.

3

Resting uneasily in bed, Zoé moaned through her soft cries. She had skipped supper because she didn't want to face Madame. Marianne brought her something to eat but her anxiety over her father's arrival left her without much appetite. Eventually, Marianne climbed into bed and curled up next to her, holding her until she fell asleep, as they'd done since they were children.

Zoé sighed, recalling the fading image of her *maman*. Capucine Draqcor was a striking, dark-skinned African. Capucine's father, Bakkir, had been captured and put on a slave ship. The ship's captives overtook it and found amnesty in France. Several Africans chose to settle in the French fishing town for its prosperous shipping trade. Bakkir took on the name Draqcor after arriving in Narbonne. Little was known about him after that. However, it was common knowledge that he fathered three girls and that he died shortly after his wife, Lindewe, gave birth to Capucine. Many had told a young Zoé that her grandfather was considered a leader among men.

Capucine was considered the most daring and free-spirited of Bakkir's daughters. Rejecting what was expected of her, she fell in love with the wealthiest man in the village and gave herself to him. This broke her mother's heart and her bond with her family was forever severed.

ZOÉ

That was basically all that Zoé knew of her *maman's* past. She was only six when Capucine succumbed to tuberculosis. Madame had forced her to work in a torrential storm, bringing in all the ripe vegetables from the garden. *Maman* had never seemed right after that and died some short months later.

Papa had her *maman's* portrait painted and kept it in the cellar where Zoé could go and gaze at it for hours. Zoé savored all her memories of her *maman*. She could vividly recall getting out of her bed, a side drawer with a fluffy mattress which pulled out of baby Marianne's bed. Sometimes she would walk eagerly down the dark halls in bare feet in search of her *maman*. With her long black curls in her face and her thumb in her mouth, she would step down the marble stairs, careful not to lose her balance on her way to the servants' quarters. *Maman* would leave the door cracked for her if she was alone and Papa was with Madame.

Zoé would ease open the door, step inside to see her mother waiting for her. Capucine always wore her thick, black hair in two long braids down her back. *Maman* had the deepest, most caring eyes, and they sparkled like black diamonds when she saw her baby. Zoé would rush into her arms, and snuggle her breast, loving the warmth it offered. *Maman* loved to run her fingers through Zoé's ringlets and sing to her, either in French or, more frequently, in the words of her native tongue.

It was her most cherished memory. Zoé understood that her mother was Papa's mistress. Capucine had never said a bad word against him. As much as Zoé loved *Maman*, she couldn't understand how she could love a man who kept her in the lower part of the house like a dirty secret.

Other servants told Zoé that, at one time, *Maman* had been the lady of the house. They said Papa had stood his ground with *Grand-mère* and gone public with his torrid affair with Capucine. Then something happened and it all changed. To this day, Zoé didn't know what caused the reversal, but sometimes she would go to the cellar and find her father in front of the portrait, weeping like a baby.

The extreme guilt he carried was evident, and Zoé was given every privilege his child could receive. No matter how much Madame or *Grand-mère* protested, he remained solid in his love for Capucine.

Turning over in bed, Zoé wept in her sleep. "Oh, Papa," she moaned. "I am so sorry, *Maman*."

La Roque was in his bed also, staring at the draped ceiling of his canopy. Candles lit his room, casting a soft glow and throwing flickering shadows. He knew that Zoé had not left her room since they'd returned from their ride. He asked Marianne before she retired if her sister was unwell, but Madame interjected, assuring him that it was a simple headache and that Zoé would be good as new tomorrow. La Roque knew better.

Why was he so drawn to her? Especially when he so coveted being a bachelor. There was her beauty, of course. Ah, he could dwell endlessly on her charms, but he knew that her beauty didn't fully explain his attraction to her.

After all, he had loved women from all over the world. They had all shared his bed, whether Occidental, African, Asian, Indian, or Arabian. He enjoyed possessing exotic things, thus his obsession with the wildflowers that bloomed in his conservatory. There was a freedom in their uniqueness that helped him see past the complacency that often followed wealth. Zoé possessed those qualities, plus a uniqueness of her own. It wasn't just their differences that entranced him. It was the way she existed freely in a world that insisted she be constrained. His desire for her intensified each time she withdrew from him or when she stood firm in her convictions. He had to have her. When he took her into his chamber, he thought corrupting her would satisfy this thirst, but it had done the opposite. It had torn open his cold heart.

His father, Count François Julien La Roque, had suffered tremendously because of his love for a woman who was not meant to be his. The demoiselles had no idea that the château he had shown them and the story he'd told were so personal. Marcela, though beautiful, had been a villager of the most common sort. She worked as a chambermaid for his family. As a young lad, La Roque watched as his father's obsession with her destroyed his family.

The La Roque family held the most powerful office in Toulouse and Julien Charles La Roque was, from birth, destined for greatness. His mother nearly died giving birth to him and had been unable to have more children. After she became bedridden with depression over her native Italy, François promoted Marcela from being a maid to an "Abigail," a woman who worked as a close companion and personal assistant to the lady of the house. He hoped it would bring his wife around, but nothing seemed to work.

It was then that François, pained by his loneliness and being forced from his wife's bed, became infatuated with the dark-haired, beautiful Marcela. At first, he found stolen moments to make advances toward her, but when she refused him, his obsession drove him to take her by force. Something in Marcela broke after the rape. She responded to his advances with a sense of apathy. He had her in any way he chose after that.

By the time Comtesse La Roque recovered from her mysterious ailments, François had placed Marcela in separate quarters, and spent many days away from his family, indulging in his never-ending obsession with her.

But Marcela was restless and by no means in love with François. She hated him for what he had done to her and punished him by using his desires against him. It drove his father to madness; murdering her was his final act of that insanity.

Of course no one questioned the fire, but La Roque was present the night of the argument and witnessed what had pushed his father over the edge. The son vowed never to give a woman that kind of control in his life. His view of love was tainted forever that fateful night.

Closing his eyes, La Roque thought of Zoé. He was hiding behind beliefs he didn't necessarily share in order to protect himself from giving in to true love, a concept foreign to him. As much as he desired and intended to have her, he was terrified of his feelings for her. She'd been in his presence for barely a day, yet she already consumed his thoughts. He'd even missed a meeting with his banker to take the girls riding. He was acting like a lovesick schoolboy, and it infuriated and frustrated him.

Emotionally spent, he laced his fingers behind his head, thinking of what Zoé had said in the cottage. Her words echoed that he would never have access to her heart. It was only in that moment that he had realized it was what he wanted. He thought it was merely lust that drove him, but there was more. There was something in the way she bloomed in a garden webbed with thorns. She flourished in the French culture, even though her physical features were a permanent reminder that she was also *une femme de couleur.*

Yes, his Zoé was unlike any other. The more life pushed her, the more she pushed back. The way she stood her ground with him was proof of that. He envied her strength and craved her favor. He wanted to possess her heart as she now possessed his.

He justified the offer to be his mistress. Doing so had restored a sense of control over the situation. He hoped it would protect him from falling deeply in love with her. Yet, knowing how badly his father's affair had ended, he still worried that he stood to lose greatly in the end. He didn't understand why he would employ his father's tactics with this woman, at this stage in his life. All he knew for certain was that he was determined to have a different outcome.

The next morning, Beauregard Bouchard rode in the back of a horse-drawn carriage, en route to Chatêau La Roque. He was in extreme distress, for his financial interests in the shipping trade were failing. It took everything he had to hold onto Marianne's dowry so that she might wed. He hoped that pairing Marianne with La Roque would forge a relationship that could help him salvage his small empire.

It was his wife's suggestion that she take the girls to meet La Roque. She was confident that he would take one look at Marianne and want to make her his bride. At first he'd balked at the idea. He loved his girls, and would rather see them grow old as spinsters than be married off and snatched away from him. Yet, it was well expected that they should wed.

He had even found a proper suitor for Zoé, which would be his surprise for her. The fisherman overseeing his business had been asking for her hand. He was a young, handsome man, and not the least bit bothered by her color. He wanted to take her to England to wed, where it was legal. Bertrand had even found the means to put together a modest dowry. It wasn't much, but it would make his acceptance of Claude Chafer's proposal respectable.

Sighing, he looked out the window and thought of his sweet, dear Capucine. She was in Heaven, proudly smiling down on him at how well he had protected their child. It could not make up for the horrible way he'd failed her, but it was a start. The driver veered off the country road toward the city, and Bouchard relaxed. He couldn't wait to see his daughters.

Zoé opened her eyes to the bitter smell of black coffee. Turning her head, she saw Marianne smiling at her while filling her cup.

"Are you feeling better today?" Marianne asked, placing the cup next to her on the small bedside table.

Rising on her elbows, she smiled back at her sister. "Much better."

"*Bien*. I hear that Papa will arrive this afternoon. Isn't that great news?"

Zoé chewed on her bottom lip. "Yes, *Chérie*. It is."

Marianne climbed onto the bed and reached for her sister. Zoé lifted the blanket, and made room for Marianne. She climbed into the bed and hugged her sister tightly.

"I don't want to leave you, Zoé. Papa will soon marry us both off, and we won't be together anymore. Not like this," she said softly.

Zoé stroked her sister's hair and thought of what Madame had proposed. If she were to do what was demanded of her, she would become a whore to Marianne's husband. Closing her eyes, she sighed. "Maybe, we won't be separated."

Marianne frowned. "What do you mean?"

She struggled to find her voice and managed a weak smile. "You will need an Abigail, won't you? Perhaps I could stay on for the first years of your marriage to make sure that your needs are attended to."

"As my servant?" Marianne said, disgusted.

"No, as your *lady-in-waiting*."

Marianne shook her head. "No! You must go and have your own life and marriage. I would never impose that on you."

The door flew open and Madame strutted in. "Why are you girls still in bed?"

"We were talking," Marianne said with a hint of irritation.

Madame glared at Zoé. "You rudely missed supper last night. I expect you at the breakfast table."

"*Oui, Madame,*" murmured Zoé.

Madame eyed her. "Are you feeling better?"

Zoé nodded.

"Very well. Get dressed now. Both of you are to look your best. Wear the dresses I brought you from Paris, and make your father proud of you when he arrives." She flashed Zoé a meaningful look to remind her of their conversation and of what was expected of her.

Zoé averted her eyes and Marianne burst into giggles.

"Really, *Maman*? We can wear them?" She hopped off the bed and ran to her mother and hugged her.

Madame touched her daughter's face and kissed her forehead. "*Oui*. Now hurry."

Marianne raced from the room as Madame lingered at the foot of the bed. For a long moment, she studied Zoé.

"This must be your idea," she said finally. "If your father is to be convinced, then you must do the selling."

"I could tell Papa what you are trying to do and take my chances."

Madame nodded. "Yes, but we already discussed that. As far as I'm concerned, you would be doing me a favor. It would ensure that Marianne sees you for what you are and that my husband finally sends you away to America to pick cotton."

Zoé sat up. "Why do you hate me so? What makes me so unlovable to you? You are the only mother that I've known since I was six, and you treat me worse than one of the servants."

Madame took a long look into Zoé's eyes. "Sometimes you remind me of your mother," she said softly. "But I don't hate you."

She turned to go.

"Please wait!" Zoé called.

Madame froze, but did not turn around.

Zoé pulled her knees up to her chest, then locked her arms around them. "I will do what you ask of me if you do one thing for me."

Madame gave a slight turn. "And what is that?"

"Tell me the story of my mother. I want to know the true story of what happened to her. If I am to suffer her fate, I would at least like to understand it."

Madame swallowed hard, as if her throat had gone dry. "I... I can't," she said, her voice cracking.

"Is it that painful for you, too?"

Madame opened her mouth to say something, but then apparently thought better of it. "Get dressed," she snapped. "I want you present at that breakfast table." Then she walked out.

Tears welled in Zoé's eyes and slipped down her face. She lay back on her pillow, closing her eyes. Today she would betray herself and her father with this lie. Even worse and even more painful, was that she would betray her dear, departed *maman* as well.

❦

La Roque sat at the head of the table, watching the doorway for Zoé to appear. He had resisted the urge to go to her bed in the middle of the night, but if she did not appear at breakfast, he would hold back no longer.

"Julien, may we discuss my business proposal?" asked Sheridan, interrupting La Roque's thoughts.

"You mean your attempt to extort money from me?"

Sheridan laughed. "We are friends. Are we not? Closer than blood? If I am in need of financial assistance, shouldn't I come to family?"

La Roque smiled grimly. "How much?"

Sheridan sat back with an audible sigh of relief. "Like I said earlier, things are sure to change for the Carolinas. We are organized, and ready to take on John Quincy Adams as well as Congress, to nullify the tariffs that have stripped us of our riches. As you know, friend, prosperity comes at a price." Sheridan walked around the room with his hands clasped behind his back. La Roque regarded him with suspicion. His friend only took the long route to a point when there was another agenda at play. "I am unable to provide for my slaves as well as run the harvesting on what I am producing. Furthermore, the plantation next to mine is to be auctioned off. They weren't able to survive the death of the father in that family, and his widow is desperate. If I can purchase it and secure labor to work it, I am sure that I can turn it around."

"How much?"

Sheridan took a seat next to La Roque. "It's a good deal, Julien, and it will make both of us rich. I just need to be able to purchase and sustain it for a year before you can see a return on the investment."

"I will ask you one last time. How much?"

Sheridan cleared his throat. "Five thousand American dollars."

La Roque laughed. There was no way that a small rice plantation would cost that much. "You can't be serious!"

"It's a fair price and you have to keep in mind that I have to repair my own plantation as well. We suffered rainstorms that have all but ruined my crop."

"I can give you three."

"Three! What can I do with three?"

"It's all that I will give on this. Consider it a gift, not a loan."

"You insult me, sir."

La Roque gave Sheridan a cold gaze. "I will remind you of where you are. Control your tone or take your leave."

Sheridan reddened with anger. "It's that girl. Isn't it? She's got you all turned around."

Now, it was La Roque's turn to flush. "How dare you! I make no financial decision based on the turn of a skirt. What I have decided, *c'est bon sens, simplement*. And if the amount is too little for you, then you may go."

Sheridan opened his mouth to reply, but Gérard entered the room.

"Madame Bouchard," he announced.

She appeared in a tangerine-colored dress, her red hair pinned up in tight curls. Both men rose when she entered, watching as she took her seat. Sheridan slumped back down in his chair, fuming. La Roque nodded at Madame.

"Are the girls joining us?" he asked.

"*Bien sûr*," she said.

La Roque glanced at Sheridan and saw his smoldering resentment. The count gave an inner shrug. He'd never denied his friend's request for money before. He wasn't happy to do so now, but he would. And what little chance Sheridan might've had to convince him otherwise was gone. The American had made a foul error in blaming Zoé. Of course, he also didn't like the way Sheridan looked at her. This was true. But the one had nothing to do with the other. He would never make a business decision based on common jealousy and he was infuriated that Sheridan would accuse him of doing otherwise.

The girls were announced and entered. La Roque felt his heart lift at the sight of Zoé. She was so breathtakingly beautiful, he had to control the urge to walk over and embrace her. She stood before him in a blue gown with light blue stones interwoven in the corset. Her long dark ringlets were pinned back to set off her lovely face. She wore a teardrop necklace and matching earrings in the same shade of blue. They sparkled when she moved. Marianne was dressed similarly in a soft pastel pink gown, but he barely noticed her.

Zoé avoided the count's eyes as she walked to the table and was seated.

"Are you feeling better this morning?" he asked.

"Oui, mon seigneur," she answered with her head lowered.

La Roque frowned. The fire that he loved in her had dimmed. She seemed changed to him, and that didn't sit well with him at all.

Breakfast was served and the tension at the table was thick. Between Zoé's evasiveness, Sheridan's anger and Madame's nervousness, Marianne seemed to be the only one enjoying the conversation. La Roque wished he could reach out to Zoé. He desperately wanted to talk to her, but she gave him no opening. He fell more in love with her as he watched her eat in silence.

"My husband should be arriving shortly after noon today," Madame announced.

"Really?" Sheridan said, with a noticeable hint of interest in his voice.

La Roque glanced at him. Why should he care about Bouchard's arrival? Perhaps, Sheridan hoped that once Bouchard fetched his daughters, then he could once again have La Roque's full attention and pressure him for more funding.

Madame nodded. "He will be entertaining Comte La Roque's offer."

Sheridan looked at La Roque with an expression of new comprehension. "So is that why you so rudely dismissed me this morning?"

Infuriated, La Roque slammed his fist on the table. "Enough!"

Zoé looked up, as did Marianne and Madame. Sheridan stood, excused himself and stormed out. He paused just long enough to give Zoé his now familiar glare. She paled, her face showing confusion—and a new sense of fear.

A moment of stunned silence followed Sheridan's departure. Then Madame Bouchard cleared her throat.

"*Mon seigneur*," she said, "Zoé has something that she would like to discuss with you."

La Roque raised a surprised eyebrow. Marianne looked puzzled, then fearful. Her eyes darted between her mother and Zoé, who put on a small smile. Madame rose and grabbed Marianne's hand. "Come. We will leave them alone."

Baffled, La Roque watched them leave, and then returned his gaze to Zoé. She remained at the other end of the table, looking into her plate.

"Will you speak at last, and tell me what's on your heart?" he asked.

Struggling to find her voice, she raised her head and looked straight ahead. "I was told that you intend to ask for my sister's hand in marriage today."

"*Mais non!*" he said, both surprised and relieved. If her sadness was due to this simple misconception, then it should be easily remedied.

But to his great dismay, Zoé turned to him and said, with even deeper sadness, "Oh, but you will, *mon seigneur.*"

"I will do what?"

"Ask for her hand. And I..." Zoé choked on her words and closed her eyes.

"You will what?" Frowning with worry, he leaned on the table with hands clasped.

"I shall stay behind as her Abigail... and your mistress."

"What on earth are you talking about?"

Zoé stared at him for a moment. "I am talking about the best of both worlds for you. A beautiful bride to give you an heir and a whore to warm your bed!"

His heart sank at the bitterness in her voice.

"But I don't want you to be my whore."

"I am already. You yourself said so. Don't you remember?"

"I never said—"

"I think your exact words were, 'Would my dream suitor want me knowing that I am no longer intact?' Isn't that right?"

He shook his head. "No, this is not an arrangement that I shall abide by."

"It is the only one being offered. Any other would break my father's heart, and I won't let that happen to him again. I care less what you do to me. I just want to keep my family's honor *intact*."

Looking into her full brown eyes, with sweeping lashes, he saw her resolve.

"You hate me," he said.

"I feel nothing for you. I guess I am more like Marcela than I thought."

He blew out a frustrated breath, stung by her last comment. Seeing her harden herself for a fate not of her own choosing made him ache with regret. He had never wanted to hurt her, but by trying to possess her, he had done exactly that.

"I shall speak to your father and clear this up. The offer I was to make was to ask for you, as my maîtresse, but I have no intention of marrying anyone."

Zoé shook her head. "Therein lies the problem. I won't have it. I won't let him be hurt by my actions. I won't have him humiliated in front of you. He will think that this is my choice. I will convince him of that. I just ask that you make sure that he's well taken care of."

"But I only want you, Zoé. Only you."

"And that is all you care about, isn't it? What you want."

He felt reduced under her words, realizing the truth in them, but he couldn't find words to answer her.

"Look at it this way," she continued. "You shall have me. I will not fight your advances any longer. You shall finally have your *mistress*."

She pushed away from the table and rose. "Now, if you will excuse me, I must prepare for my father's arrival."

"Zoé, wait."

La Roque got up, went to her and took her hand. "If I withdraw my offer to your father and let you leave, will that give you back what you lost?"

She shook her head. "I have nothing to offer a husband. Madame reminded me of that. If my father tries to pair me off, and my suitor discovers our secret, then he will be ruined. If you don't accept my offer, then I will be forced to tell Papa the truth, and I will probably be sent to America to experience a worse fate. So it is up to you, *mon seigneur*, because I no longer care what happens to me." She withdrew her hand from his and went out.

La Roque ran his hand through his hair and sighed deeply. He couldn't let her go, but to keep her this way would be worse than losing her. It would be destroying her. He wanted her heart more than anything, and now he had done the very thing that would steal it away from him. Furious, he kicked over a chair. He couldn't decide who he was angrier with, himself for falling in love or her for bewitching him the way she had.

Walking with her head down, Zoé hurried away from the salon. She wasn't in the mood for Madame and Marianne now. She needed to gather her strength in order to stand before Papa and lie. How could she tell the man that she respected more than anything in this world that she had no respect for herself? That all she wanted out of life was to wait on her sister. How on Earth could she sell him that lie?

Lost in her thoughts, she didn't hear the stealthy footsteps behind her. Before she knew what was happening, someone had grabbed her by the arm and yanked her into a room to the left of the corridor.

It was Sheridan.

Pushing her inside, he slammed the door. Zoé fell across the arm of a sofa. Breathless with shock, she straightened up and brushed aside the hair that had fallen across her face.

"What is this?" she asked, her thoughts racing and her gaze shifting between him and the door.

"It's about that apology you owe me," he said, advancing toward her.

She ran around the table, using it to block him. "I will ask that you leave me at once or I shall scream."

Sheridan laughed. "You scream and I will tell dear old pappy the truth about his nigger whore of a daughter."

Her eyes grew wide. "What?"

"You heard me. If you can give yourself to Julien, why not me?"

He licked his lips and moved around the sofa. Zoé backed away. Her heart raced and the tears that she'd vowed to hold back now fell from her lashes. She didn't know what to do. He crept toward her. She took two more steps back, pinning herself against the wall behind her.

"Please," she begged. "Don't do this."

"Now it's please, eh? Before, you sneered at me and disrespected me. Give me my apology!"

He made a grab for her. She slipped around the side of the sofa and made a dash for the door, but he caught hold of her long curls and yanked her back. She screamed in pain and terror. He clamped a hand over her mouth and wrapped an arm around her waist. She fought and kicked, to no avail. He was stronger, much stronger, and emboldened by malice. Standing behind her, he whispered into her ear, his voice filled with lust.

"I will say you are a tasty dish."

He licked her cheek and forced a hand down the front of her tight corset.

"No," she whimpered and squirmed to avoid his rough probing.

He yanked her around and shook her. "Don't you tell me no! Don't you ever dare utter those words to a white man!"

He slapped her. She fell across a table, her hip connecting painfully with the hard wood edge. The heavy brass candelabra on the table fell and she grabbed it and held it out in front of her. Her hair hanging in her face, she breathed through it and tried to focus on defending herself.

Sheridan laughed. "Are you really going to fight me on this? Exactly what are you protecting? You're lower than a common street walker."

"That very well may be, but even the lowest wretch of a woman would bite through her wrist and rip open her own veins rather than allow herself to be touched by a pathetic scoundrel like you!"

ZOÉ

"I shall teach you something about respect!"

He lunged for her. She swung the candelabra and felt it connect with his shoulder. He roared in pain, knocked the candelabra from her hand and grabbed her by the throat. Forcing her back against the table, he put both hands around her throat and squeezed. She clawed at his hands, twisting and kicking, but couldn't loosen his grip. She felt her vision darken. On the verge of slipping away, she realized that his hand was under her petticoats.

Zoé thought of her *maman*, of how strong Capucine had been, and how it would've broken her heart to see her daughter die this way. Without thinking, she prayed, *"Help me, Maman! Please, help me."*

For a moment, there was nothing, just the deepening dusk of her dying vision. Then a wave of strength surged through her. She gave one last mighty kick. Her knee connected with the soft underparts of Sheridan's manhood and he gave a guttural cry.

Then his touch was gone. She dropped to the floor. As from a distance, she heard the sound of a struggle.

Blinking through tears and gasping for breath, she found the strength to sit up, and was stunned at what she saw.

La Roque had Sheridan pinned to the floor, pummeling him with blow after blow. Sheridan had his hands up, trying to protect himself, and begging for mercy, but La Roque kept inflicting his powerful punches.

"Arrêtez! Arrêtez!" Zoé cried. "You will kill him! Stop!" Zoé ran to the count and grabbed his arm.

Feeling her touch, La Roque lowered his bloodied fist. He got to his feet, took another look at Sheridan and gave him a kick for good measure. The plantation owner rolled over on one side, coughing up blood. La Roque dismissed him with an expression of contempt, turned to Zoé and pulled her into his arms.

"Did he…?" He couldn't bring himself to say the words. "Are you hurt, *Chérie?*"

"No." she said as she shook her head and held onto him.

He cupped her face and brought it to his to see if she were truly unharmed. She gazed up at him, her heart grateful. With a sigh, he crushed her to him and kissed her, pouring all of his desperate longing and fear of losing her into his embrace. They heard Sheridan scuttle out of the room and ignored him.

Zoé held tightly to the count's neck and kissed him back. His embrace felt like the safest place in the world. He had saved her life and defended her honor. No man other than her father had ever gone to such lengths to protect her.

La Roque lowered one arm and pressed a kiss into the palm of her hand. "I am so sorry," he whispered. "So very sorry that you were hurt."

She ran her fingers through his long mane, savoring his affection. She could feel his sense of guilt and regret. But more than that, she felt his need and desire and knew that she wanted him just as badly. He was her prince, and he had slain the dragon. His gallant efforts had won her over and had awakened a sense of not only gratitude, but also adoration. These feelings only made her more aware of her heart's desires. She was in love with him and she could no longer deny it.

La Roque walked her backward. She found herself between him and the wall. At first his kiss was soft and apologetic. She quivered under the sweet tenderness, and her passion, mixed with his, grew. There was a dreamy intimacy in the kiss they shared, a kiss so intoxicating that she lost her head. When he buried his face against her throat, he left her mouth burning for more. Summoning what little resistance she had left, she pressed her hands against his chest and pushed at him.

"I can't. My father will be here soon," she panted.

He blinked and she could sense the fever leave him. "I'm sorry," he mumbled again, smoothing her long ringlet curls.

"This is my fault. I should never have—"

"Shh," she said as she hushed him with fingertips on his lips. "I am not hurt. This is not your fault."

His gaze scanned every inch of her. It was as if he was trying to impress every bit of her image on his mind. It was the look of someone who feared losing someone that was so dear to him.

He took her hand and they turned to go. They paused, however, at the sight of the blood smears on the floor. She could feel the count's rage coming back.

"He will be made to answer for this," La Roque said. "I will call him out publicly for violating your honor."

"*Non,* you can't!" she cried, grabbing his arm.

"Why not?"

"He knows. He is threatening to tell Father. Please. I don't want my father to know." She blinked back tears.

"Zoé…"

"Please, honor our agreement. Give me this much, for it will kill him to know what has become of me. I beg you." She waited for his answer, openly fearful.

"To listen to you beg me for this," he said, "makes me feel like a monster."

Her only answer was the pleading in her eyes. After a moment, he gave a nod of consent and she exhaled a sigh of relief.

"I must go to my room and freshen up," she said. "I can't let Papa see me this way."

Without another word, he escorted her to her room and saw her inside. She sensed him waiting outside and then realized why he was waiting. She turned the key in her lock, and then she heard him walk away.

Gérard gave a welcoming bow, and then accepted the guest's hat and cloak. "Everyone is in the parlor room to your left, Sir," he said.

Bertrand Bouchard nodded and walked down the hall, pulling off his gloves. As soon as he turned the corner, he heard his baby, Marianne, squeal "Papa!" She came running into his arms, as beautiful and adorable as always. He hugged her heartily and kissed her soft cheek. Looking into her clear green eyes, he saw the jewel in her that warmed his heart.

"How is my sweet *Chérie?*"

"I missed you so much, Papa!"

Bouchard nodded and looked across the room. His wife sat near the fireplace, but he saw neither his host nor his beloved Zoé.

"Where is your sister?" he asked Marianne.

Madame Bouchard rose to her feet and smoothed her dress. "She was just up the hall—"

"Here I am, Papa," said Zoé from behind him.

Turning, he saw her in the doorway and beamed. She was as radiant as ever. Letting go of Marianne, he opened his arms for Zoé. She rushed into his arms and held onto him tightly.

Bertrand was puzzled by the intensity in her embrace as she clung to him. She had always desperately needed his love, the feeling of being in his arms. Normally, he attributed it to her mother's death and her feeling of insecurity about her place in the household, if not the world, in general. But now, he sensed something more.

Stroking her silky curls, he looked over at his wife, slightly confused.

Madame smiled, walking over to them. "She's been sick since we arrived."

Marianne nodded. "*Oui*, Papa. She's not been right since we arrived."

Zoé lifted her head and glared at her sister.

Bouchard touched her forehead. "Are you better now?"

She looked up at him, smiling. "Of course, I am so much better now that you are here."

Bertrand extended his arm and took Marianne into his embrace as well. Madame rolled her eyes, strolled back to the sofa and sat down.

"Monsieur Bouchard, welcome," said La Roque as he entered the room.

Bertrand released the girls and bowing, shook La Roque's hand. *"Mon seigneur,* it is a great pleasure to see you again."

"I trust that you had a pleasant journey?"

"I did, and I trust that my family hasn't caused you any trouble?"

"They have been an extreme delight."

Bertrand smiled, turning to look at his girls again. "They are my jewels," he said proudly.

Sheridan came into the parlor. His lip was cut and his eyes blackened. Marianne gasped at the sight of him; Zoé stared in shock and Madame put her hand to her breast. He ignored them and walked up to the newcomer.

La Roque grimaced, then hid his reluctance and performed the job that was expected of him.

"Monsieur Bertrand Bouchard, may I present my friend Flynn Sheridan, from the States."

"Greetings, sir. I had to come down and meet you," said Flynn, extending his hand. Bertrand shook Sheridan's hand, but couldn't help wondering at the man's obvious injuries.

It was Madame who blurted out the obvious question, *"Monsieur* Sheridan, whatever happened to you?"

He touched his blackened eye gingerly. "Oh, I got kicked in the face by a jackass—excuse me, ladies—by a mule in the stables. I was contemplating a ride on a wild buck, but things didn't go as well as I had anticipated."

Zoé flushed and La Roque gave him a look of fury. With a grim smile, the count put a hand on Sheridan's shoulder and gave it a squeeze.

"Serves you right," La Roque said. "Next time, ask before riding anything in my home."

Sheridan fumed but remained silent. Witnessing the exchange, Bertrand's gaze shifted back and forth between the two men. He glanced at his wife, but saw no answer there. La Roque turned back to his guest and Bouchard put on a smile.

"Would you like some brandy?" asked the count.

"No, thank you. However, I would like to speak with you now, if that's acceptable to you."

La Roque glanced at Zoé and then smiled at her father. "*Naturellement*." To the others, he said, "You will please adjourn to the drawing room while *Monsieur* Bouchard and I have a little chat."

Marianne curtsied and walked out, followed by Madame Bouchard. Zoé hesitated, however. Her father turned and looked at her. "Go ahead. I shall join you soon."

She kissed his cheek. "I am so glad you are here."

Bertrand smiled at her but felt a deeper stirring of unease. Watching her as she turned to leave, he saw how Sheridan smirked at her, and heard how La Roque told him, "I would ask that you leave as well."

Sheridan ignored La Roque. He turned to Bertrand. "I have had the divine pleasure of entertaining your lovely daughters. At the conclusion of your business with Comte La Roque, may we have a chat as well?"

Bertrand narrowed his eyes, less than charmed by Sheridan's bruised grin. "You say you are from America, *Monsieur?* May I ask what part?"

"Why, from Carolina, to be exact."

Bertrand's demeanor turned cold. He had ugly run-ins with Southern 'gentlemen' where his girls were concerned, especially Zoé. He wouldn't entertain any offers this man had to make, but he found it wise to play along. Something was going on in this house and he had a terrible sense that this man, as distasteful as he was, could help him learn the truth.

"We shall speak," he replied.

La Roque walked over to a chair and sat down, with Bertrand seated across from him.

"Your home is grand."

"Thank you Monsieur. I'm glad you were well received."

Bertrand cleared his throat. "My wife…"

"With all due respect, your wife has been brazenly out of line since she arrived. She has on several occasions tried to speak on your behalf." La Roque observed the flushed, embarrassed way Bertrand averted his eyes.

"She did?"

"Indeed. I am only speaking to you on this matter because I respect you as a gentleman. I wanted you to know how far out of line she was."

"So this summons is not your idea?"

"*Non*, quite to the contrary. I am absolutely taken with both of your daughters."

"Both?"

"Yes, they are exceptional."

"I was told that you wanted to speak about Marianne."

La Roque read the suspicion in Bertrand's now pointed stare.

"*Oui*, Marianne. I offer my hand in marriage," he finally heard himself say.

He could see Bertrand's elation, and further realized how much he would wrong this family.

"Marianne is a sweet girl and very trusting. She will make a good wife. I would ask, however, that you be patient with her. She has been very sheltered and is not experienced in worldly matters."

"And Zoé?" La Roque asked, looking into Bertrand's eyes.

The smile faded quickly from Bertrand's lips and La Roque saw the same suspicion return. He imagined that Bertrand had to have turned away many a gentleman suitor with ill intentions toward young Zoé. It was probably why he was so defensive at the mere mention of her name from any man's lips.

"My daughter has a suitor at home," he said proudly, announcing that Zoé was just as much a prize as Marianne was.

La Roque blinked, then recovered. "She does? Is she aware?"

"It's my surprise for her," Bertrand nodded.

La Roque had to digest the news. There was no point to this farce any longer. Set to inform Bertrand of the truth, he opened his mouth to speak. Yet he held back. Zoé would never agree to the marriage. To do so could defraud and ruin her father. In the meantime, as she said, he could have the best of both worlds. Though he was growing increasingly aware that the only world he preferred would be one with her in it.

He saw Bertrand growing puzzled over his hesitation and gave him a polite nod. "About Marianne's dowry—"

"I know that you own land in our village, and wish to acquire the estate in her dowry. I have a proposition for you as well. Investment within my business."

La Roque barely heard him. He could only process how far he had gone over his desire to possess Zoé. "Whatever your company needs, you shall have. Think nothing of it. Keep the land as well."

"Well… that's too generous, *mon seigneur*," Bertrand stammered.

"I said, think nothing of it!" La Roque's voice sharpened, breaking his control.

"Have I offended you?"

La Roque stroked the silken hairs on his chin. "No. I am just not at my best today. Forgive me."

"Is everyone coming down with something here?"

La Roque saw the older gentleman look around, puzzled, and he knew his father's intuition had him sensing the secrets within his château.

He rose. "It is that time of year…"

Bertrand nodded up at him. "I need to speak to my girls."

"I shall fetch them for you," La Roque offered, ready for the escape. Never had he gambled so much for the small sum of one, one woman who had him now hopelessly ensnared. Bertrand rose and bowed slightly as La Roque left the room. And La Roque felt the man's eyes on him and didn't dare look back. He contemplated removing them all from his home in order to regain his sanity.

Zoé, waiting in the salon with Marianne and Madame, hurried quickly to the parlor to meet with her father. She was desperate for the protective cover that his love for her always brought. Once inside, she stopped to see him smoking his pipe, staring up at La Roque's portrait. Marianne caught up and breezed right in.

"Papa!"

Zoé smiled and followed.

"Sit down, girls," Bertrand said, gesturing to the *chaise longue* in front of him.

They did so obediently and Zoé relaxed under her father's warm stare. She watched as he then looked to her younger sister with just as much love. "How do you feel about Comte La Roque?"

"I like him, but I don't think he likes me…"

Zoé tensed.

"You don't?" Bertrand asked.

Clearing her throat, Zoé found her voice and immediately spoke up. "Marianne isn't aware of how taken he is with her. Just the other day, he took us for a ride, and although we shared a horse, he peppered me with questions about her."

Marianne frowned. "He did?"

Zoé smiled. "*Oui…* he did."

"I thought—"

Zoé grabbed her hand. "Trust me. He has fallen for you."

"*Really*? I thought I noticed how he looked at me at breakfast today. He is so handsome, Papa. I really do like him."

Zoé looked up into her father's eyes and saw he was not as easily fooled by her performance. She put on her sweetest smile for him, hoping to not draw further suspicion.

"Zoé, are you saying that you believe his intentions are honorable?" Bertrand asked.

Zoé nodded. "*Oui*, Papa. He's a good man from what I can see. I think he will make a good husband for Marianne."

"Then it's settled. You are to be married."

Marianne squealed with delight and hugged Zoé tightly. Zoé held her close, allowing the finality of her actions to sink in. "I am so happy for you," Zoé said, kissing her cheek.

Zoé opened her eyes to see her father wearing a smile he'd reserved for the Christmas morning when he unveiled the grandest of surprises for his girls. Curious, she let go of her sister and stared at her father.

"I have a surprise for you, Zoé."

"A surprise?" Zoé asked.

"Do you remember Claude Chafer?"

Zoé smiled. "Yes. He has always been so nice to us when we visit your docks."

"Well, he has asked for your hand in marriage."

Marianne squealed and Zoé went numb. Her sister's hugging her and her father's grin did nothing to ease the shock and dread that gripped her in that moment. Her father, soon recognizing that the elation wasn't shared, looked into her eyes with concern.

"What is it?"

"I can't marry him, Papa," she said, pushing her way out of her sister's arms.

"What?" her father asked.

"I can't marry him!" Zoé said again, her eyes welling with tears.

"Of course you can!" Marianne interjected.

Zoé rose, nervously twisting her hands. "Chérie, please leave. Papa and I need to speak."

She saw the surprise in their faces and chose to ignore it.

"What's wrong?" Marianne asked in a small voice.

"Chérie, please join Madame so that I can speak with Papa!" Zoé snapped, losing all patience. When Marianne rose and sulked out, Zoé regretted her tone. Silently she vowed to apologize later. For the moment, she had more pressing concerns. Taking a seat next to her father, she dropped her head.

"What is going on around here? Truth, Zoé!"

"It's Marianne, Father."

"What about Marianne?"

"Look at her, Father. She's so trusting and naïve. She has no idea of the ways of the world."

"And you do?" he scoffed.

"More than she does. If she is to be married, then she will need me, at least in the beginning. I need to help her."

"Help her? Help her how? You are making no sense."

"Papa. I want to stay with her… to *assist* her." Zoé chose her words with care.

"Absolutely not! You are no one's servant. I forbid it! I didn't raise you for this!" Bertrand stood quickly, infuriated that his daughter would even suggest such a thing.

Zoé swallowed at the rare sight of her father losing his temper. She was losing this battle, and didn't know what to do.

"This is Madame's doing! Isn't it? She convinced you to stay and become a servant to your own sister!! Answer me, girl!"

Zoé could not contain the lies that escaped her. She couldn't face her father's anger without revealing her shame. Keeping her head bowed, she spoke in a low, resolute tone. "No, Papa. I am telling the truth. This is what I want."

"You will be married to Claude Chafer. Your dowry is being prepared."

Zoé's head rose and her eyes widened with awe. He had a dowry for her? His love for her knew no bounds, and it broke her heart. It was because of that love she'd sacrifice anything to protect him. He must never know her sins. Rising, she faced him.

"Papa, what if I could postpone marrying for just one year? Just until Marianne is settled in her marriage. She needs me. You have to see that."

His hand went to her cheek, and he gave her the look she assumed he once gave her mother. The one of undying commitment to their child's well-being. He'd told her that the day they placed her in his arms, he vowed she would have a better life. Zoé was beginning to realize the unyielding force of that vow.

"I can't allow you to sacrifice your chance at happiness for anyone, *ma fille*."

"This is not a sacrifice. It is an act of love," she said, wrapping her arms around him. She hugged him tightly. Lifting her eyes, she saw they were being spied upon. La Roque held his pipe, watching her closely. Closing her eyes, she sighed.

"Trust me, Papa. I know what I am doing."

⚜

Madame sat in her room wringing her hands as she waited for her husband. She knew that Zoé must be telling him now, and knowing Bertrand, he wasn't going to take the news well.

She stood and began to pace. She was doing a horrible thing to a girl who was as close to her as her own blood. But damn it, Zoé had brought this on herself. She was the one foolish enough to bed Julien La Roque. Madame had paid her debt back to Capucine for the horrible things she'd done to her. She had given Zoé every advantage, yet the girl still acted impulsively. Sighing, she thought about her husband's health. She wouldn't allow the truth to destroy him.

Besides, Marianne was the one that was to have a proper wedding. It wasn't her fault that society placed such constraints upon them. She was doing what any mother in her position would do.

Madame told herself these things and more, but the truth was seared in her memory. She had wronged Capucine all those many years ago, and had stolen the life that she should have had. That guilt would forever haunt her.

The door opened and her husband walked in. He didn't see her at first. Coming further inside, he looked up, and the scowl on his face confirmed her fears.

"What have you done?" he asked in a low, angry tone.

"I—"

He slammed the door and glared at her. "Why is Zoé asking to remain here and wait on Marianne?"

"She loves Marianne. You know that."

"I want the truth! Why is Zoé asking to be a servant to her own damn sister?"

Madame jumped. She'd never seen him so angry. She stared at him with fear in her eyes. "Listen to me. Please, calm down. You can't be upset."

She was a fairly decent wife, and he felt that she had given his daughters the upbringing they deserved. But he saw her jealousy of his Zoé. He saw her constant desire for him to love Marianne more than Zoé, and it infuriated him.

He'd known that she would pull something, but never this. No matter how much she wanted Zoé to be considered second-class, she had no influence over his daughter. Zoé had stood up to her tyranny for years, confident that he would protect her. What could have happened to make her succumb to Madame's demands now?

"I mean it. What's going on?" Bertrand said through clenched teeth.

"We arrived here and Marianne was terrified. Zoé had to hold her hand through most of the courtship. Zoé came to me and said that she was fearful of just passing her sister off. You know how naïve Marianne is. She just wants to help her transition into the marriage."

Bertrand looked at Madame. "Zoé is to be wed to Claude Chafer," he said.

Madame's mouth fell open. She couldn't believe her ears. Claude Chafer wasn't a wealthy man, but he was modestly comfortable and quite sought after by the women in their village. Madame had even considered him for Marianne at one time. Why on earth would he choose a *mûlatresse* as his wife?

"Are you serious?"

Bertrand smiled. "Yes, wife. I am serious and very proud. She shall be married to him. After Marianne marries, of course."

Madame stared at her husband. If he married Zoé to Claude under the pretense of her virginity, it could ruin them. It would be considered fraud, and their reputation would not survive. "Husband, there is something I—"

"She will marry Claude. You will talk to her and convince her to let go of this crusade to sacrifice herself for Marianne and undo whatever evil web you've woven around her. Because if you don't, I shall make you pay in ways you can't even imagine."

"You hate me, don't you?" she whimpered.

"I feel nothing for you, Élise. You know that."

Madame let the tears fall. "You never let go of Capucine! She is long dead and buried. Yet you still carry her around in your heart!"

"And why is she dead and buried?"

Madame shook her head. "Don't blame all of that on me. It was your lust and arrogance that took her from you. It was not entirely my fault."

"I won't do this with you!"

"Why not? It's hung over us for a dozen years now. You wear it as armor over your cold heart, keeping me shut out!" said Madame, crying.

Bertrand glared at her. "My heart was not what you desired when you plied me with wine and seduced me. Oh, I know you had my *maman's* help. But my heart was the last thing that you wanted when you showed up pregnant, demanding that your honor be restored! It was my money, you wretched cruel woman, that made you feel all warm and loving inside!"

"I love you, Bertrand. Stop this!"

"Capucine trusted you. You befriended her and worked your way into my home. Then you and my mother sent her and my daughter on a fool's errand so that you could seduce me and destroy my world!"

"If you loved Capucine, then you should have married her."

Bertrand laughed a painful laugh. "How? How! She was forced t—"

The rest of the painful story caught in his throat. He clutched his chest in obvious pain. His face began to crumple and his knees gave way. Madame ran to him, held him up and walked him to the bed.

"Where are your pills?"

"My bag…" he wheezed.

Madame fished out his silver pillbox, and then returned with a single pill in her hand. Bertrand swallowed it, trying to breathe.

"You can't get yourself exhausted like this," she said.

He pulled away from her. "Then stop trying to destroy my child."

She was hurt. She wanted to tell him the truth, and expose that tramp for what she was, but it would kill him. She needed to keep the truth from him in order to protect him. He may never have loved her, but she had always loved him and always would.

She had watched Capucine with envy as the African moved into his home, and was shown around the village as his wife with no legal standing. And it was true that she had befriended Capucine to gain her trust. Élise had stayed at their home, dining each evening with them both, all the while secretly lusting for handsome Bertrand Bouchard.

But Bertrand had eyes for no one but Capucine. When his mother approached Élise about the seduction, she jumped at the chance. She had thought herself triumphant when she learned that she had conceived.

She would always remember the day she appeared on his doorstep, pregnant and demanding to be married. Capucine had been there, holding Zoé in her arms and looking broken-hearted to learn that her lover, her prince among men, had betrayed her.

When he'd conceded defeat and told Élise he would marry her, she assumed that Capucine and her bastard would disappear. Days later, she was stunned when his mother told her that her son was desperate. He would do anything to keep Capucine and the African had agreed to stay at his side.

But this was only under one condition.

If Zoé were recognized and raised as a Bouchard, then Capucine would remain as his new bride's slave.

At first, Élise had been furious. She wanted Capucine as far away as possible. But his mother had convinced her otherwise. Wasn't it better to have your enemy under your heel where you could grind her down, than far away where she could plot and undermine you in all secrecy? Finally, Élise had agreed and regarded the day she would become Madame Bertrand Bouchard as the happiest in her life.

In the end, of course, her trickery had backfired. She was treated like a stranger in her own home. The servants knew what she had done and took her orders with barely concealed contempt. She wanted to fire them all and hire new people, but Bouchard wouldn't let her. Even worse, he spent more nights in Capucine's arms than in hers and he barely gave their new baby a second glance.

Her jealousy made her cruel to Capucine, who never complained. All Capucine wanted to do was protect her daughter and her lover. She took the horrible things heaped upon her with a smile. So Madame pushed Capucine further and further, hoping that the woman would snap and do something punishable, or run away.

Neither was to occur.

When Capucine came down with tuberculosis, Bouchard struck his wife for the first and only time. In his rage, he almost took her life. It took several servants to pull him off of her.

The day they buried Capucine was the day Madame's fate was sealed. He never visited her bed again. Madame focused her energies on the girls and tried to ignore her heartache. But no matter how much cold antagonism her husband showed her, she never stopped loving him.

Bertrand had also paid a high price for that one-night lapse in judgment. "I betrayed my Capucine twice," he once told her. "The first was by planting my seed in you and the second by allowing her to become your servant. You came into our home and destroyed our happiness." Over the years, Madame had seen how his sense of guilt ate away at him. Capucine's ghost followed him everywhere. He couldn't escape the sorrow of his betrayal.

Now looking at his pain, she wanted desperately to comfort him. But he was still closed off to her. He'd taken his pill, but then turned away from her. Unable to think of anything better to do, she offered him water—and a lie.

"I shall speak to Zoé, but I have no influence over her."

Bouchard accepted the goblet of water and swallowed. "Leave me while I rest." He handed her the goblet, stretched out, and closed his eyes.

She stood there for a long time, viewing him with a mixture of affection, irritation and resentment. He was tired from the long trip, and their fights drained him, but that wasn't all of it. His health was failing, and the reality was that he might soon leave her. She loved him and didn't want to lose him, but she had to be realistic. She had to make sure that Marianne married, and that neither he nor Zoé ruined her future.

It was Marianne's survival she was fighting for— Marianne's and her own.

❦

La Roque walked out to the open veranda to find Sheridan standing in the yard, smoking his pipe. Sheridan saw him approaching, put up his hands defensively and backed away.

"Wait, Julien. Let me explain."

La Roque grabbed him by his collar and lifted him from the ground. Sheridan dropped his pipe and clawed at La Roque's hands.

"Let me explain!"

"Give me one good reason why I shouldn't snap your neck like a twig."

Sheridan's eyes bulged. His face turned a deep shade of red and spittle bubbled from his lips. La Roque shook him like a rag doll and then threw him to the ground. Sheridan grabbed his throat, gagging and backing away.

"I want you out of my house," La Roque said.

Sheridan struggled to get up. "Wait!" He put a hand up, still gasping for air.

"I want you gone," La Roque said.

Sheridan appeared to be shocked. "I'm sorry. After years of friendship, allow me the opportunity to make amends."

La Roque shook his head. "I won't have a friend like you. I have misjudged you. I thought your narrow-mindedness was a cover. I had no idea it was actually who you are."

Sheridan got to his feet, dusting himself off. "I was wrong to take liberties with her and I beg your pardon. Please don't send me away. Your friendship means a lot to me."

"My money means a lot to you."

"No! We're like brothers. We've been through worse situations than this. Why are you being so irrational?"

"You tried to violate her!"

"She attacked me!"

La Roque felt a new surge of fury and reached for Sheridan again. The American fell back.

"Very well," Sheridan said. "I tried to hurt her. I was wrong."

"You owe her an apology."

Sheridan was stunned. "What? Are you serious?"

"You give her an apology, or you will meet me at dawn to settle this as men."

Sheridan stared at him. "I've never apologized to a woman in my life. Not even my own mother. So I won't apologize to her. I have my honor, too, you know."

"You mean the honor that makes you brutalize young girls to make yourself feel like a man? That honor?" He gave Sheridan another shove.

"Or is it the honor that makes you say vile things to people you deem beneath you? Is it that honor?" He pushed Sheridan again, forcing him to step back, fearful.

"Or, wait. Is it the honor that brings you to my home to scheme me out of my money because you can't maintain your own fortune? Tell me, my friend. Is it that honor you speak of?"

"That's enough!" Sheridan shouted. Trying to recover his dignity, he straightened his topcoat and gave La Roque a haughty scowl. "You win. I shall apologize to her. Just don't throw me out. I don't have anywhere else to go," he added.

La Roque frowned. "What do you mean you don't have anywhere to go?"

Sheridan rubbed his jaw. "I lost it all. My plantation and my fortune: it's all gone." Sheridan dropped down onto a bench. He steadied his breathing and told La Roque the humiliating truth. He said he was ashamed, desperate to hold on to his family home. He had worked his own rice fields at the side of people he once enslaved. Eventually, unable to farm and unable to purchase slaves, he had sold off most of them but he was unable to pay the mortgage. The bank tossed him out. He had to borrow the money to pay for his passage aboard ship.

La Roque listened with astonishment. He'd heard stories of fortunes being lost before and so Sheridan's story was nothing to new to him. He wasn't bothered by Sheridan's loss of wealth but of something far more significant: the loss of trust and honesty.

"You lost your home and you couldn't tell me that?"

"Pride, Julien. You know what that is. It's the same thing that keeps you locked in your own hell. Well, I have pride, too, old boy, and I couldn't come here groveling." Sheridan's cheeks burned a scarlet red.

La Roque ran a hand through his thick hair and blew out a heated breath. "This day just keeps getting better and better."

"May I stay?"

"Apologize to her!" La Roque snapped and walked away.

Zoé sat at the piano in the salon, playing as Marianne stood next to her singing. La Roque walked in to see them and Marianne smiled, singing directly to him. He looked past her to Zoé, who also smiled at him and kept playing. His anger lessened and he came further into the room, taking a seat. Marianne rose, turning from side to side, her soft pink gown swaying at her feet as she sang from her heart out. Sheridan entered the room, his expression revealing his surprise at how wonderful her voice was.

The song resonated with both men, but their attentions were divided. Zoé looked over to La Roque, whose gaze dwelled on her, and she blushed. She could still feel his lips and hands. Despite her fear and resentment, she longed to feel his touch again.

Madame walked in as Marianne ended her song. She smiled at her daughter, delighted to see her happy. Incurring the wrath of her husband had drained her, and as always she sought solace in the unconditional love Marianne gave her.

Everyone clapped at the end of the song, and Marianne curtsied. With her eyes, she asked permission from *Maman*, then walked over to La Roque and took a seat next to him. "*Mon seigneur*, was that pleasing to you?"

He was a little surprised. "Yes, a very nice song."

Marianne beamed. "Papa told me of your news. I have to say that I am overwhelmed with joy at the prospect of becoming your wife."

He glanced at Zoé, who nodded, encouraging him, desperation in her eyes. He looked back at Marianne. "Well, I think you are a special girl. I am honored you would have me."

"Bravo, old boy!" Sheridan clapped. "You didn't tell me that it was official!"

La Roque gave him an angry look. Sheridan ignored it and approached Zoé, who looked up at him with disgust.

He gave a little mocking bow. "*Mademoiselle*, I fear that I was quite rude to you earlier. I would like to offer you a sincere public apology for my behavior."

Madame lifted an eyebrow.

Zoé felt the sting of his mockery but remained polite. "*Merci*," she said softly.

Sheridan winked at her, and she shivered in revulsion.

Marianne asked her mother, "Where is Papa?"

Madame forced a smile. "He's worn a little thin from his travels. He shall join us for supper."

Zoé resumed playing the piano, pointedly ignoring Sheridan. He poured himself a glass of wine from the decanter. Marianne chattered on about what her life would be like living at the château, but La Roque ignored her. He watched Zoé play, and everyone in the room disappeared but them.

She sat with her baby blue gown spread across the piano bench. Her dark hair, wound in curls that cascaded down her back, was pulled back from her shoulders to reveal her delicate throat. The light sparkled off the blue teardrop jewel hanging from her ear, giving her the appearance of someone magical.

She glanced over at him, her long lashes making her doe-like eyes hypnotic. They shared a knowing look that made them both tense under the desire that bound them. She started to sing and even Marianne was silenced by the sound of her voice. La Roque believed that Zoé sang only for him. He was transfixed as her soft lips parted, and the song floated out of her in an enchanting way. He'd never heard such a melody before or the language of its lyrics but he understood her song and its beauty, like hers, captivated him.

Marianne touched La Roque's hand and giggled. "She's singing a song taught to her by her real *maman*. It's in some African language."

La Roque gave her an absent-minded smile and patted her hand. Her innocence was endearing, but he couldn't imagine babysitting her as a wife. His attention returned to Zoé. Strange, how he couldn't get enough of it. He understood his father's obsession with Marcela now. He was powerless to control his desire for her.

Madame watched. She saw how Marianne held La Roque's hand, happily believing that she was embarking upon some adventure, unaware that her husband-to-be lusted after her sister. She watched Zoé playing and Madame grew angry. It was that girl's fault. That girl and before her, her mother had destroyed dreams. Capucine had ruined Madame's chances of a happy marriage and now Capucine's daughter would do the same to Marianne. History was indeed repeating itself.

Her jaw clenched and her hands curled into tight fists. How could she make this right without revealing painful truths? Exposing Zoé would destroy Marianne and kill Bertrand Bouchard. It was an impossible situation.

Sheridan listened to the wicked song the temptress was singing. He recognized it from the chants of his plantation slaves. The song was evil! He seethed with resentment. She had no right to be treated as a lady, much less an aristocrat—and La Roque was wrong to have demanded an apology from him.

Sheridan's gaze moved from Zoé to his old friend, and envy deepened his resentment. Since La Roque would be marrying the blonde twit, he wanted a consolation prize of his own. Zoé seemed consumed with protecting that father of hers, and he could use that to turn things to his favor. He needed to be smart, not brutish. He needed to gain La Roque's favor. If he bided his time and remained patient, he could accomplish both.

None of the others noticed Bertrand Bouchard when he stepped into the room and paused. His heart swelled, as it always did when he heard Zoé sing like her mother. His gaze shifted from Zoé to Marianne and back, and he beamed with pride. Both of his daughters were blossoming into such beautiful women.

When Zoé finished her song, Bertrand was the first to applaud, alerting everyone to his presence. He went to Zoé, clapping, and Zoé rose from the piano. Embracing her, he kissed her face. "That was beautiful, as always."

"*Merci beaucoup,*" she said, hugging him tightly.

La Roque rose, letting go of Marianne's hand. Gérard appeared, giving him a slight nod.

"Everyone, I believe it's time for supper. Let us adjourn to the dining room."

Bertrand put his arm around Zoé, and extended a hand to Marianne, who accepted it as they walked out. La Roque smiled at their closeness. He understood Zoé's need to remain golden in her father's eyes.

Madame watched them, too, and felt a familiar pang of sorrow and embarrassment. Her husband hadn't even acknowledged her with a glance. After all these years, his indifference still hurt, especially when it was displayed before strangers. It was good that he loved the children, but it would have been nice, if only for once, he'd...

She heard La Roque sigh, and her momentary preoccupation with her own regrets evaporated into a new surge of anger.

"He adores his girls," Madame said.

La Roque turned around to see Madame glaring at him. He smiled at her. "Indeed, he and I share that in common."

"You've threatened everything. You've ruined Zoé. I suspect that you will be compensating us for our loss!"

He was amused. "Again, you overstep your bounds. It's a wonder your husband doesn't put a muzzle on you."

Madame gasped and watched in shock as La Roque strode out. What nerve! Maybe she was wrong even to consider him for her baby. She stood there for a moment, perplexed and torn. Then she felt a delicate touch on her elbow. She was startled to find Sheridan standing at her side.

"May I escort you?" he asked. Before she could answer, he continued. "I think, *Madame*, that we each have a problem to which I may have the solution."

She was so surprised that she didn't know what to say. She disliked Sheridan and was suspicious, but something in his eyes—perhaps a reflection of her own battened-down anger and desperation—urged her to listen to him.

She gave a barely perceptible nod. He offered her his arm, and she folded hers around his. The moment she touched him, she became fully aware of his virility. It had been a long time since a man—any man, much less a young, strong one—had shown her this simple civility. She glanced up at him; her gaze traced his profile.

She could guess what he wanted. He was handsome. He had money. He had a certain *je ne sais quoi*. She would feel no guilt, no guilt at all over what she was about to do.

Together, they walked through the door.

4

The night was chilled with the secrets of Château La Roque. All of the guests had retired for the evening, leaving the things unsaid to haunt the empty halls. Marianne slept peacefully in her room, dreaming of the pleasures of becoming a wife and eventually a mother. Bertrand Bouchard lay next to his wife, content that he had finally found a way to preserve the sanctity of his family and provide a happy future for his girls, but harboring the secret of his failing health.

They at least were able to sleep, comforted by illusion. The other guests, however, didn't fare as well. Madame lay awake, staring into the darkness. It had dawned on her at supper that she had cursed her daughter with the same fate that she'd endured—to be married to a man who wanted another, a *mûlatresse* at that. All she'd ever wanted was to protect Marianne, but the web of lies that she and Zoé had woven would do the exact opposite, and she was helpless against it.

Flynn Sheridan sat in a chair in his room, smoking a pipe and stewing in hatred. How he'd suffered when his slaves walked away from his plantation and the bank took his property. What humiliation he'd endured. But that would soon change. He had a plan, one that would allow him to return to his former status, to claim his property again. He'd show them all, and that mulatto was the key.

On the east wing, La Roque suffered under a different burden—the burden of discovering the depths of his own heart, and how much he wanted to share it with the *mademoiselle* up the hall.

Turning over, he exhaled again. He grew increasingly uncomfortable in the large canopied bed. Restless, he sat up and stared into the dark candlelit room. Down the hall from him she slept, locked away from him, from his desires for her.

He pushed back the covers and threw his legs over the side of the bed. For a moment, he sat there, reflective. Supper had been painful for him. This game they were playing was pushing him almost to the brink of madness. He couldn't go through with it. He needed to talk to Zoé. He couldn't let her pass up a chance at happiness and he wouldn't take a wife. The idea of marriage terrified him no matter who the bride was.

He twisted his neck from side to side, working out the kinks. Then he got up, took his robe from the chair and covered his nakedness. He left his chambers and went out into the dark, silent hallway. Passing through the corridor, he glanced out one of its cathedral-sized windows. A three-quarter moon hung low in the evening sky. It cast a silvery light across his face. It must be well past midnight, he thought. It was no time to wake a lady.

But he had to. He had to free himself from this hold she had over him and free her as well.

A sudden thought caused him to pause. Had she locked her door? Once more he felt a surge of anger toward Sheridan. That brute threatened to ruin everything.

He continued down the hall, worried now, desperate.

But no! Blessed relief. When he closed his hand around the cool brass knob of her bedroom, he found he could turn it easily.

Pushing the door open, he stepped into her room. Her suite had a window that faced south, showcasing the moon and lighting the room in an unearthly glow. He closed the door, turning the key and locking it with care, before approaching her bed. At first, he saw only the tangle of her locks and the contour of her body under the sheets. Pausing to take in her beauty, he smiled to himself. Going closer, he saw her more clearly. She was on her side, her hair in her face. The covers, pulled up to her neck, prevented him from seeing much of her.

He convinced himself that all he wanted to do was talk. He wanted to tell her that he was sorry and that he didn't know why he had set about to destroy her when all he ever wanted was to know her. He brushed some of her long, tangled tresses from her face. She frowned and turned over, causing the sheet to slip and reveal the top of her gown.

La Roque watched her chest rise and fall. He recalled the exquisite beauty of her breasts. He should go. Seeing her like this was making him forget the reason for this visit.

As if his hungry stare had burned through her, she blinked and opened her eyes. Turning her head, she looked at him but showed no surprise. She stared at him, confused, and wiped at her eyes. He smiled, realizing that she thought she was dreaming.

When she realized that he was actually in her room he saw her frown.

"*Mon seigneur*, why are you here?"

"I need to talk to you."

Zoé propped herself up on her elbows. The sheet slid further down her body, and he noticed the points of her nipples through her gown. She followed his gaze, saw what he fixed his eyes on and drew the sheet upward.

"Is something wrong?" she asked.

La Roque was afraid to move. If he made any move it would be to touch her and he didn't want to impose. In fact, he *did* want to impose and that was why he held back.

"I can't do this," he whispered.

"Do what?"

She sat up, pulled her hair from her shoulders and lifted the curls to free them from the collar of her gown. The movement revealed the graceful design of her neck and showcased her delicate features. Bathed in moonlight, her beauty took on a dreamlike quality. He swallowed hard, finally accepting the fact that she meant the world to him.

"I can't marry your sister. Your father must be told the truth. I shall compensate him for his troubles, but I can't play this game with you and your mother."

"But you promised!" Panic swept across her face.

"It won't work. Besides, it's not fair to your sister."

Her expression became knowing. "What do you need?"

He frowned. "Need?"

"You did not come to my room in the middle of the night simply to watch me sleep. I wake to find you hovering over me and I see a need, a need I don't fully understand, but if you tell me I will oblige. I will give you whatever you want to save Papa."

He couldn't speak. Her question was too direct and a truthful answer would be too revealing.

"Why must matters be so complicated, *mon seigneur*? When I think of how you defended me, how you held me, the words you said. You confuse me. One moment, you are cruel—yes, cruel—and demanding. The next, you gaze at me as if I am your long-lost love. I don't understand. I know I am young. Perhaps, you could explain."

She was right. If he wanted her, really wanted her, then he could easily make it happen. He could take her as his. They could be together. Something was wrong in the way that he hid from her, but reached out to her when she turned away.

"I was wrong to come here," he said, and turned to leave.

"Wait."

She pushed back the covers and got up. The stream of moonlight pouring into the room revealed the silhouette of her body in the thin gown. "Before you go, I must ask you again: please, please don't tell my father about us."

He waged an inner battle. He could see her lips moving, but couldn't hear her voice. All he could hear was the beat of his own heart. She ran nervous fingers through her hair and kept talking. He watched her sweet lips move and felt his desire rising. No longer able to resist her, he reached for her.

Caught off guard, she looked surprised, but her body was compliant as he drew her to him. She did not fight as he kissed her. Instead, she yielded her soft lips and returned the pressure. But when he ran his hands over the light fabric of her gown and gathered it up, drawing it up, she stepped back out of his embrace and regarded him with sadness.

"I can't do this with you. Not now, when my papa is down the hall."

"You asked me what I need. *Bien,* I need you."

She looked shaken, but backed away. "We have an agreement, and I will honor it, but we must..."

"This is about us."

He reached for her again, but she put a hand on his chest to stop him.

"Then what prevents you from having me?"

"Quoi?"

"Ask for my hand in marriage," she said.

He stared at her. "I can't."

"Because I'm a Mûlatresse?"

"Yes—no!"

"You were willing to ask for Marianne's hand to have me."

"That was your idea. I agreed in order to help you."

"You sent for Papa——"

"To ask for you."

"To be your mistress."

"Yes."

"Why?"

He stared at her. "What do you mean why?"

"Why do you want a mistress and not a wife? If you find slavery deplorable, then why do you wish to participate in it?"

"A mistress isn't a slave!"

"Even your friend *Monsieur* Sheridan was honest enough to say that it's indentured servitude with a jeweled collar. Is that all that you want from this world? A beautiful woman to dress up in jewels and make love to in the moonlight, but no one to share your life with?"

He struggled to respond. He didn't know what he wanted. All he knew is what he feared: marriage and surrender. He feared being vulnerable. By having a mistress, he could keep everything on his terms. How could he explain that to her without her seeing it as slavery?

He touched her face. "I just need to be near you."

She put a hand over his and held it to her cheek, giving him hope.

"You want me," she said, "because I resist you. If I submit to your advances, will this burning need to possess me be extinguished?"

"I don't know."

She drew away from his hand. For a moment, she studied him. "I have put myself in an impossible situation. To make matters worse, I have developed feelings for you."

"As I have for you." He wrapped his hand around her neck, and pulled her to him, trapping her with his gaze.

"My papa is down the hall," she protested, but her voice was weak.

"I can't help that. I have to be near you again," he said in a hoarse whisper and kissed her, softly at first. His kiss grew stronger and she opened her mouth to receive his probing tongue.

With a groan of passion, he swept her off her feet and carried her to the bed, her arms linked around his neck. Gazing down at her, he nodded at her gown.

"Take it off."

She searched his gaze. He could see in her eyes that she felt her fate was already sealed, that she had little left to fight for. Obediently, she pulled her gown over her head revealing a body that was even more beautiful than the first time he saw it. Gently tossing her gown to the floor, she lay down and watched as he untied his robe. He could see her interest at the sight of his nude body, and yes, see her hunger, as her gaze traveled over his body that was now also hungry with desire.

But the moment he entered her bed, he saw fear grip her again.

"Maybe, we should rethink this," she said. "I mean… it is very disrespectful—"

He put a finger to her lips, silencing her. He lowered his head to her abdomen and ran his tongue across her navel. With a moan, she lay back onto the pillows and surrendered to the pleasure of his touch.

He kissed her stomach, and then inched upward. She felt the fire of his tongue on her breast, playfully teasing before devouring the entire nipple. His long hair fell across his face and grazed her skin, sending tiny sparks through her veins. The bristles of his pubic hair brushed her intimately as she moved her hips slightly, satisfied in ways that she didn't know existed.

"N'arrête pas," she murmured, begging him to continue.

Hearing her plea made him want to be a part of the warmth inside of her immediately. As he kissed her throat, he reached down and parted her thighs. He sensed her body tense and remembered that for her their first experience together had been painful as well as erotic. As the tip of his penis pushed through the tightness of her, she gripped the sheets and bit down on her lip.

He stopped kissing her and gazed at her face as he nudged aside her left thigh to gain greater access. Thrusting into her, he heard her gasp and then relax as the wetness of her greeted his entry.

"Are you all right?" he whispered gently.

She gave a little nod as she surrendered to the unknown feelings her body was experiencing.

"Open your eyes, beautiful."

He enjoyed how tight a fit they were. He was giving her his full length, now, feeling her sheath him like exquisite velvet. Pushing in and out of her, he stared into her amber-brown eyes. "I am falling in love with you and that scares me."

He had not planned to say those words. He had not planned to say anything. They had slipped out of their own accord and now he couldn't take them back. Caught by surprise, he realized that he didn't want to.

Her eyes widened. He could understand why. No doubt, she had imagined a lot of things with him but his using the word *love* was never one of them. She didn't know what to say, which was acceptable. At the moment, they had another way of communicating their forbidden bond.

He thrust deeper into her and her eyes closed, caught up in the moment.

"Open your eyes," he said.

With a moan, she swallowed and looked at him.

"I can't marry you," he whispered, "but I can't lose you either."

She frowned, but then he pounded into her again and she shuddered in ecstasy. Now, her hips rose to receive each passionate thrust. Panting, she dug her nails into his back. He lowered his face to kiss her and lick the curve of her throat. He gripped her hips so he could drive himself in deeper.

"*Ma chère,* you feel so good."

Still unable to speak, she could only moan in response. He slipped his tongue in her ear and she smiled at the feeling. "You taste so good," he whispered and felt her shiver under him.

He quickened his pace and bit softly into her shoulder. He slid his hand between her thighs and massaged her while he continued to thrust. He sensed her mounting excitement as she vibrated beneath him. She bit down on her lower lip, trying to hold back her cries from the orgasm she didn't fully understand. He smiled down at her and whispered, "Give into it. I have to feel you let go. Feel it as you become mine."

She closed her eyes and arched her back. As he felt her climaxing, he too let go and exploded inside of her. He collapsed on top of her, feeling her breathing. He felt her turn her face to his, but he couldn't see her because his hair hung wildly over his face.

As he slid out of her and rolled on his side she rose up on her elbow and moved his hair from his face. He was still breathing hard but those deep mysterious eyes of hers glowed in the moonlight and stared into his soul. He was overwhelmed.

"You said you loved me," she whispered. "Is that true?"

He felt a last urge to resist, but it died away.

"Answer me," she said. "Is it true?"

"Yes," he said softly.

"So you love me, but you can't marry me?"

He looked away.

Zoé pulled his face back to hers. "What is going on? What are you so afraid of?"

"I don't want to discuss it," he snapped.

"So, instead of facing it, you want to push me away?"

"Let's not do this."

"Too late, *mon seigneur.* Too late because I love you, too. Now we have to find a way to make this right for us."

He reached for her curls. "You are so beautiful."

"Don't change the subject."

"There's no point to the subject."

"I plan to tell Papa the truth. I won't have my sister marrying a man who doesn't love her and I won't make this easy for you. I will trust in my father's love for me."

He shook his head. "I won't let you go."

"You can't make me stay. This has turned into a nightmare for so many. You were right to want to put an end to it."

"He will send you away!" he said.

"Maybe, or maybe you will face whatever keeps you from me and prevent that."

"What are you saying?"

"I'm saying that if you love me, if you can't live without me, then you will have to find a legitimate way to have me."

He pushed her away and sat up. He was silent. After a moment, he got up and retrieved his robe. Shouldering into it, he went to the door. Before leaving, he turned back to her.

"Don't tell your father anything, yet. Give me time to decide what... what I can offer you."

"How much time, Gianelli?"

"I don't know. Just time."

"We are set to leave in two days and Marianne's betrothal will be announced then. You have until then to decide if you want to live in fear or in love. If I must, I shall leave here and face whatever lies ahead for me. But I won't regret anything that happened between us. I shall never regret giving myself to you."

He looked unhappy. "I don't want to fail you."

"Then don't."

He turned to leave and looked over his shoulder to see her one last time. He felt humbled. He had taken advantage of her, yet she had forgiven him. Despite everything, when he looked into her eyes, he found only trust there. It was the same trust that he'd seen in her eyes when he asked her to come into his room that night. He had set a trap for her, only to become caught in it himself.

Yes, he loved her. And the realization terrified him.

After he left, Zoé lay awake, her gaze on the ceiling. Such passion. She had never experienced anything like that in her life. Why wasn't it like that the first time? Was it different like that because they were in love?

In love?

He said that he was in love with her.

She reached down and pulled up the covers. She understood now that being a woman was not losing her virginity. Being a woman meant understanding her heart.

Comte Julien La Roque was her heart and no matter where she went from here on, this night had been a magical one for her. This night, she fell completely in love. Turning on to her side and savoring the lingering aches from their lovemaking, she closed her eyes and welcomed sleep.

La Roque rode in his carriage making a familiar journey. Silently, he looked out of its small window at the sunrise. The orange orb rising in the distance kissed his cheek with warmth, the same warmth he felt in her arms. His eyes dropped away. He'd left word for his guests that he would return around midday. It was a trip he had to make. The night before, he'd touched an angel and she had changed him. His feelings were so strong that he found himself rethinking every notion he'd held dear. He'd refused to allow love into his life and now it was consuming him. A visit with the devil that haunted him might free him from the hell that kept him from his beloved.

The horsemen yelled at the horses to pick up speed and the carriage swayed as they rode through the countryside. He had not visited *L'Endroit Aliéné* in more than six months.

The insane asylum was on the outskirts of Toulouse. Quite isolated, it housed some of the most pathetic and tortured souls in all of France. None could be more tortured than Count François La Roque, Julien's father. His affliction was the source of Julien's greatest turmoil. If Julien La Roque had any hopes of understanding his fears and desires, he would have to start here.

The carriage pulled up to the main entrance of the asylum, a four-story stone building punctuated by small barred windows. The handsomely dressed horseman opened the door for La Roque to step through.

La Roque exited with the stance of one whose appearance reflected his wealth and position in life. His long mane was held in a queue with a silk ribbon that matched the dark color of his top coat. The men working turned at the sight of him and flashed him a curious look.

La Roque ignored their questioning eyes and tried to mask his terror. Each time he visited this place, fear and anxiety ruled over his emotions and he struggled to remain in control. Walking down the dark corridor with his coat tails flapping behind him, he felt as if his heart would leap from his chest. The asylum's head-master came rushing out to greet him.

"*Mon seigneur*, we wish we had known of your visit in advance. We could have—"

"Just take me to him," he said.

"*Oui, mon seigneur,*" the head-master said, nearly running at La Roque's side to keep up with him.

They turned the corner and he was confronted with the wails and screams of some of the most insane. He passed those that were crippled and quadriplegic. He stayed focused on his mission and tried to deafen himself to the pleas of the patients, who reached for him as he walked by. Outwardly, he remained calm, but inside he wanted to scream. This would never be his fate. The thought was so painful, he fought against displaying the intense emotions that engulfed him. He would not end up here!

Arriving at his father's cell door, he looked at the headmaster and nodded for him to open it.

His father's accommodations could be considered some of the most comfortable. La Roque spared no expense in making sure, at least in this self-imposed prison, his father was afforded the luxuries that his stature required.

The guard pulled the large circular key ring from his belt, unlocked the iron door, and drew it open. La Roque walked in to see his father sitting in a chair facing a window. His hair, long and grey, hung down his back, making him appear to be more advanced in years than he actually was.

La Roque cleared his throat. "Papa?"

François said nothing and La Roque knew this visit would be a difficult one. Some days were better than others. He grabbed a chair and pulled it near his father. There were so many emotional reflections of pain in his father's face, the face that, once, so resembled his own. The burn marks on the side of his face were evidence of the sad tale of what drove him mad, and made him look more like a wicked warlock instead of a heartsick man. His hands were arthritic and gnarled. They had the same horrendous burned tissue as his face and were pinkish and wrinkled. His long silver beard matched his hair and added to the illusion of him being ancient and lost.

"Papa, it's me, your son. Can you look at me?"

François turned to his son and La Roque saw the only sign that indicated mental acuity: his father's blazing blue eyes shone with recognition and sadness. At times, François seemed to be painfully aware of his lot in life and struggled for escape. It was his eyes that revealed this truth.

"Julien?" he whispered.

"*Oui, c'est moi.*"

The old count reached out and caressed his son's face. He gave a weak smile, and La Roque realized his father was lucid enough to talk. "How are you?" he asked.

"They won't let me see her," his father said, his gaze dropping to the floor.

La Roque felt his chest tighten. No matter how much his father progressed, he never let go of Marcela. "She's not here."

"I hear her, at night. She cries for me. She tells me that she's changed her mind and to come to her. She tells me that she was wrong and that she loves me. But they keep her from me. They think I'll hurt her again. Please, Julien. Make them let me see her."

"All right. I will speak to them and tell them to let you see her."

"Thank you. Thank you, Julien."

La Roque hesitated. "I need to ask you a question, one I've never asked you before."

"Quoi?"

"Did you love *Maman*? Was it choice or circumstance that caused you to marry? Was your marriage at any point satisfying for you?"

"I loved only Marcela. I was bound to your mother by obligation and duty. Marcela was all I wanted and I thought I was all she wanted. That is, until she taunted me with her affair and told me she would never love a man who had violated and enslaved her. It was your mother that enslaved me. It was my marriage that kept me trapped and made me treat Marcela as nothing more than a mistress. It was my own foolish greed that made me think I could have it all." François closed his eyes. "Love is dangerous, Julien, especially for a man. You love a woman, you lose your soul."

"Father, I saw you."

François opened his eyes and frowned. "What did you see, Julien?"

"I saw you strike her when she told you of her affair with Jean-Luc. I saw her fall back against the hearth and the hem of her dress caught fire. I saw you step back and watch her burn."

"*Non*! I tried to stop the fire! I tried to save her!"

La Roque didn't respond. He remembered that horrible scene so clearly. After his father's wanderings kept his mother weeping, Julien decided to seek him out. Following him to the forbidden lair where he kept Marcella, he hid at the side window. When brave enough to peer inside the glass, he lay witness to his father's greatest crime.

His father had stood there, transfixed, as Marcela ignited in flames. She beat at her skirts, terrified, then ran through the room, screaming in agony, knocking over furniture that ignited as well. François didn't move, perhaps also prepared to die. La Roque had run into the burning house to pull his father out. When François saw his son, his trance broke and he threw himself on Marcela to try to extinguish the flames, burning himself in the process. Julien dragged him from the house, kicking and screaming.

If the events of that night weren't enough to traumatize young Julien, what ensued certainly did. His mother's subsequent cover-up and disposal of his father clued him in to the coldness of their marriage. Then a few months shy of his majority and soon to be the man of the house, Julien La Roque fought not to have his father sent away, but even he had to admit that the man was broken and catatonic. The bond between mother and son was forever broken. He didn't even weep at her burial, just years later. Yet he missed and longed for her still.

And thus, he had seen the cruelty of women. How dangerous it was to give your heart or trust to them. Both women in his father's life cared little for his well-being. The one woman he'd chosen to love had pushed him beyond his breaking point by her salacious behavior. And his mother's offense was far greater. For when Julien had hoped to care for his father at their home, she had him committed to this cage and left him to rot in his insanity.

Now La Roque looked around the dark room that housed a cot against the wall and a small reading table on the other side and shivered. He vowed to never suffer the same fate. He would never be his father. Eventually, he might be forced to marry in order to preserve his line, but he would never allow a woman to destroy him this way. He would never trust in something as dangerous as love, believing that it brought about happiness. He was stronger and more in control. He had desires, yes, and he was in love, but to continue would only further empower his Zoé and that would be a dire mistake. He could never give her power over him. Never!

François looked over at his son. "Are you happy?"

"Assez bien." Well enough.

Francois, imprisoned in his mind, probed further. "Have you seen her?"

His father's moment of clarity had passed. He was again asking for his dead mistress, still haunted by her screams. La Roque rose from his chair ready to end the visit. "She's dead."

"No, she can never be dead! She's to be with me always. If you see her, tell her that I love her. I will always love her."

La Roque patted the old man's shoulder. "I will."

"Thank you," his father said and turned back to the window.

La Roque walked toward the door and looked back at his father. He didn't know why he had come. He'd gained nothing new and only worsened his fears. He guessed that a small part of him wanted to believe that all was not lost, that somewhere his father still existed outside of his pain and guilt.

Now he knew that he was wrong.

Zoé sat in the parlor, listening as her father and Flynn Sheridan discussed politics. She watched as the snake with two black eyes charmed her father by romanticizing his life in America. Sheridan even said that the South was changing and that *Negroes* were progressing, with some of them able to buy their freedom and own land. He said that he heard that in New Orleans an entire faction of *le gens de couleur* known as Creoles owned property and even held political office.

The tall tales fascinated her father, but they didn't sway Zoé. Sheridan would look at her from time to time and give her a smug smile. She could only grit her teeth and wish that La Roque would return and end the tiresome charade.

"*Monsieur* Sheridan," her father said, "I have to say I misjudged you and your intentions. It's been my experience that Southern gentlemen were not adaptable to change."

"Completely understandable, and I will admit it took some time for the evolution, but I have learned so much in the past years."

"Wouldn't it be nice if we all went to America as a family after the wedding?" Marianne said. "I want to go."

Bouchard touched his daughter's hand, painfully aware that his failing health would consume him before any of that could happen. "Maybe your new husband can take you."

Madame shifted uncomfortably in her chair and turned to Zoé. "We must speak." She paused for Zoé's nod, and got to her feet. "Gentlemen, excuse us. Marianne, why don't you entertain your father and Monsieur Sheridan with a song?"

Obedient, Marianne went to the piano while Zoé followed Madame out of the salon. They walked down the corridor in silence and stepped into the salon for privacy. Madame closed the door and Zoé braced herself. Madame had been flashing her hateful looks all morning and Zoé had no idea why. She had tried to follow Madame's orders. Now it didn't matter. She would tell father the truth soon and she needed to make Madame aware of that as well.

"Sit down," Madame said pointing to a sofa seat.

Zoé, in her lavender gown, walked over and sat down. Madame paced in her long black gown. She looked as if she were in mourning.

"Your father is not buying your act, Zoé, and I think that is your intention."

"Papa just wants what's best for me."

"So you know of his plans to marry you off to Claude Chafer?"

"*Oui.*"

"And?"

"Madame," Zoé hesitated. "I plan to tell Papa the truth. This is my fault and I would never let him be humiliated by my deeds."

Madame gasped. "You can't be serious."

"But I am. I want Papa's respect. A lie on top of my foolish indiscretion only cheapens me and destroys the trust we share."

Madame laughed. "You foolish girl! Do you think that telling the truth helps you reclaim some of this so-called 'respect'? You're a stupid, insolent, naïve, and reckless wench. If you cared for your father's respect, you wouldn't have given in to La Roque. There is nothing you can do now to redeem yourself."

Zoé winced and looked at the floor. "That may be true, but I still plan to spare Marianne the humiliation of marrying a man who doesn't love her."

Madame drew in her breath. She walked over to a window, and stood there, looking out. "There is something you should know."

Zoé felt the stirrings of a new unease. Was it possible that something else had gone wrong?

Madame turned around with tears in her eyes. "*C'est ton père. Il est malade.*" It's your father. He's ill.

"*Quoi?*"

"He has a heart condition. He's been taking medication for it for a year, now. That's why he is working so hard to secure a future for you and Marianne."

Zoé felt her chest tighten. She rose from her seat. "You're lying."

"*Non. C'est vrai.*" Madame straightened up and blinked back her tears. "If you tell him of your indiscretion, you could very well kill him."

"*Mais—*"

"Listen to me. I won't lose my husband to your foolish deeds. You will find a way to convince him of this arrangement."

"But it is too late. Comte La Roque has told me that he will not marry Marianne. Whether I tell Papa the truth or not, he won't marry her. If he doesn't marry her, then Papa will pair me off with Claude Chafer and the scandal alone could kill him."

"Then you find a way to fix this. You find a way to make the count marry your sister. It's the only way."

"I can't. It's beyond me now. His heart is not in it. He will not do it."

"If you don't, your father's death will be on your hands."

"There may be another way," Zoé implored.

Madame frowned. "What other way could there be?"

Zoé hesitated. "We are in love. The count might ask for my hand instead."

Madame was so startled her jaw dropped. Then she erupted in laughter. Zoé blushed. Madame laughed so until she could barely catch her breath.

"Are you mad?" she gasped.

"No!" Zoé jumped to her feet. "*Le Comte* and I are in love!"

Madame's laughter vanished. Her eyes narrowed as she advanced toward her stepdaughter.

"Are you stupid enough to still be in his bed? *C'est ça, n'est-ce pas?* He tells you pretty words and you sneak around in the night, pleasing him. You're denser than I thought."

Zoé slapped Madame across the face. For a moment, there was a shocked silence at the abrupt rebellion. Zoé was stunned at what she had done, but she knew she would not back down. Madame held her jaw and looked at Zoé in horror.

"You dare strike me?"

Zoé screamed hysterically. "I won't allow you to talk to me like that. I won't take it from you any longer!"

"I ought to tell your father, just to see you suffer his death, and then ship you off to America with that creature in the parlor."

Zoé paled. She realized that she had declared war on the woman who controlled her fate. If anything ever happened to Papa...

"Please, no! I—"

"Save it! You will regret the moment you dared raise a hand to me. You either barter the marriage of your sister to La Roque or I will barter you!"

Madame turned and stalked out.

Zoé buried her face in her hands and wept. She was lost and had no idea how to save herself and her father. With each day, the aftershocks of her love affair with the count rippled through her world, threatening to destroy everything she held dear.

La Roque arrived home to find everyone entertained. Bouchard and Sheridan were playing a friendly game of chess while Madame sat reading her Bible. Marianne sat at the piano, playing a sweet but forgettable melody. It was she who first noticed him standing in the doorway. She jumped up and ran to greet him.

"You've returned!" she cried.

"Indeed," he said to her, and then gave everyone else a nod and greeting. For a moment, his gaze dwelled on Bouchard and Sheridan and he felt a distinct prickle of anxiety.

"Where's your sister?" he asked Marianne.

Madame looked up from her Bible. "The last time I saw her, she was in the library. She had found a volume of poems she wanted to ask you about. Perhaps, you might retrieve her."

"Yes, let's join her," Marianne said, slipping her hand around his arm.

Madame spoke up. "But Marianne, dear, you must finish that lovely song you were playing."

Marianne pouted. "But I will only be a minute."

"Marianne!" Madame snapped.

Bouchard looked up from his game, startled and concerned. Marianne dropped La Roque's arm and flounced back to the piano. The count made his excuses and went in search of Zoé.

He found her walking down the corridor toward the east wing. He loved the way her hair, which was pinned up away from her shoulders, cascaded around her face. Recognizing an air of loneliness about her, he hesitated to approach her, as he was no closer to offering her a solution than before. When she turned the next corner, he followed her. She paused before a window and stood looking out. The window gave her a beautiful view of his land, but from her preoccupied expression, he doubted that she saw any of it. For several seconds, he simply watched her.

"Zoé?" Her name left his lips without his even realizing it.

She blinked, as though coming back to herself, saw him and forced a smile. "Oh, *bonjour*."

He walked up to her and caressed her cheek. "You are very sad," he said. "I never wanted that."

"We need to talk. Something has been brought to my attention and I need your counsel."

He frowned. Had something occurred in his absence? He led her to a room off the side of the wing. "What is it?"

"My papa…"

"What about him?"

"He's sick."

"Sick?"

"He has a heart problem, and he's not to be stressed." Tears welled in her eyes.

"I am so sorry," he said, taking her into his arms.

She rested her head on his chest. "I can't tell him about us, not unless…"

His jaw clenched and he closed his eyes. "I don't mind telling your father my feelings for you but… he will expect me to make a commitment."

She straightened up and gazed into his face. "You're still afraid, aren't you?"

"You said you would give me time."

"Well, time is short."

"I won't be pressured."

He walked away, clenching and unclenching his fists. Zoé went to him and took his hand. She placed it on her warm, soft breastbone, letting him feel the strong heart beating underneath.

"Don't you understand? My heart beats for you, and you only. I want to be with you always. I want to protect you, to love you. I want to have your babies and tend to your needs. You have nothing to fear in my love."

He snatched his hand away. "Why do you keep saying that I'm afraid?"

"Because I know fear. I have lived with it all my life: fear that my *maman* would be taken from me, fear that my papa would one day give into the demands of his wife and send me away—and that may happen. Fear is something that I am very familiar with and so I know you are terrified."

Hesitant, he reached out and touched her face. "How did you become so wise?"

"I'm a woman now, and a woman knows her own heart. She also knows the heart of her lover. You can push me away but

I see through your actions. I won't let your fear keep us from the truth."

He searched her eyes and saw that she meant it. With a groan, he pulled her into his arms and kissed her, surrendering to his need to hold her again.

Neither La Roque nor Zoé had seen Sheridan peek around the corner to witness them enter the room. Nor had they seen his evil and calculating smile. He'd followed La Roque from the parlor. Now he returned to it with a sense of malicious glee.

He found the others much as he'd left them. Bouchard had fetched himself some reading, but Madame continued poring over her Bible and Marianne was still at the piano.

"Marianne," he said, "your sister asked me to bring you so we can go riding again. The Count is excited about taking you on another tour of his land."

"How exciting!" she cried.

Madame frowned. "Where are they?"

"Waiting for us near the stables. Don't worry. Your sweet Marianne is safe with me."

Bouchard frowned. "Just the same, Marianne is not to be in any man's company without a proper escort."

ZOÉ

"Bertrand, they've been riding. *Monsieur* is a fine gentleman; Marianne is well in his care."

"She is safe with me," offered Sheridan with a curt bow. Bouchard looked to his wife who nodded and he gave his permissive nod as well. "Not too long. You girls are to return shortly."

"*Oui,* papa"

Zoé moaned as La Roque's breath and kisses warmed her neck. His nimble fingers began to untie the ribbons at the back of her dress.

"Gianelli, what are you doing?"

"Must I explain it?" he whispered.

Zoé tilted her head back as his kisses traveled to her collarbone, then to the swell of her breast. She desperately wanted to repeat what had transpired between them last night. Never in her life had her body felt so hot and eager for anything or anyone. She rubbed her thighs together as the fire he ignited made her wet with anticipation. At the same time, she could not forget that their love was not only forbidden, but dangerous.

"I'm loving you," his voice sang through her veins and pierced her heart.

"We shouldn't," she groaned.

He paused, kissing her. "You said you wanted to take care of me. Right now, I'm suffocating from my need to have you. Put me out of my misery. Let me have you once more." He gripped her hips and pressed her to him, making her aware of his throbbing manhood.

She gasped.

Unable to resist any longer, she pushed his topcoat from his shoulders while kissing the side of his face.

"You take my breath away," she whispered.

"As you do mine," he said, kissing the curve of her throat and struggling to unravel her corset lacing.

"Let me help you."

Reaching behind, she unhooked the straps in the back of her corset to loosen it. She then popped the buckles and freed her breasts.

La Roque stepped back and feasted on her beauty. She had perfectly round breasts with perky dark chocolate nipples that called out to him.

Smiling, she untied her skirt and let if fall slowly to the floor. She hooked her thumb into the waistband of her decency slip, also letting it drop to the floor and stepping out of it. That left her in her ruffled knickers and stocking legs. The knickers fit her thighs snugly. They were connected to single straps that adjusted to the band around her waist. This offered him an inviting view of her treasures.

She kicked off her shoes and reached for the top of her waistband to remove her knickers.

"Leave them on," he said, aroused by the way they fit her hips and connected to her stockings.

As she stood before him, exposed and vulnerable, she saw wonder in his eyes. It was as if he questioned how he deserved her affections, and what he could do to preserve them. Why did he fear their love so much?

She removed the pins from her hair, freeing her locks and allowing them to fall down her shoulders, the picture of perfection now complete.

"Do you know how exotically beautiful you are?" he asked. "I have never known a woman more captivating than you."

He fingered her long tresses, played with them. He draped her long ringlets across her breasts so they were partially covered. She heard him whisper that she reminded him of paintings of Eve in the garden of Eden. Her skin, a golden honey color, was smooth and silky to the touch. He said she smelled of lavender and she saw his arousal intensify by just being near her.

She smiled at him, sliding her hand up his chest and unbuttoning the top button to his ruffled collar. She reached behind his head and pulled the gentleman's bow from his hair. His dark brown mane fell loose and framed his handsome face.

He allowed her to continue unbuttoning his shirt as he gazed into her eyes. She finished undressing him, and the heat between them made everything happen fast. He carried her to the other side of the room and laid her on the chaise longue, then lowered himself down upon her, kissing and positioning himself to possess her. Zoé surrendered to him, allowing his passion to consume her as she blocked out the rest of their world.

When he eased into her, her pelvis quaked and she arched her back, opening her mouth in a silent cry of ecstasy. He kissed her chin before slipping his tongue between her parted lips and twirling his tongue around hers. As he ran his hand down her smooth thigh, she locked her right leg over his hip and threw her left leg over the top of the chaise, giving him all the access he sought.

He moved in and out of her with a precision that allowed him to go as deep as he could before pulling back. Looking down at her beauty as she sweated and twisted beneath him, he saw her breasts bounce perfectly. With a groan of total surrender, he buried his face between them as she grabbed the back of his head.

He could make love to her like this for an eternity, and she would oblige.

"This is not the way to the stables," Marianne said, walking down the corridor. She cut her eyes at her escort, leery of his intentions and thinking that she'd made a grave error in trusting him.

Sheridan smiled in a way that was apparently meant to be reassuring, but she shivered at the look he flashed her through his swollen black eyes. "You see that door right there, sweet Marianne?"

She stopped with him and looked at the door, frowning. "*Oui.*"

"They're in there, waiting for you. I was to bring you. I'll meet you all in the stables soon."

Marianne was relieved. "*Merci,*" she said. She let go of his arm and headed toward the door.

Sheridan smiled as he watched her hand clasp the doorknob. Turning on his heel, he whistled and walked away, looking forward to the fireworks that would soon begin.

"*Je t'aime ma jolie,*" Gianelli whispered in Zoé's ear as he pushed his way deeper inside her. She shivered with delight at the warmth that enveloped them. Bracing himself with his hand on the arm of the chaise, he kept grinding his hips, pumping his love into her while kissing her. She pushed her leg up higher, eventually throwing it over the back of the sofa again in response to his passionate demands.

"Oh, *mon Dieu*," she moaned.

Vaguely, on the edge of her consciousness, she heard the sound of a door opening, of tentative steps. And then she heard a small voice, an unmistakably familiar voice.

"Bonjour? Qui est là?" Hello? Who's there?

The effect was immediate.

Gianelli lifted his head in surprise and Zoé slunk into the pillows of the lounge, covering her face. So shocked was she, she forgot her leg was thrown over the chaise. That leg could belong only to her, betraying her attempt to remain unseen.

There was Marianne, standing in the middle of the floor, her face as white as chalk, her eyes wide. Zoé looked up at La Roque to see the blood drain from his face. Somewhere in the back of her mind, she was gratefully aware that the back of the sofa blocked her nudity, because in her heart she knew.

"Mon Dieu!" Marianne whispered, confirming Zoé's fear that it was one of her own family that had discovered them.

Marianne covered her mouth in horror, stumbling backward.

"Marianne!" Zoé yanked her leg back from over the sofa.

"You whore!" Marianne screamed, then turned and ran from the room.

"No! Wait!" Zoé shouted. She jumped up, ran to retrieve her clothes, tripped over her shoes, and struggled into her slip and skirt.

"Calm yourself. I will help you fix this," La Roque said. He too was hurrying into his clothes.

"I have to stop her before she gets to Papa!"

She struggled to hook up her corset. Her hands were shaking so badly she couldn't do it. His pants done, he went to help her.

"Zoé, please, we can fix this."

Tears filled her eyes. "You don't understand. I have killed my Papa," she cried and raced out, her corset still partly undone.

Forgetting his jacket, he grabbed his shirt and chased after her. Her fear and desperation matched his sense of guilt and regret.

Blinded by rage and sorrow, Marianne ran down the hall at breakneck speed, holding the front of her skirt and trying to keep from falling. She would never forget the memory of walking into that room, of seeing those clothes on the floor. Hearing moans, she remembered looking to the sofa in the middle of the room to see La Roque's backside rising and falling, along with a caramel-colored stocking leg thrown over the side of the chaise. She would never forget the pain of her sister's betrayal.

Marianne stumbled into the salon where her parents sat, talking. Seeing his daughter in tears, Bouchard jumped up to ask her what was wrong.

"Qu'est-ce qui c'est passé?"

"Papa! Papa!"

Bouchard ran to her and grabbed her. "What is it? What's happened?"

Madame dropped her Bible. "Are you hurt?"

Marianne wailed into her father's shoulder and he held on to her, his face growing pale, his chest tightening. He exchanged glances with his wife, both wondering the same thing. What had Sheridan done to their child?

Bouchard was trying to coax Marianne into her mother's arms, so he could track Sheridan down, when Zoé ran in.

Both parents were stunned. Zoé's dress was half undone; her long locks were loose and hanging wildly around her shoulders. Their shock deepened when La Roque ran in seconds later, his shirt open and his hair free.

Bouchard took one look at them and saw the truth. His face darkened with anger. Zoé looked into her father's eyes and saw not only rage, but disappointment, humiliation and a profound sense of sorrow.

"Oh, Papa," she breathed.

Bouchard pushed Marianne into her mother's arms, advanced on Zoé, and delivered a blow across her face that sent her reeling against the doorway. La Roque grabbed Bouchard by the throat and slammed him against the wall.

"Unhand me," Bouchard sputtered, pounding La Roque's arm.

"Calm yourself and I will," he said, but his anger was so intense, he wanted to murder the man.

Madame released Marianne and went to help her husband. "Please," she cried. "Let him go! He has a weak heart!"

Bouchard clawed at La Roque's hands, swinging at his face and head. "Let me go!" he sputtered.

"Do you promise not to strike her again?" La Roque asked. The lack of answer from Bouchard only furthered his anger.

Bouchard's face turned a dark shade of pink from the strain.

Marianne sat weeping in the corner, too lost in her own pain to realize the danger her father was in. Zoé realized it, however. She picked herself up and ran over to them. She, too, tried to free her father from La Roque's furious grip.

Bouchard was now gagging, not from La Roque's hold, but from the piercing pain in his chest.

"Gianelli, please!" Zoé shouted, tugging at La Roque's powerful hands. "Please let him go. He's sick! Don't you see? You're killing him!"

Her words got through. La Roque released Bouchard, who slid down the wall. La Roque looked down at the wheezing, sick man as if seeing clearly how ill he was for the first time.

"I didn't realize," he muttered. "Oh dear God. What have I done?"

Zoé dropped to her knees at her father's side and tried to help him stand. With a weak hand, he tried to push her away.

"No, Papa, please! I can explain!" she cried.

Madame shoved Zoé aside and took him in her arms. "Step away. You have done enough! You are killing him!"

La Roque backed up further and looked at his trembling hands. He was shocked by the rage he'd displayed, fueled by his passion for his mademoiselle. It was the same intense rage his father had felt when Marcela rejected him. La Roque realized now how great a hold his love and desire for Zoé had over him, and the thought of it terrified him.

"Papa, please," Zoé wept, her hair falling in her face and her body racked with sobs.

Bouchard looked up at her with bleary eyes, and then closed them. "The numbness," he whispered. "My arm."

Madame snapped at Zoé. "Go upstairs and get his silver pill case from the vanity. Go! Now!"

Zoé scrambled to her feet and ran out, desperate to help, to make everything right again, to find the medicine that would save her father.

La Roque took her place at Bouchard's side. Madame moved to protect her husband. "No—"

"It's all right," said La Roque. "I won't hurt him."

He slipped one arm under Bouchard and helped him to his feet, then half-carried the man to the sofa. There he eased him down. The older man tugged at his collar, fighting to breathe.

La Roque ripped the collar open, but still Bouchard struggled; now clutching his chest. Madame had dropped down next to him on the sofa. She reached out to stroke his brow.

"I'm afraid he doesn't need love, *Madame*. He needs help," La Roque said. "There's whiskey over there, on the table. Pour him a glass."

Madame gave him a cold look. "Thank you for your kindness, *mon seigneur*, but it comes a little too late. Don't you think you have done enough to damage our family?"

Stung, La Roque straightened up. He looked at Bouchard and realized that for once she was right. This was his handiwork, the result of his obsession with a woman, the same kind of obsession that had driven his father to madness. La Roque backed out of the room, horrified. Then he turned and fled, trying to escape what he believed to be the beginning of his own insanity.

Marianne finally seemed to realize that her father was in a dire situation. She ran to his side. "Papa?"

"Maybe the whiskey will help," Madame said. "It's in that bottle, over there."

Marianne rushed to pour him a glass, nervously spilling some. Her shaking hands extended the glass to *maman*. She took the goblet and held it for her husband to drink. Trembling, Bouchard sat up enough to take a sip, but then fell weakly into the arms of his wife.

Zoé ran in with the pills. Madame snatched the case from her hand, opened it and handed a pill to Bouchard.

All three women watched him, praying that he would survive whatever had him in its grip. Zoé was crying so much that she didn't even realize her tears had all run out. Marianne stared at her father, terrified as she watched his chest rise and fall.

Finally, Bouchard's breathing eased. He opened his eyes and still panting from exhaustion, managed to sit up. He looked at his daughters.

"I want you both… I want all of you… to get our things. We are leaving now!"

"Papa please," Zoé began. "I have to explain. It isn't—"

"Tais-toi!"

He said it quietly, but with such restrained anger that Zoé snapped into silence.

"Girls, get your things," said Madame. "I will summon a carriage."

She rushed out, but the girls hung back, both afraid to let him out of their sight. Zoé felt sick to her stomach. Her father wouldn't even look at her, much less speak to her. Marianne was another story.

She glared at Zoé. "I hate you! I shall never forgive you!" she said through her tears.

Zoé opened her mouth to respond, but Marianne stood and stalked out. Zoé realized that it was time, too, for her to leave. She made it to the doorway and then paused, to glance back over her shoulder.

Her father was looking at her, but with such despair. She could see that, in his eyes, she was now stained in some way.

She turned away, feeling exposed and vulnerable. Why had her lover fled? Why, instead of attacking her father, had he not stood by her side, stayed to defend her honor? Why wasn't he here, in spite of the terrible position in which they'd been found, to help her explain that they were in love?

Why had she been left to face this alone?

They were all packed and ready to go within the hour. The attack left Bouchard so weak that the footmen had to carry him to the carriage. Marianne avoided Zoé and Madame ignored her, leaving her to feel cast aside. As the carriage rode away, she thought of La Roque and silent tears slipped down her face. She felt the acute sense of his abandonment. A stab of guilt lay buried deep within her breast. She now faced a lightless future without his love or her family's respect. It was over. She no longer believed in love or hope. She no longer believed in him.

There had been no sign of the count since the events in the parlor. She made a quick, desperate attempt to find him but couldn't. Instead, she saw Sheridan lurking in the shadows. At the sight of him smirking, she felt her world crumbling. She could not help but feel that somehow the American would be a part of her fate.

Was La Roque's decision to run a message that he would not honor their love? He would not make her his bride.

Before climbing into the carriage, she gave one last look at the château. Her eyes found the windows of his chambers, and she stared hard, hoping to see him. But there was nothing. It was as if he'd never existed, leaving her more alone than before she'd met him—and with significantly fewer chances in life. Heartbroken, she climbed inside.

La Roque stood at the attic window, watching Zoé being helped into the carriage. He was hiding and it killed him that he had resorted to such cowardice. He saw her look up, searching for him, and the pain on her face made him weaken. He dashed out of the attic, desperate to save her, to hold her again. Running down the long spiral steps, he fell and went tumbling down the stairs. The fall didn't injure him, but it did leave him momentarily dazed. Coming to himself, he jumped up, raced through the main hall and out of the foyer.

The carriage was already gone.

He paced the dirt path in front of his home, breathing hard and cursing himself for being a fool. His hands hung in fists at his sides, a sense of madness settling over her leaving. He thought fighting for her would drive him insane, but losing her was even worse.

Sheridan came out of the front door. "Are you all right, old boy? What on earth is going on?"

"I failed her."

Sheridan masked his amusement. "Failed who? Marianne?"

"No, Zoé."

"Oh, so you did have an interest in her?" Sheridan asked. He looked La Roque up and down. "You are very serious, aren't you? Well," he looked down the road, squinting, "Why don't you go after her? They couldn't have gotten far."

La Roque shook his head. "Her father is ill. If I stop them and engage him, I could make matters worse."

"This is true," Sheridan said, nodding and watching him pace.

"What will become of her? What will become of me without her?"

"Are you prepared to make her your wife?"

"I…" La Roque looked back at the road. "I don't know. I guess I can fix this. I'll just have to—"

"Listen, old friend. I know you care for the Negress, but its better this way. Remember your father and the insanity in your family. You are too attached to her. That's not love. That's obsession. It'll drive you mad. Plus, you stand to lose your position in society if you marry a–if you marry her. There's no way to correct this. No way."

La Roque looked at him and confessed, "I love her."

"There is no such thing, remember?" Sheridan said and gave La Roque a pat on the shoulder.

La Roque looked down. "I don't know what I'm doing anymore."

"Come inside. Let's talk this out."

La Roque allowed Sheridan to lead him. He wanted to believe that Zoé would be all right, that she would marry her suitor and have the life she deserved. He needed to believe that. He couldn't expose her to his madness. Letting her go was for the best.

That was the lie he told himself. That was the lie he so desperately needed to believe.

5

The journey home was difficult. Bouchard suffered tremendously from discomfort and complained of numbness on his left side. Marianne barely spoke two words. The tension between them pained Zoé. She sat with her head down in shame, and the family acted as if she weren't there.

The staff greeted them upon their arrival and Zoé's childhood companion, Marguerite, who acted as an Abigail to both daughters, was waiting with a joyful smile. That smile disappeared when she saw Bouchard being carried in and the solemn look on everyone's face.

Zoé was so heartsick over her father's disappointment and her lover's betrayal that she barely noticed anyone as she hurried to her chamber.

Madame had grabbed her arm and said, "You are not to leave your room until you are sent for. Your meals will be brought to you."

Zoé paused long enough to cast one look over her shoulder and catch a final glimpse of the men carrying her father to his wing. He gave her a pained smile. It was enough to give her hope. The events of the past hours had her completely disoriented.

Now alone, Zoé sat staring out of the frosted window in her room. She thought of the count and how the sweet taste of forbidden fruit had soured for them both. She wiped away her tears as flashes of their last passionate moments together played over and over in her mind. She could almost feel the soft touch of his hair as it traveled down her body while he rained kisses between her breasts and over every part of her. Closing her eyes, she fantasized that she was of nobility, or simply of a different skin tone, someone who could have love and happiness without stigma. She fantasized that La Roque loved her enough to want to share in all the desires she had for him.

She went to her small bureau, sat down and opened the tiny drawer where she kept her stationery and inkwell. Taking up her feather quill, she set about writing the goodbye that she hadn't been able to say to him.

Mon Amour,

For me, our time together was a dream, a fantasy that even now I wish were a reality. I can hear you reciting passages from Victor Hugo. I can see you walking through my boudoir door, daring me to toss all caution to the wind just to relive that dream once more. Last night I lay in your arms. You whispered your love for me in my ear. Now all of my hope and your promises have disappeared. I don't blame you, for your world is a place in which I would never find acceptance. I embrace the belief that if our circumstances were different, our love would have had a much more deserving end.

I know not what is to become of me, but without your love and that of my dear father, it matters less. All I know is that for a small moment in time I was not Zoé Bouchard, fille mûlatresse of Monsieur Bertrand Bouchard and Capucine Draqcor. For a small moment, I was your mademoiselle, free to love you and experience your love without constraint. I will cherish that memory always, and I will carry you in my heart forever. I pray that whatever haunts you, whatever keeps you tortured and locked in fear, is exorcised, and that someday you will find the love you deserve. Remember me always and know that I will never forget you.

> ~ *Zoé*

Resting her quill in the inkwell, Zoé read what she had written, unaware of the tears that slipped down her cheeks. Before La Roque, she had known little of matters of the heart and just wanted her father's love. Now she had discovered how deeply fulfilling it was to have experienced love, only to have that joy ripped from her heart.

"*Mademoiselle?*"

Zoé looked up as Marguerite entered the room, carrying a silver tray. Zoé smiled at the sight of her and got to her feet. Marguerite had been there since Capucine's time.

"Madame asked that I bring you your dinner."

"*Merci.* How's my father?"

Marguerite was grave as she set the tray on the table near the window. "They have sent for the doctor. The journey home exhausted him."

Zoé felt another surge of sorrow, felt tears slip from her eyes. With a shaking hand, she wiped them away. Marguerite's kind face puckered with worry.

"What's happening? Marianne is locked up in her room, refusing to come out. You have been banished to yours. Monsieur is gravely ill and Madame is in the meanest mood I've seen in years. Tell me your troubles."

Zoé dropped her head and wept. Marguerite took her into her arms and held her as the young woman shared the details of her lost love. The story told between desperate breaths and lonely tears freed her in many ways of some of the burden and heartache.

Marguerite led her mistress to the bed and sat her down. She drew Zoé's hair back from her face, cupped her chin and turned her face to her. "You are in love and there is nothing scandalous or wrong about that."

"But Papa…"

"Your father has experienced this pain and much more. Trust me. He will not abandon you for your lapse in judgment. Love makes us all reckless."

Zoé closed her eyes. "The Comte doesn't want me."

"Then it is his loss! Do you hear?"

Zoé opened her eyes and nodded. She went to the bureau and folded her letter. She slipped it inside an envelope, dipped the feather quill in the ink and scribbled La Roque's address.

"I need you to get a footman to deliver this letter," Zoé said, handing Marguerite the missive. "And I would ask that you do me another favor."

"Of course."

"Can you find a way to get Papa to request to see me? I desperately need to speak with him."

"Bien sûr," Marguerite said and left.

Zoé felt her first small sigh of relief since it all began to fall apart. Would the letter help? Would it make a difference? And suppose she did get in to speak with her father? Would he listen?

Her gaze fell on the dinner tray and her stomach soured at the sight of it. She went to her bed and stretched out on it. Burying her face in the pillow, she gave vent to a silent scream, succumbing to her pain.

"Here you go, old boy," said Sheridan, passing the whiskey to La Roque.

The count had been sitting in his study, drinking for hours, still in shock over his failure to protect Zoé and ashamed of his cowardice. He was quite inebriated and could barely hold the glass.

"I need to return to America," Sheridan said. "I was wondering about the loan we discussed."

La Roque's hand shook as he raised his glass and took a sip of the pungent liquid.

Sheridan leaned closer. "I know you said three thousand, but I need ten. I can't live like a pauper."

La Roque looked over at him, his eyes red and heavy. "You dare ask me for money when my world is coming apart?"

Sheridan rolled his eyes. "You are the wealthiest man in Toulouse. You can have any maiden in this village. Hell, in all of France! What is so fascinating about her?"

"You have no idea what it's like to be loved by her. You have no idea."

Exasperated, Sheridan ran a hand through his hair. "About that money…"

"*D'accord!* Take the damn money! Take as much as you want!"

La Roque threw the glass across the room. It shattered against the far wall, staining the patterned silk with amber-colored whiskey.

Sheridan raised an eyebrow.

La Roque pushed himself up from the chair. Unsteady on his feet, he had to grab the back of his chair to balance himself. He staggered to his writing desk, flipped open his ledger and made out a cheque. When La Roque straightened up and turned with the cheque in hand, he found Sheridan already standing there, grinning. Sheridan reached out to take it, but La Roque snatched it back.

"Hear me well," he said. "Let this finish things between you and me. I have not forgotten the way you hurt her. Take this money and leave my country, never to return. We are no longer friends."

Sheridan stared at him. "You would end our brotherhood? All because of her? Her father will probably sell her to the next man who makes an offer."

"Watch your step. I give you this money because of that brotherhood. But this fountain of finance has just run dry. I want you out of my home before sunrise or we shall settle this like gentlemen."

Sheridan opened his mouth to say something, but then thought better of it. He licked his lips. "I beg your pardon," he began. "This is an emotional time for you and I am being insensitive. I'm sorry for what you are going through, and I shall return home immediately. I can only hope that with time we can find our way back to the brotherhood we once shared." He once again extended his hand.

La Roque looked at the proffered hand and softened. He had no more fight in him. Money meant nothing. All he wanted was to be left to his misery. He slapped the cheque into Sheridan's hand, and pushed past him. Then he sank back down in his chair and buried his head in his hands.

"Farewell, dear friend," Sheridan said.

ZOÉ

La Roque moaned. He wanted more liquor to numb the pain. He got up, stumbled to the cabinet, and grabbed the spirits that were stored in a wooden cask. He poured some into a drinking glass. Then he upended the glass and drank from it, determined to drink until he felt nothing.

⁂

Zoé sat on her bed, reading a classic that her father had given her on her tenth birthday. She loved the story and had read the book more than a hundred times. Hearing her door open, she looked up to see Madame step through. Zoé lowered the book and looked into her stepmother's hateful face. She wasn't expecting a visit from her so soon and was terrified as to what she wanted.

"Madame?"

"Your father is asking for you."

Zoé's eyes grew wide. She was off the bed in an instant, ready to dash off.

"*Un moment,*" said Madame.

Zoé stood still, waiting to bear another onslaught of insults and taunts. None of it mattered if father wanted her. Everything would be all right once she explained herself.

"He's dying," said Madame.

Zoé blinked. She felt as though she'd been punched in the chest.

"He's dying," Madame repeated, "and we all have to make our peace. I thought you should know what your selfish, foolish deeds have cost us."

Zoé felt a wave of guilt. She began to shiver all over. Her stepmother kept talking but Zoé registered little of it. She couldn't get past the word dying.

"*Non…*" she moaned and clutched her chest.

Madame had tears in her eyes. At the sight of Zoé's distress, a flicker of compassion lit her eyes. She actually made a move toward Zoé, to take her in her arms, but the girl stepped back, shaking her head no, and Madame's eyes filled once more with resentment and frustration.

"Fix yourself up. Don't go in there making matters worse."

"This can't be. Papa can't die!"

"He can and he will. I, for one, don't think you deserve a moment of his time, but he is insistent upon seeing you. So swallow it and face what you've done to him and yourself," Madame snarled.

But Zoé was so stunned she couldn't move.

Madame's eyes blazed. "Don't you ever think of anyone other than yourself? I am battling my own hell. I want to spend time with my husband, but all he wants is to see you two. Marianne is with him now and he keeps moaning for you. I must honor his wishes—and for once, so will you. It's your fault he's on his deathbed. Yours and yours alone. Now, come!"

Zoé was so stunned she couldn't react.

Madame grabbed Zoé by the arm and dragged her from the room and down the hall to the stairs. Tearful and consumed by guilt, Zoé could barely keep up. She stumbled down the stairs, lifting the front of her skirt to keep from tripping on it.

Madame pulled her to his doorway and pushed her through. Zoé's long curls covered her face and fell around her shoulders. She looked upon the scene with a face drawn by sorrow. Her father lay in his bed, ashen and obviously very weak. Marianne knelt at his bedside, her long locks wild, her face pink and streaked with tears. Madame beckoned her daughter from the doorway. Marianne gave her father one last longing look, then reluctantly got to her feet. She kissed his hand, and then bent over his bed to hug him and kiss him on the cheek.

"Marianne?" called Madame.

With a cry, the girl pulled herself away and ran past Zoé out the door. Bouchard's gaze followed his youngest daughter, then moved to Zoé. He gave her a look of great love and smiled weakly.

"Ne pleures pas, ma fille," he whispered, asking her not to cry.

Zoé ran to his bedside and fell to her knees. She grabbed his hand and pressed it to her face. "No, Papa. Please, no…"

With visible effort, Bouchard extended an arm to stroke her silken curls. He hushed her, trying to get her to calm down, but nothing he said or did silenced her wails. She'd rather he hate her and send her away than see him die because she broke his heart.

"Zoé…" he whispered, but she was so hysterical, she didn't hear him. So he struggled to speak louder. *"Zoé, écoute!"*

She looked up, eyes brimming with tears, her hair in her face and lips quivering. "I'm so sorry—"

"No!" He shook his head. "Listen."

She swallowed and nodded. He smiled at her and his fingertips cleared the hair from her face.

"You are my Zoé, the beautiful daughter of Capucine Draqcor who was the love of my life."

"I didn't—"

"I am no fool. I raised you to be strong and independent. I encouraged that flame in you that burns so bright even now. I knew how dangerous it was to shelter you from the evil of men and make you believe that everyone had goodness in their heart.

I want to apologize for striking you. You are young and innocent and that man took advantage of your trust."

Zoé looked up at him, wild-eyed, and shook her head. "But Papa, he loves me."

"No, he does not. But I see that you love him."

"Yes," she whispered, "I do."

"We all do impulsive things for love. Some of us even destroy the ones we desire the most. I loved your mother most of all, but I was arrogant, and selfish. I made her suffer because of my mistakes. I took your stepmother to bed, causing her to bear me Marianne. Your mother was forced to play mistress in a home she thought was hers. I was thoughtless, and I will forever regret how we both suffered because of it."

Zoé had heard rumors that Madame had tricked him into marrying her, but she'd never believed them, not because she thought Madame incapable of such trickery, but because she didn't want to think that he could have betrayed her mother so horribly. To hear the truth deepened her sorrow.

Bouchard sighed. "I want you to know that I don't blame you or love you any less because of this."

"Oh, Papa…"

"This is not your fault. My health has been failing for years. You must know that you did not do this. I don't want you ever to carry one ounce of guilt or regret for daring to be you.

My only regret is that I didn't protect you from that man, that I was unable to defend your honor."

Zoé gripped his hand. She had to make him understand. "Papa, please listen. I know that what Gian— what he and I did was wrong. We should have come to you with our feelings, but he is a good man. He is just tortured like most men. I don't blame you for *Maman's* death. She was happy loving you, and told me many nights how wonderful you were to her."

She was overjoyed to see how her words, and the memories they evoked, brought a smile to his face.

"You're a woman now," he said, brushing his fingertips against her cheek.

Zoé kissed his palm. "I love you so much."

"I love you, too. I've told Madame to take care of you. I don't have much to leave for you three. Our business is not profitable, but there's a policy on me and Madame should be able to sustain you."

Zoé nodded, knowing full well that once he died Madame would expel her from the household, but she didn't dare tell him that. She wanted him to have peace.

Bouchard gestured for her to come closer. She climbed into bed and snuggled beside him, her wide skirt fanning across his legs as she nestled into his arm. The door opened and Marianne appeared, still crying. Bertrand looked up and beckoned for her as well. She ran to the other side of the bed and climbed in to hug him.

He smiled. "I love you."

Marianne's hand slid across their father to Zoé, who accepted it and squeezed it as they both rested their heads on their father's chest. They were both so choked up with emotion that they could hardly speak. Snuggled up next to him on either side, they listened to his weak and erratic heartbeat. When they heard the final thump of his heart, when they saw that his chest rose and fell no more, Marianne screamed and Zoé clung to him. Shattered by their loss, they clung to his lifeless body, shedding the most heartbroken tears of their lives.

Their father was dead and their world would never be the same.

They buried him on a Sunday. The sky, ash gray and cloudy, offered no hope of sunshine or joy. The grass in the private graveyard was wet and muddy from the morning rain, which continued to fall in large droplets around the mourners. All of Narbonne was in attendance to pay its respects to one of the most beloved men in the village.

The Bouchard family had always been generous and supportive of the villagers who worked in its fishing trade. This was especially true under the leadership of Bertrand Bouchard. It was why the family fortune was all but exhausted. Bouchard could never turn away anyone in need.

Standing two steps back from the grave, Zoé wore a long black velvet gown with a matching black rain cape around her shoulders. A mink cuff concealed and warmed her trembling hands. On her head was a black bonnet with a net veil that shielded her tear-stained face. Marianne and Madame were dressed in similar fashion and all three ladies were locked in their own personal hells.

Under a darkening sky, the priest spoke of God and heaven, telling the surviving souls that death was all a part of the Almighty's plan. Zoé took in each word with bitterness. Her father deserved better than this. He should not have died broken and poor. Nor should he have suffered even a minute of discomfort because of her recklessness. He'd told her that his illness and impending death was not her fault, but it was.

Gazing down at the casket holding his remains, her vision became blurred. Vaguely, she noted that the air had gotten heavier. Thunder could be heard at a distance. Tears slipped her from eyes and an irrational resentment swelled in her breast.

How could he die on her? How could he leave her? He was all she had left in the world.

Marianne stood next to her, weeping softly. After he died, the two girls had refused to leave him. After several hours, Madame had gotten the staff to carry the girls away. In the middle of the night, Zoé awakened to find Marianne standing by her bed, her long blonde locks tangled and disheveled. It occurred to Zoé that her younger sister was carrying her own load of guilt. After all, it was she who had told their father of Zoé's indiscretion.

Zoé pulled back the covers for her sister to climb in. Marianne lay in her arms as she had when they were little girls after Zoé's mother died. When Zoé was six, Marianne was four and they were inseparable.

Whatever anger and disappointment the sisters felt toward one another died with their father. Zoé extended her hand to her sister and Marianne accepted it. The contact brought about the comfort that only sisters could give to one another.

"Ashes to ashes, dust to dust…" the priest intoned.

Zoé let her gaze drift over the crowd. The grief-stricken faces of the villagers, men, women and children representing a range of social classes and occupations, impressed upon her how widely loved her father had been. She was grateful that Madame, who was always so conscious about status and matters of propriety, had opened the funeral to everyone, and not just the established class.

As her eyes passed over the familiar faces, she wondered if this would be the last time she saw them. How long before Madame—

Suddenly, she drew a sharp breath.

There, standing among the mourners under a large old olive tree, was Sheridan. He tipped his top hat to her and her blood ran cold. What was he doing here? For a moment, one very brief but intense moment, she felt a surge of anger. But then it died and she returned to her grief.. It didn't matter why he was there. Nothing mattered, now that the two men she loved more than life itself were lost to her forever.

Madame stepped forward to toss a lily into the grave. Marianne did the same. Then it was Zoé's turn. She put all thoughts of Sheridan out of her mind. It was time to say good-bye to Father. She stepped up to the graveside.

There was a clap of thunder overhead and heavy rain burst from the dark clouds, causing many to take shelter under umbrellas and coats. Madame and Marianne rushed back to the family carriage, but Zoé didn't flinch. She looked down into the grave, rain pouring all around her, and whispered.

"I love you, Father. I'm so sorry I failed you."

Her gaze went to the neighboring tombstone. It marked her mother's grave. Bouchard's will had been specific. He was to be buried next to his beloved Capucine. Zoé was surprised that Madame had honored his wishes. Glancing up at the carriage, she saw that Sheridan was in conversation with Madame. The sight penetrated her despair and grief, reawakening her sense of unease. Again, she wondered, what was he doing here?

No doubt she would soon find out.

Her attention returned to her father's grave. A thought had come to her in the middle of the night, in those long hours between dusk and dawn, when neither her exhausted heart nor fretful mind could find peace. It was the only thought that had given her a measure of comfort or eased her guilt.

She would make her father a promise, a final promise, and she would make it now. As her tears mingled with the rain, she fell to her knees. Ignoring the beating rain, she raised her head to the sky and spoke to her beloved papa.

"One day, I shall make you proud of me," she whispered.

Strong hands gripped her by her left arm and pulled her to her feet. She turned to find Sheridan standing next to her.

"Zoé, I—"

With a cry, she wrenched herself away from him and ran to the carriage, stumbling as her heeled ankle boots sank in the wet marsh and the bottom of her rounded skirt dragged across the earth. By the time she'd covered the short distance to the coach, she was out of breath. The footman bowed and opened the door, and she climbed in.

"You will catch your death of cold," Madame scolded.

Zoé was horrified to find that Sheridan had climbed in behind her. She glanced at Marianne to see that she, too, looked stunned.

Sheridan smiled at her as the carriage pulled from the graveyard. "I am so sorry for your loss, ladies."

Marianne regarded him with unconcealed resentment. "What brings you here?"

Zoé's lips parted in surprise. Marianne had never spoken out of turn and she had never spoken with such venom.

Sheridan ignored the two girls and addressed Madame. "I am on my way back to America and when I heard of your husband's death, I just had to come. He was a great gentleman."

Before Madame could respond, Marianne spoke up.

"Now that you've had your say, I trust that you will be leaving us soon?"

"Marianne, bite your tongue!" Madame said.

Marianne reached for Zoé's hand. "We just lost Papa. We need no company at this time. We need to be alone, as a family, to heal."

Sheridan nodded, as though this made perfect sense to him. "Oh, I don't want to impose. I actually came with news."

Zoé's heart skipped a beat. Was she about to hear news of her beloved?

"I would like to take a bride," Sheridan announced.

Two shocked faces looked back at him.

"I see?" Madame asked.

Sheridan put on a magnanimous smile. "Madame, you have just lost your husband. I don't want to add to your grief. Far from it. As I said earlier I am here to ease your situation, to make your burden easier."

Marianne narrowed her eyes. "And how do you propose to do that?"

Madame again hushed her, but Sheridan took no offense. He continued merrily.

"Why, by making a handsome offer of marriage."

"I don't think so," said Marianne. "I have no desire to marry you."

"*Bien.* It is your sister's hand I seek."

Zoé felt a cold sense of danger grip her. She'd known. She'd seen him under the olive tree and a part of her had known what he was up to. He smirked at her and she had to fight an urge to slap his face.

"Absolutely not!" Marianne cried.

"Marianne! That's enough!" Madame declared. "I understand that you're under duress, but you will stop with this rudeness."

Marianne turned to her sister. "He's not to be trusted! He sent me to find you. He knew what I would walk in on."

Zoé was shocked. She looked at Sheridan and her anger flared. *"C'est vrai?"*

Madame raised her hand. "Nothing Monsieur Sheridan did compares to what you did. I am your guardian and I shall speak on your behalf."

"Maman!" Marianne cried, "There is no way Papa would have approved—"

"Enough, I said! We won't have this discussion now."

Marianne swallowed, her cheeks flushed pink. Zoé looked from her to Madame and Sheridan, and felt chilled to the bone, certain that her fate had already been determined.

Madame gave Sheridan a smile. "We shall discuss your offer over tea."

The carriage fell silent. The girls watched Sheridan in disgust the rest of the way home.

"I won't let her do this to you, Zoé. I swear it!" Marianne said, tears in her eyes, as they climbed the stairs to their rooms.

Zoé shook her head. She didn't care what happened to her, anymore. She had nothing to offer anyone, anyway. When her father died, she assumed that this would be her fate. The thought of being held captive by that monster did sicken her, but she was resigned to it.

"Marianne, you have no say in this matter and neither do I. Madame will never allow me to stay and I can't marry now."

Marianne stopped in her tracks. "Are you saying you will give up? Have you not told me that you and La Roque are in love?"

Zoé had shared that with her sister that morning as she pinned her curls. She explained how she had succumbed to her passion with La Roque and why she had no regrets. She just wanted Marianne to know that they never meant to hurt her.

"He doesn't want my love. I can't force him to face what he dreads."

"How do you know that? Shouldn't you find out before you let yourself be sold off into servitude with that man?" Marianne gestured down the stairs, toward the parlor, where her mother and Sheridan had gone as soon they reached the house.

Zoé closed her eyes briefly and sighed. She saw no point in arguing; she was sick with grief and guilt. She just wanted to get out of her heavy, wet dress and crawl into bed.

⚜

"You have a lovely home," Sheridan was saying. "It must cost a small fortune to keep it up." He gave Madame his most charming smile, but it was lost on her.

Madame had learned to despise him. She now knew that it was his conniving ways that had pushed her husband into an early grave.

"I need the truth," she said, taking off her wet rain cape and draping it on a chair. She unpinned her hat, freeing her red and gray spiral curls.

"Truth?"

"Why do you want Zoé? Is this some sick game between you and Comte La Roque?"

"Why do you care? I've asked my questions and I know that you are in financial ruin. There is no way you can sustain all three of you. I offer you a way out."

"By betraying my husband and selling away his child?"

Sheridan shrugged. "Those are matters of guilt that don't concern me. I am prepared to give you 50,000 francs. That should more than sustain you and Marianne until you're able to handle your affairs."

"Fifty thousand? That is quite a generous offer, Monsieur Sheridan."

"Extremely."

"You would give us that kind of money for Zoé?"

"Yes."

Her husband had made her swear to take care of Zoé and not ship her off, but he'd left no money or resources. Her only hope was to marry Marianne off, but acceptable suitors were few and far between, with so many men lost to their village after the Napoleonic wars. She would have to put her own child first. Zoé was Capucine's daughter and a woman now, and a brazen harlot at that.

Madame felt a moment of old guilt at the thought of Capucine, but quickly cleared her emotions. She had long ago repaid her debt for her trickery. It was time to move on.

"How soon will you be taking her?"

"Tonight."

"Marguerite! Marguerite!" cried Marianne, rushing into the servants' quarters.

Marguerite turned around from the laundry, worried. "What is it?"

"It's Zoé! We have to help her! *Maman*-she plans to sell her!"

"Mais non!" gasped Marguerite. "I knew this day would come, but I had no idea it would be the same day as the funeral. Your mother… has she no respect for the dead? But what can we do? We can't stop her. There is no way."

"We must get word to Comte La Roque," urged Marianne.

Marguerite shook her head. "Marianne, dear, that won't make a difference."

"It will! I saw them together. He loves her. It's her only hope."

Marguerite studied her words. *"Bien…* I sent Jean-Claude on an errand yesterday. He should be back. Maybe I can send word through him."

"Oh, yes! Hurry, please! Take me to Jean-Claude."

It was well past midnight when the Bouchards' fourteen-year-old gamekeeper, Jean-Claude, reached Château La Roque on horseback. He had traveled all day to deliver his mistress'

letter and was exhausted. He hitched the horse to the post at the side of the gate, thinking of his mission and its urgency. He knew this was an inappropriate time for a visit, but Marguerite had said it was for sweet Zoé.

He had carried a secret torch for her for years. He would do anything to lessen her pain. He knocked on the door and stood back. His white wig was crooked from the ride, so he reached up, adjusted it and brushed himself off. He wore a standard footman's uniform with a blue topcoat and tail, white tights and black pointed pumps.

After several minutes with repeated knocks and no response, he was wondering what he could do. He dare not return without having fulfilled his mission. Suddenly, the small panel in the door was unlatched and a man's face looked out.

"Yes? Who goes there?"

Jean-Claude identified himself and explained that he had an urgent message for the count.

"Are you aware of the hour?" the voice snapped.

"It is from Mademoiselle Zoé Bouchard."

One could immediately hear the gasp from person behind the door. The face disappeared from the panel, which was slapped back into place, and a moment later, the door itself was unlocked and swung open. An older servant stood there, holding a candelabrum and urging Jean-Claude to hurry up and get inside.

Jean-Claude walked in and looked around. This château was much more lavish than the one in Narbonne. At the thought, he remembered the reason for his presence.

"Is *le seigneur* awake?" he asked.

The servant hesitated. He seemed to be struggling with some inner decision. After a moment, he said, "Follow me. I will take you to him."

As he led the way up the marble spiral stairway, his candelabrum held high, the old man said, "I am Gérard, the count's manservant. I have served his family for more than forty-five years, and I have seen much, but I have never seen my master in such a state."

"Is he not well?" Jean-Claude inquired.

"You shall see," Gérard said. "You shall see."

The flames of the candles cast flickering shadows on the walls as they walked down a long, lonely corridor. Gérard led the boy to the very last door at the end of the hall, pushed it open and stepped inside. He crossed a magnificent sitting room to the inner chamber door on the other side. This door, too, Gérard entered without the usual knock. Jean-Claude was amazed: Gérard hadn't even bothered to announce their presence much less ask permission to enter, but the moment the boy stepped into the room, he understood why.

Julien La Roque lay on his bed, sprawled on his stomach, his long hair tangled and covering his face. Overturned goblets littered the floor and the room reeked of whiskey and soiled linen. Jean-Claude could see La Roque was completely drunk and thought it would be a hopeless cause to try to wake him, but when Gérard grabbed La Roque by the shoulder and shook him, La Roque moaned and rolled over, on to his back.

"What is it?"

"A messenger has come," Gérard said. "It is urgent."

La Roque managed to lift his head and squint at Jean-Claude. Apparently unimpressed, he yelled at Gérard. "Why in hell would you bring him to me in the middle of the night?"

"The message, it is urgent," Gérard repeated. "And it's from Mademoiselle Bouchard. *Zoé* Bouchard."

La Roque sat up, breathing hard. He swiped a tangle of thick dark hair back from his forehead. His eyes were red and shadowed. A scraggly beard was forming around his face. His skin was pale and pasty. Jean-Claude had been told of the love his mistress bore this man. He couldn't understand it. How could she love someone so broken?

"*Mon seigneur* Comte La Roque," he said, then walked over and offered the letter.

La Roque snatched it out of the boy's hand. He tore open the envelope, unfolded the page and read it with shaking hands. He blinked rapidly and Jean-Claude realized that the count was fighting back tears.

"How is she?" La Roque asked in a shaky voice.

"Not well," Jean-Claude said. "The doctor told the family that her father would not survive this night."

La Roque closed his eyes. "Tell her I'm sorry. Tell her—"

"*Mon seigneur,*" said Gérard, stepping forward. "Forgive me for speaking so directly, but a gentleman must deliver his condolences himself."

La Roque gave Gérard a look meant to silence him, but the servant stood his ground.

"*Mon seigneur—*"

"Leave me!" La Roque snapped.

Jean-Claude turned and left. Behind him, he heard Gérard say, "This has gone on long enough. This business is killing you. You must make it right."

"Leave!"

Jean-Claude waited in the antechamber. Gérard stepped out, closing the count's door behind him. Jean-Claude looked at Gérard, confused. The manservant shook his head, his face expressing both sorrow and frustration.

As they started out, there came from within La Roque's room a cry of great anguish. The two servants paused and exchanged looks. Then, of one accord, they continued out the door, leaving the count to his misery and madness.

Marianne walked with Marguerite to the rear of the stables and approached Jean-Claude. He was tending to a horse as they approached.

"When did you return?" Marguerite asked.

"I just arrived." He glanced at Marianne and his eyes widened at the sight of her black gown. "Monsieur Bouchard?" he asked with a shaky voice, noticing her attire.

"Papa is dead," Marianne said, "and if you don't help me, Zoé will be sold off to America, which will kill her and me for sure!"

6

"I don't understand. America? Why is she being sent to America?" Jean-Claude asked.

"*Maman* is entertaining an offer from a horrible man named Flynn Sheridan," said Marianne, pacing.

Marguerite looked at Jean-Claude. "Did you deliver the letter to le Comte? What was his response?"

Marianne stopped her pacing to hear his answer. The limp blonde curls hanging around her face made her appear vulnerable, but the blazing fire in her green eyes revealed her determination to protect her sister. "Is he on his way?"

Jean-Claude shook his head. "No, I don't think so. He's a drunkard."

Marianne frowned. "A what?"

"A drunkard, *mademoiselle*. He was barely awake when I saw him last."

"Don't be absurd."

Jean-Claude stood his ground. Marianne stared at him for several minutes, and then ran her hands through her hair, still damp from the rain.

"I don't care!" she cried. "He must be told that my sister needs him. If he knew that his friend was trying to take her to America, then he would come."

Marguerite nodded. "Jean-Claude, you will have to go back to Toulouse. We will try to stall Madame, but you have to get word to La Roque!"

"I am telling you that he is not well. The man is drinking himself to death."

"Then you pour him some tea and drag him here," Marianne said. "I won't lose my sister. Do you hear? Now go!"

Jean-Claude bowed and readied his horse for the ride.

Marianne turned to Marguerite. "We need to find a way to stall Monsieur Sheridan!" she said, putting her hand to her head.

❦

Madame knocked on Zoé's bedroom door but got no response. She opened the door and saw the girl stretched out on her bed. "Are you ill?"

Zoé said nothing and closed her eyes.

Madame walked into the room and saw several large trunks already packed and lined up at the door. "I need to talk to you," she said, surprised that Zoé had already packed everything she owned.

Madame watched for a reaction but still saw nothing but the back of Zoé's black curly head. Walking over to her bed, she sat down at the foot of it, putting her back to her stepdaughter. "I know that your father told you our history."

Zoé stared at the window in front of her and said nothing.

"I would like to say that he exaggerated or that my intentions weren't so malicious, but that would be a lie. We are well past lies now," Madame said, her hands in her lap, wringing them over and over in her own guilty grip.

She looked back at Zoé, who still hadn't moved, and sighed. Through the years they'd had their problems, but overall Zoé was a good girl, very good up until her fall from grace, and the subsequent destruction of their family.

She remembered how protective Zoé was over her little sister, how Zoé, only two, would pull baby Marianne from her cradle and hold her in her tiny arms, talking to her in baby talk. At first Madame had been shocked at the sight and afraid for her baby, but then she saw how smart and protective Zoé was.

Even then she saw the beauty and innocence in her stepdaughter. She was bold and daring, qualities that Capucine possessed, the qualities that Madame envied most of all.

"I want to do right by you and for years, I have tried," she now said. "You have to know that."

Silence.

"We have nothing," Madame continued. "I know that you think that I've always wanted this fate for you and I will admit to threatening you since you were small enough to understand. I can only say that I never really intended to follow through."

Madame began to pace. "He's offering me and Marianne a chance to survive. Without your father we have no way to manage. I can't run his business. Listen to me. This is for Marianne, as well as me. I know that you love Marianne and want her happy. I think you should——"

"I want to go with him," Zoé said in a voice stripped of emotions.

Madame was stunned. "What did you say?"

Zoé turned to face Madame. "I said I want to go with him. I'm dead anyway. I don't care what happens to me."

Madame's eyes watered "Oh, *ma chérie...*" She walked over to the bed, ready to reach for Zoé, but the contempt in the girl's eyes stopped her.

"It's what I want, so let's just be done with it. When does he want to leave?"

"Now."

Zoé sat up. "*Bien.* Please excuse me while I dress."

Madame turned her head in shame. Walking to the door, she thought of all that was transpiring and her role in it. How long would it take before she forgot about Zoé? She prayed that it would be soon. She couldn't bear more guilt.

Standing before his mirror, bare-chested and in long pajama pants, La Roque had just finished receiving a fresh shave. He looked at his face in the mirror and smiled grimly at the familiar man staring back. The mustache and thinly-lined beard that framed his lower jaw and connected to his sideburns was perfectly trimmed. He wanted to look his best. He was going to bring her home, after he begged her pardon for all the ways in which he'd failed her. She would be his wife and the lady of this château, which without her had become his mausoleum.

He read her letter over and over and drank and drank until his tongue and brain were numb, yet her face and smile still remained. No matter how much he drank, no matter how much he tried to forget her, his pain and desperation grew. He had to stop it and the only way was to reach her and make things right for them both. He realized that her love was his salvation, and that if he were to continue on with life she would have to be at his side. He believed that reclaiming his love would keep him sane. Madness came only when you allowed fear to rule your actions. He would do that no longer.

He knew that her father's impending death would leave her in peril. Bouchard would have to listen to him. He had to get to his bedside, beg his pardon, and ask for her hand in marriage.

"Mon seigneur?"

La Roque turned to see Gérard stepping in the room. "What is it?"

"News from Narbonne. It just arrived." Gérard shuffled over with a folded message.

La Roque had asked Gérard to have the local postman relay any news of Bertrand Bouchard. Now, as he read the message, he felt his chest tighten. Bouchard was gone. The funeral was to have been held that very day. La Roque crumpled the paper.

"Saddle my horse!" he snapped, snatching the hand towel from his shoulder and wiping his face of shaving soap. He had to leave immediately.

❦

Marianne came back inside to see several footmen carrying out large trunks from upstairs. *Maman* and Sheridan stood in the foyer, talking. Marianne approached them, Marguerite two steps behind her.

"What is going on?" Marianne asked.

"Zoé and Monsieur Sheridan will be leaving soon," Madame said.

"No!"

"Marianne, it's—"

Holding her dress, Marianne rushed toward Sheridan, glaring at him. "You will not take her from this house! Do you hear me? She is not your property. Take your uncivilized tactics to that cesspool of a country you came from! Leave my family in peace or I swear upon my father's grave, I'll–"

"Marianne!" interrupted *Maman*.

Sheridan smiled at her. "I think you should ask your sister what she wants."

Marianne stepped closer. "I know what she wants, and it's not you! Now get out of my house!"

Maman had never seen Marianne so enraged and could do nothing but stand there, speechless. Sheridan was tired of her defiance and ready to pounce on her when he looked up to see his chocolate bride coming down the stairs. She was again dressed in all black with her cape around her shoulders. Her hair, raven black and shiny as always, hung limply down her back in deep waves, the vibrant curls now gone.

"That's enough, Marianne," Zoé said.

Marianne frowned to see her sister coming down the stairs. "This will not happen. Where are you going?"

Marguerite looked confused as well.

Zoé looked into their faces and smiled sadly. "We need to say our good-byes."

"*Non*!" Marianne shouted, rushing to the stairs.

Zoé continued down, and Marianne threw her arms around her neck. Unable to watch, Madame left the foyer and headed to the parlor for some brandy to steady her shaking hands. Sheridan smiled triumphantly as Marguerite glared at him.

"Marianne, listen to me," Zoé said, cupping her sister's face. Marianne was crying and shaking her head. "Listen. This is my choice. I want to go."

Marianne screamed, wrenched herself away from Zoé and went for Sheridan. Before he could protect himself, she attacked him, scratching at his face. A couple of the footmen removing Zoé's things converged on Marianne and pulled her from him. Madame came running out of the parlor to see what the ruckus was all about. Zoé ran to her wailing sister.

"Marianne, please, please calm down!"

"You won't take her! I won't let you! He will stop you! He's on his way!" Marianne screamed at Sheridan.

Sheridan paled.

Zoé saw his reaction and looked at Marianne, confused. "Who is on the way?"

Sheridan grabbed Zoé's arm. "You're making this more difficult by staying. Come." He pulled her away as Madame watched in shock.

Marguerite called out to Zoé. "You must listen to her. We have sent word to Comte La Roque!"

But before Zoé could respond, Sheridan had pushed her out of the door. Marianne's screams followed them outside. Sheridan tried to shove Zoé into the carriage.

"Get in!" he shouted in her face.

Zoé bit her lip and started to take the steps to the carriage, but the sounds of a struggle caused her to turn around. Marguerite had run out the door to try to stop Zoé, but Madame had grabbed her and was trying to pull her back into the house.

Sheridan shoved Zoé into the carriage, pushed his way in behind her and screamed at the driver. *"Allez! Allez vite! Maintenant!"*

Zoé barely had time to sit down before the driver cracked the whip and the carriage took off. From her window she saw Marguerite turn on Madame and attack her, hitting her across the face and forcing her to let go. Madame stumbled back, shocked, as Marguerite rushed out to see the carriage pulling away. She ran after it screaming.

The sight broke what was left of Zoé's heart.

"This is for the best," Sheridan said.

She turned to look at him. "What did they mean? Are they speaking the truth? Will Gianelli come?"

Sheridan laughed. "Come, now. *Julien* wants nothing to do with you. When I told him that I was coming to collect you, he bade me well. As a matter of fact, he paid for our passage to America."

His words re-opened her barely-healed wounds. She closed her eyes, summoning her strength. No matter what happened to her, no matter how she suffered, she would not cry. Her father would be the last person to witness her tears.

She swayed from side to side as the carriage rocked on its wheels, racing them to the docks. She felt him studying her face. He wanted her to be his. He wanted her to serve his needs and satisfy his desires. What he felt had nothing to do with love. She closed her eyes against the sight of him.

For a long moment, there was an almost peaceful silence. But then she felt fingertips touch her hands as they rested in her lap. Her eyes popped open and she looked at him with a mixture of fear and disgust.

"Such an expression," he said. "It hurts my feelings, but I will allow it. We will have plenty of time on the ship to get acquainted, and you will see. It won't be all bad, being with me."

Her large doe eyes glistened with sadness. "I won't be your wife, will I?"

He leaned back and laughed. "Of course not. It's illegal to marry *niggers* in the States." He caught how she flinched.

"Don't like that word, do you?"

"No, I prefer that you use it. It shows what you think of me, and my kind. If I ever suffer a lapse in judgment and start to believe that you're human, your crass remarks will remind me what a monster you really are."

He reddened with fury. "This is going to stop!"

"What should stop?"

"Your defiance, the way you mock me! When we arrive home, you will learn to temper your tongue or suffer the consequences."

"Oui, monsieur."

Apparently, he missed the scorn in her voice because he appeared mollified. "You will love Carolina," he said. "Of course, you will stay in the big house with me, but you will be expected to handle your chores."

"And, may I ask, what else is expected of me?"

She could see his face become suffused with desire. His eyes raked up her and down. She wasn't dressed in the dainty corseted gowns he'd seen her in at La Roque's château. The black dress she wore now was buttoned all the way up to her chin, with lace around the bodice, its long sleeves puffed out at the shoulders. Still, it revealed the swell of her breasts and her tiny waistline. She could sense his desire to see more.

"I expect you to satisfy and obey all of my wishes," he said. "If you serve me well, then I may grant you certain privileges, but make no mistake about it. You're a lowly nothing, and that's what you'll always be. The sooner you realize it and accept it, the happier you'll be."

Zoé allowed a grim smile to curve her beautiful lips. "Does it make you feel powerful, *monsieur*? I really want to know."

"Does what make me powerful?"

"Dominating others. Persecuting those who are different from you. Why do you enjoy it so?"

He shrugged. "I believe that we all have our place in the world, and women of your kind are here to serve men of mine."

She stared at him with pity. "I feel sorry for you."

He threw his head back and laughed. "You? You feel sorry for me? This ought to be good. Tell me, why do you feel sorry for me?"

"Because you will never know love. You are filled with hatred, envy and greed. That's no way to live."

She said it softly, and then turned her attention to the view out the window, dismissing him. She felt him watching her, but pointedly ignored him. Her gaze was fixed on the blood-red sun outside of the carriage. She wanted to imprint it on her mind and always remember it. She was certain she would never see the sun set in Narbonne again.

Perched atop a reddish-gold Palomino, La Roque raced down the road toward Narbonne. He wore a standard Frenchman's suit and his topcoat and tail blew behind him as he leaned into his horse, making it quicken its pace. His hair was loose and blowing as the wind combed through it.

The hooves of his charging horse kicked up the wet marshy ground and he narrowed his blue eyes on the path, determined to get there in time to see his Zoé. She had lost her father and he knew that loss, compounded by what they had done, could destroy her. He had to keep her from slipping away as he almost had.

Barely able to make it out, he thought he saw another rider coming toward him at a rapid pace. Increasing speed, he navigated his horse to the right to allow the other to pass. When they raced past each other, Jean-Claude recognized him immediately.

"*Mon seigneur! Mon seigneur!*" Jean-Claude cried out in excitement, hailing him to stop. "Are you on your way to *Maison Bouchard*?"

"I am."

"Thank God," sighed Jean-Claude. "It is I, Jean-Claude. I was sent to deliver a message to you. It's urgent. An American has come for Mademoiselle Zoé. She's being forced to leave with him."

"American?"

"*Oui*, a Monsieur Sheridan," he panted, pulling his horse in closer. La Roque felt as though the wind had been knocked out of him. Without saying another word, he kicked his heels and raced away, with Jean-Claude close behind him.

7

The *Aventine* was the largest ship docked at the port. The vessel stood over one hundred feet in length and twenty-five feet in width. It loomed over the other, smaller fishing boats as if it were some large sea monster set to devour them all, glowing in the moonlight with a mystical bluish hue.

The wooden planks that framed the outer hull of the ship were a deep glossed brown with portholes every few feet across. The bow was graced with a carving of a woman clutching her breast and looking upward to the heavens. Above, sixteen large and small sails fanned out, the rigging flapping in the night breeze and connected by coiled rope that attached to the lower flanks.

Zoé had visited the port many times with her father to check on his shipments to and from Narbonne. She had seen many boats arrive off the Mediterranean Sea and had even boarded a few, so she had no fear of ships in general. However, ships such as the *Aventine,* headed to America and used in the slave trade, terrified her.

Captain Delaflote stepped down the wooden plank to where she and Sheridan stood on the docks. He was no more than Zoé's height. He wore a captain's blue topcoat trimmed in gold and yellow ties and a coiled belt, dingy and faded. Any regal presence it might once have had was lost in the shapeless way it hung from his shoulders. His sword rested on his hip, its golden handle glowing in the moonlight.

Zoé recoiled at the awful scar that ran from the left side of his forehead over his eye, which was covered by an eye patch, and down to the middle of his cheek. His working eye had a cold, serpent-red cruelty that sent shivers up Zoé's spine. His beard, long and scruffy, was knotted at the end from his constant twirling of the wild spiral hairs. He smiled, revealing a few rotted stumps for teeth.

"*Monsieur*, will you be sailing with us?" Delaflote asked.

Sheridan stepped away from Zoé and handed Delaflote their papers, along with a small fortune in francs to secure plush accommodations on the ship. The captain pocketed the cash and scanned the papers.

"South Carolina, huh?"

"Yes. How soon before we sail?"

Delaflote cast an eye at Zoé, who averted her gaze. "And is she your slave?"

"Yes," Sheridan smiled. "I guess you could call her that."

Slaves don't sail in the staterooms. She will be housed in the gully."

"I want her in my quarters. She is to be at my beck and call."

Delaflote gave Zoé another look. He licked his lips and asked Sheridan, "Will she be able to service the men as well?"

Zoé's heart raced upon hearing those words. She was in much greater danger than she'd realized.

Sheridan glared at the captain. "Absolutely not! She's my property. If anyone dares touch her, I shall hold you personally responsible."

Delaflote gave a dirty laugh. "Don't worry. We have other slave girls to entertain the men on the voyage. Now, please come aboard," he said, stepping aside.

The night wind blew at Sheridan's coat as he edged past Delaflote and headed up the gangway. Zoé grabbed her long skirt with both hands as the wind licked at her face and ruffled her hair. She kept her head bowed as she passed the captain. He leaned over and whispered in her ear.

"Très belle."

She cringed, kept going and fought off a wave of revulsion. The deep blue ocean waves lapped at the boat and whiffs of the smelly seawater assaulted her senses as she stepped on to the ship. With everything she had been through today, the danger of this journey with these crude men turned her weariness into terror. Knowing that she would have to depend on Sheridan for protection provided no solace.

She went to Sheridan's side. All around them, crewmen yelled out to each other as they prepared the sails. Zoé watched them carry her trunks with a sinking sense of finality. She couldn't believe that she'd been so wrong about La Roque. She'd desperately wanted to hold on to the love she thought they shared. She wanted to believe that it was fear that kept him from her, not the circumstances of her conception. But the fact that he had given Sheridan money to take her away had shattered her faith in him. Now she knew that her submission to his desires had been for nothing, and that her father had died because of her foolish choices.

Sighing, she lowered her head and silently prayed that the ship would sink before they ever reached America.

La Roque followed Jean-Claude, who now led the way along a dark path to the maison Bouchard. The moon shone brightly overhead, but the overhanging trees blocked most of the moon's glow, keeping them in darkness. La Roque knew they were riding dangerously fast with such limited night vision, but he didn't care.

He had to find her.

They turned off the path up to the maison and he felt his chest tighten. Sheridan had tricked him and used his own money to buy his beloved. The thought of her being victimized because of his callous treatment of her made him crazy. He wanted blood—Sheridan's and Madame's.

He jumped down from the horse and dashed up the stairs to the entrance. Jean-Claude grabbed the reins of La Roque's horse to secure it and looked back to see the count pounding on the door.

Marguerite opened the door, holding a lit candelabrum against the dark. Before she could open it fully, La Roque pushed his way past her, storming inside. Marguerite gasped and stepped back.

"*Monsieur!*"

"Where is she?" he cried, and raced toward the stairs.

She ran after him. "Are you Comte La Roque?"

"Where is she, damn it?" He was taking the stairs two at a time, his hair blowing light around his shoulders and his face twisted in rage.

"Attendez, mon seigneur! Attendez!"

But La Roque didn't wait. He ran up the stairs, shouting Zoé's name. He threw open door after door and Marguerite struggled to catch up. Finally, he barreled into Marianne's room. There he was confronted with the sight of the girl lying prone in bed, red-eyed and pale, with her mother sitting at her bedside.

"Where is she?" he demanded.

Madame's mouth dropped open in surprise but Marianne raised her head from her pillow. With a cry of both relief and misery, she jumped up and ran to him. He instinctively opened his arms to her and she clung to him, crying. Her sobs were so loud and desperate that La Roque felt a new sense of panic. What had become of his Zoé?

"What are you doing here?" asked Madame. She looked terrified.

"Tell me where she is."

Marianne raised her head. "He took her! He took her to America."

La Roque gripped her by the shoulders and held her away from him. "Where did they go? When did they leave?"

ZOÉ

Marianne tried to answer, but she was so hysterical her blubbering made no sense.

Madame stood and faced him. "Are you considering her as a bride? She is already promised to him. I accepted his proposal. I had no idea——"

"I ought to snap your neck," La Roque said. He pushed Marianne into Marguerite's caring arms and advanced on Madame. "You wretched woman. Your husband isn't even cold in the ground, and already you defy his wishes."

Madame tried to stand her ground. "You know nothing of my husband's wishes."

"I know that he loved Zoé, that he wanted her married. This is all your doing!" He grabbed her roughly by one arm and jerked her toward him. "You tell me where she is now or I'll make sure that you're reduced to cleaning fish at the port by sunrise. I'll turn this little palace of yours into your mausoleum and bury you in it!"

Madame's eyes widened and her mouth went slack, but at first all she could do was stammer.

"I–I had no idea. I didn't know. I thought you only took her for your amusement, *mon seigneur*. I had no idea you felt this way. I——"

"You're wasting time," he said through clenched teeth. "Tell me, or——"

"She's at the port and sailing on the *Aventine*."

La Roque threw her to the side. Her boot heel caught on the long hem of her skirt and sent her falling to the ground. He barely noticed. Marianne let go of Marguerite and raced to La Roque as he turned to leave.

"Please! Oh, please bring her back! Your friend *monsieur* will do despicable things to her and she has no will to fight!"

He was worried, but tried to be reassuring. "I won't let that happen. I'll kill him if he lays one finger on her. I promise," he said, touching her shoulder gently.

Then he was gone.

Zoé followed Sheridan into their quarters, ignoring the comments she heard in her wake. The men took extra pleasure in whispering vile things to her in French as she passed them. Sheridan turned on them, frowning. Zoé blushed deeply, and the fear in her eyes only fueled their meanness. Sheridan grabbed her arm and pulled her closer as they walked through. She was grateful for at least that much.

Once inside the cabin, she was relieved to be locked away with one monster rather than trapped with the twenty others that roamed the ship. Looking around, she saw the dark oak walls.

The room held what looked to be a full-sized bed planked out of the left wall and a table with chairs for meals. Their luggage had been piled in and the quarters were modest but cramped. She saw Sheridan grimace. He'd paid top money for this? The captain had sold a complete falsehood when he advertised this ship as luxurious.

Zoé went to the far right side of the cabin and stood there waiting for what was to come. She noticed that Sheridan looked somewhat pasty. He'd been wiping at his sweat for a while. It was as if he were coming down with a cold.

He took off his jacket and draped it over a chair. "It's so incredibly hot in here. Open that window."

She went to the round porthole and twisted the bolt, then popped it open. A gust of salty sea air came through. She looked back in time to see him unbutton his ruffled collar and pull off his shirt. Reddish splotches covered his neck and chest. He didn't seem to be aware of them. He swallowed with a grimace and rubbed his throat.

"Monsieur?" she said, going up to him.

"What is it?" Seeing her expression, he followed her gaze, looked down at his chest and saw the wound he'd tried to attend to in Toulouse. The color had changed drastically, and it oozed. "It's nothing," he added quickly, trying to conceal it.

"It looks to be infected." She put the back of her hand to his head and felt for a temperature. "How did you get it?"

"Your lover was overly rough the first time he caught us, or have you forgotten?"

Zoé grabbed his wrist and forced him to sit on the bed. "It's infected and you were foolish not to tend to it. I might be able to save you some pain. Maybe your life."

"What nonsense!"

"*Monsieur*, an infection like this with weeks on this voyage can lead to blood poisoning. It can kill you!"

"What do you know of it?" he scoffed.

"I am not some backwards animal; I've tended to sailors with the assistance of the other ladies in our village. What I know, *monsieur,* may very well save your life." She turned to leave.

"Where are you going?" he asked, panic in his voice.

"To the galley. You need treatment."

Sheridan stared at her. "Those men out there… it may be dangerous for you. I'll go." He stood up, but immediately sank back down again, gripping his temple.

Zoé shook her head. The thought occurred to her to let him die, but she could never stand by and let someone suffer, not even someone like him. Furthermore, if he were incapacitated, he could not protect her from the hateful attentions of Delaflote and his men.

She went to the door. "I will be careful," she said and ventured out.

La Roque and Jean-Claude arrived at the port, riding their horses up the flank of the pier, searching for the ship. Seeing a shipper taking down his net, La Roque approached him.

"Where is the *Aventine*?"

The fisherman looked up at La Roque and frowned. "Set sail over an hour ago."

La Roque's expression tightened. "I need a boat."

"For what?"

"To catch the *Aventine*."

The fisherman laughed. "That's Captain Delaflote's boat. Good luck finding someone to chase him and those demons he leads."

La Roque turned his horse and raced down the dock to another fisherman's boat. He got the same response. His temper boiling and time escaping, he went from one to the other. Desperate, he offered money and they laughed or shrugged or waved him away.

Finally, a young fisherman in his twenties said, "If you want to go after the *Aventine* you will need a pirated ship to do so."

"A pirated ship?"

"For the right amount of money, Captain Ferdinand will do it."

He pointed to a medium-sized ship with a yellow, black and green flag at the far end of the dock. La Roque thanked the fisherman and tossed him some coins, which the young man caught and pocketed with one graceful move.

La Roque clicked his heels and trotted down to the ship. As he approached, he saw the ship's name, *Veuve Noire,* scrawled across the belly. Several black men were lounging and drinking on the deck. One of them sat up and looked at La Roque with a scowl. He shouted at him to state his business. The tone was aggressive and no-nonsense. Everything about the man, from the fierceness of his glare to the tension in his pose, announced that he was battle-ready.

La Roque smiled. This was exactly what he was looking for.

Zoé held onto the wall as she made her way down the corridor toward the back of the cabins. She hoped the galley was nearby. Coming to the end of the corridor, she heard voices and stopped. Two men spoke of how they hated the Captain and wished that the others would consider a mutiny. She stepped back, afraid to go forward. The men laughed and their voices carried off into the distance. Moving forward again, she looked around the corner and saw them going up the stairs to the upper deck.

Finally she found the stairwell below and rushed toward it, holding onto her black skirt. After descending the stairs, she was relieved indeed to be in the galley. A short, portly white man in a grease-stained apron, with large sweat stains on his collar and underarms, looked up from cutting potatoes, saw her and gave a curious smile, revealing the fact that he was missing several teeth.

"Aye," he said with a Scottish burr. "Whom do we have here?"

Zoé saw that he was harmless. Curtseying, she introduced herself.

"Zoé Bouchard, eh? That wouldn't be any relation to Bertrand Bouchard, would it?"

"*Oui, monsieur. Je suis sa fille.*" Her voice saddened as she confirmed that she was Bouchard's daughter. She might've realized that the cook would have heard of her father. Any seaman experienced in those ports would have known of Bouchard's kind reputation.

"He died, recently, didn't he?"

She nodded. "His funeral was today."

"And now, you're here, on board this ship?" he scowled.

"Please, no more questions. Just help me. I need your help with a poultice."

"Infection, possible fever?"

"How did you know?"

He let out a hearty laugh that was so much like her father's that it warmed her to hear it. "It's the kiss of death on a voyage such as this. You look well?"

"No. My... my... *Monsieur* Sheridan has a wound that hasn't healed properly. It's infected and he suffers from fever."

The cook's puzzled frown returned. Then his eyes narrowed with sudden dark understanding. "Well then," he said, in a matter-of-fact voice. "I can make up a cabbage poultice, certain to fix what ails him."

He put down his large knife, went to a shelf and removed a crate of vegetables he'd provisioned when they'd docked. Taking out a head of cabbage, he ran a sharp blade down its center. Turning, he snatched up a rag and dipped it into the boiling water. He used a long fork to bring it back out and dropped it into a tin bowl.

She didn't mind the idea of Sheridan suffering with joint pains and fevers. She just wanted him to last long enough to keep the men on board away from her.

"Use the leaves of the cabbage to cover the wound but cover them with the hot towel," Douglas said. "How long has he had the fever?"

Zoé shook her head. "He's suffering from it now. I think this is the beginning."

"Aye, well then. He'll suffer for the next couple of days. Keep some water on hand. I'll bring you his meals and some limes for him to suck on."

"Merci, monsieur."

Douglas smiled. "Zoé, is it?"

"Oui."

"You have a friend in me. Remember that."

Zoé smiled and had to blink to hold back a sudden rush of tears. "I will."

Douglas handed her the bowl and cabbage, and she turned to go. Just before climbing back up the stairs, she glanced over her shoulder and saw the cook whistling and cutting potatoes. God was so very mysterious, she thought. She felt that her father was looking down on her. He was protecting her, too.

She took care to be silent as she went up the stairs and was relieved to find the corridor empty. Turning back to Sheridan's quarters, she felt some of her sadness dissipate. She couldn't think of her losses now; she needed to be smart and think of survival.

La Roque boarded the *Veuve Noire* with Jean-Claude on his heels. The boy had asked to go with him. Discerning how much the boy loved Zoé and wanted to help her, La Roque had agreed.

Ferdinand was at the helm. He was a free African rumored to indulge in piracy off the coast. When La Roque told him whom they were chasing, Ferdinand's eyes glistened with murderous joy. He hated Delaflote for his own personal reasons, and would enjoy battling him on behalf of the lovely Zoé. He'd seen Bouchard on the docks, conducting business, and had heard that he was a kind and fair businessman. Furthermore, he'd heard the story of Bouchard's doomed love affair with the beautiful African Capucine. That such a story should end with the daughter's enslavement enraged the pirate's unorthodox sense of gallantry.

When they found Delaflote's ship, they would have to take it by force. Ferdinand's men looked to be ready for any battle.

La Roque looked at the full moon and saw Zoé's face in it. "Hold on my love. I'm coming."

Feeling a cramp in her back, Zoé rolled over and opened her eyes. As she felt the ship sway, she listened to Sheridan's moans. She'd made herself a crude pallet on the floor at the foot of his bunk after tending to him.

Sheridan was in so much pain and sweating so badly she feared he wouldn't make it through the night. After he finally became so weakened from his ailment that he passed out, she changed into her nightgown and barricaded their door before giving into her own exhaustion. In the middle of the night, she awoke, terrified to see the doorknob being turned. The key in the lock and the chair propped under doorknob kept the door firmly in place, but that attempted break-in was enough to keep her sleeping with one eye open for the remainder of the night. While lying on the floor, she thought she heard women screaming, the sound drifting up to her. She prayed that she was wrong.

Sheridan's moans and groans grew louder. Sitting up, she saw that him shaking through his fever. He was pale and his lips looked purple. The shivering from head to toe was a sign that his fever might soon break. She got up, peeled more cabbage leaves free and repacked the infected area.

"Here," she whispered, "chew on this."

He shook his head from side to side, refusing the cabbage leaf and moaning. She saw his teeth chatter and knew he was feeling the worst of it. She grabbed his face, held it and forced the torn leaf between his lips.

"If you don't chew on it, it will get worse, and you can't die on me. We have weeks left on this horrific boat."

He gagged and she shoved the lime into his mouth. Dazed he opened his eyes and looked at her. She felt a sense of irony that she would be helping someone whose only purpose was to make her his slave.

"Look at you. I should show you no mercy for all the things you've done to me."

She reached for the bowl of water on the counter, dipped the rag in it and wrung it out. Then she went back to him, pulled back the sheets and looked at his bruises. She'd seen worse on some of her father's helpers who had returned sick from voyages. She'd assisted Madame when an epidemic struck Narbonne.

The fever and sweats were to be expected, but the bruising looked as if it was already on the mend. She looked over to the glass of cloudy liquid that Douglas made and realized that it must be responsible for Sheridan's speedy recovery.

He spit out the cabbage and turned his head. Zoé began to wipe down his face, neck, and chest, careful to soothe his bruises. He moaned and tried to twist away, but she kept carefully cleaning him and cooling his fever. Finally, she rose, grabbed the discarded cabbage and dropped it in the pail, then walked over to the table to retrieve the water for him to drink.

There was a knock on the door. She froze, staring at the door in fear. She didn't want the captain to know that Sheridan was sick; it would draw unwanted attention to them.

"Lass, are you all right?"

With a sigh of relief she realized it was Douglas. She put her tankard down, then fixed her robe.

"I brought some breakfast for you," he said.

"One moment!" she called out.

She tied her robe, removed the chair she had propped against the door, and let him in. Smiling warmly, he brought in a tray laden with food. She watched him put the tray down and closed the door. He went over to Sheridan and looked at his bruising.

"He seems to feel relief already," she said.

Douglas glanced back at her. He was dressed in the same sweat-stained white shirt and soiled apron, his belly round and pushing it outward. "He should be coming out of it by tonight. Make sure he drinks all of this: it's my own remedy," he said pointing a fat finger at the potion on the tray.

Zoé nodded, somewhat relieved. She needed Sheridan up and making appearances on the ship. She thought of how someone had turned the doorknob the night before and shivered. "Have you told the captain?"

Douglas chuckled "No, I wouldn't do that to you."

He went over to the tray of food set a plate for her at the table. "I have some fruit and bread for you. I also brought some aloe for you to put on the abrasions. It should give him some relief."

"That's very kind of you."

Douglas looked up from his arrangement of the food, with a worried expression. "So this bloke is taking you to America, eh?" He jerked his head toward Sheridan, who was asleep but still shaking.

Zoé's looked at Sheridan with unconcealed contempt. "My papa died and my stepmother sold me to him."

"I am so sorry," Douglas said.

Zoé gave him a grateful smile. *"Merci."*

"Look, we have some slave women on board," Douglas said. "They're housed in the belly of the ship. Captain Delaflote does a lot of trafficking, but those poor dears belong to the men of this ship. The things those girls are forced to endure turns me stomach."

Zoé's eyes widened. She was horrified. Those screams she'd heard in the middle of the night... they had been real.

"I'm telling you this," Douglas said, "because I want you to stay in this cabin. I'll come and check on you and bring you food, but until he is up and about, you shouldn't leave, Lass. Don't even come looking for me. The latrine for this wing is right outside your door. Be careful using it. The door does not lock."

She remembered the evil in the men's eyes as they watched her board the ship. She had no intention of wandering about on her own.

"Don't worry. I'll do as you say."

"Good. I'll be back this afternoon." Wiping his hands on his apron, he headed for the door.

"Merci, monsieur."

Douglas was grim. "Don't thank me, yet, me Lass." He glanced back at Sheridan. "I have a feeling that he's no different from the trolls on this ship. I have a daughter your age. I am disgusted by the things I've seen and I'll do my best to help you."

"You're very wise."

"And you are very special. No matter where he takes you or makes you do, try to hold on to that."

Zoé nodded, thanking him again. As soon as he left, she put the chair back in place. Then she went to the bread and broke off a piece. She hadn't had dinner last night and was starving. Sheridan writhed in pain. She hoped his suffering was great. She would never forget that his games and cruelty led to her father's discovery that she had betrayed herself. Her thoughts slowly drifted to La Roque. She looked up at the porthole window and saw the sky outside. What was La Roque doing? Anger and disappointment swelled inside her and she had to blink back sudden tears. She would cry no longer over him. He wasn't worthy of her tears.

La Roque came topside to feel the warm morning sun on his face. His thin white blouse flapped and rippled from the persistent wind. His coat was in his tiny cabin, tossed on the cot he'd slept on. As he walked up the deck, the same wind whipped his hair around his head and carried the strong salty smell of the sea to his nostrils. The ship rose and fell with the waves, making him struggle to keep balance as he observed the hustle of Ferdinand's men.

The Africans who manned the boat were an interesting lot. Their skin was as dark as coal and almost all of them wore long twisted unruly locks down their backs, as though they were in some fraternal club that required them.

Walking over to the ship's stern, La Roque spotted Ferdinand at the helm, looking north. Ferdinand wore only a pair of red tights with an orange tie around his waist. The same kind of orange bandana was tied around his head to keep his hair from his face. His skin glistened with beads of sweat that bubbled along his muscled chest and biceps.

"*Bonne matin*," said La Roque.

"Ye decided to join us, eh?"

La Roque frowned at the implied criticism.

"Look ta de sun, it's around nine," continued the captain.

La Roque glanced up at the sun. It was high in the sky, but he couldn't believe he'd slept that long.

He sensed Ferdinand's glare. The man's eyes were as dark as his skin, and his teeth as white as snow. When he spoke, the one gold tooth in his mouth sparkled as the sun caught it. "Dis for your Zoé, correct?"

La Roque nodded. "And to deliver some overdue justice to a friend of mine."

"Aye then, act like it's of major importance. Because when ye find the *Aventine,* you will have to be at the ready. We have thirteen men on dis ship, including ye and your young companion dere."

He pointed at Jean-Claude, who was helping one of the ship's hands hoist another sail so they could catch more wind and pick up speed.

"Delaflote has more than twenty," Ferdinand continued. "His ship is equipped with six-foot-long cannons that reach over 700 metres. D'ye understand?"

La Roque expressed no fear. "I know what we're facing and I don't care. My only mission is her. Saving her."

Ferdinand burst into hearty laughter. "I see you, so French, dressed in yer fancy clothes and think to meself, 'Ah, yes, this one, he thinks the fight with Delaflote's men will be according to the rules of gentlemen.' I tell you now, if you think dis, then you're wrong. I, meself, was once held captive on the *Aventine*. I will not say what I suffered. I will say that I wasn't alone. Me youngest brother died on that voyage and his ghost sails at me side."

For a moment, Ferdinand fell silent. La Roque waited. He'd wondered at the captain's readiness to go after Delaflote, a readiness that was unwavering and immediate even before they'd discussed money.

ZOÉ

"I remember it all as 'twere yesterday," said Ferdinand. La Roque's eyes followed the pirate's stare into the vast dark waters. "Dat devil ship reached the shores of Jamaica first. Dey brought on others there, men like me, who had been dragooned, and divided us up for the voyage to America. Delaflote was lucky. His ship had already set sail by the time the slaves in Jamaica revolted and killed their captors. Many of the slaves took ships and sailed into the Atlantic, lost and desperate to find dere way home."

La Roque listened, silently, as Ferdinand told how he and his band of friends took their ship and headed with the winds. They arrived in France, where they found welcome. They soon adapted to the foreign land, learning its language and customs. He had seen Jacques Delaflote several times and wanted to exact his revenge, but the pirate was always surrounded by his henchmen and unreachable. Ferdinand said he bided his time and built his crew for this voyage and battle at sea. What he planned to do to Jacques Delaflote in avenging his brother would fall under a pirate's code, he said. He'd just had no idea he would be doing it so soon.

Zoé, now dressed, sat at the table composing a letter to Marianne. She didn't know if she would be able to mail it, but she missed Marianne so desperately that writing helped her close the distance between them.

"Zoé…" croaked Sheridan.

Looking up, she saw that he was awake. She went to his bedside and touched his forehead. His fever had broken, but his linens and pillow were soaked.

"How do you feel?"

"Thirsty."

Zoé poured him a tankard of water, and then helped him sit up to drink it. He coughed as the cool water went down his throat.

"How long…?" he moaned

"It's around noon, I think, so you've been out for some time."

"And you cared for me?"

She smiled grimly. "I had little choice. We are at sea. I couldn't have you die on me."

She rose and went to the potion that Douglas had made. She felt Sheridan watching. When she brought him the drink, he looked at it suspiciously.

"What is that?"

"Something that will have you on your feet soon."

He tried to reach for it, but then flinched in pain at the attempted movement. She sighed and went to his side. She hated nursing him. It made it appear as though she excused his abhorrent treatment of her.

Sheridan lifted his head and drank the bitter thick liquid, then gagged at the taste. "Dear God, what is it?"

"A remedy that will cure you." She forced the remainder of it to his lips and urged him to swallow. Once he'd finished, she looked down at him, she asked, "Now, are you hungry?"

"Yes."

She had saved him some bread and fruit. While getting it, she could feel his eyes on her. "Something wrong?" she asked without turning around.

"Huh?"

"You keep staring at me. Is something wrong?"

"Why are you helping me? I thought you hated me."

"I'm not like you. I don't hate anyone, not even someone as pathetic and sad as you."

He glared at her and lifted up on his elbows, grunting at the residual aches he felt. "That's the second time you've called me pathetic. I won't have it!"

She turned to look at him with a mocking nod.

His nostrils flared. "I think in time we will become quite close."

That made her laugh. "Your fever has broken, but you're still hallucinating."

Some of the color drained from his face.

She grew somber again. "*Monsieur* Sheridan, why did you take me?"

"Because you were for the taking."

"Why?"

"What do you mean, 'Why?'" he asked.

"Do you like me? Do you want to know me? Or is it because you were jealous of Comte La Roque and saw that he had something you can't have?"

Sheridan gritted his teeth. "I'm doing you a favor. No one would take you, and your stepmother and sister needed money."

"Please, don't pretend that you care for my family. You did this for some sick kind of revenge. It was your twisted way of getting back at the man you wish you could be."

"You hold your tongue!"

He got out of the bed grimacing from the pain, and straightened up. He walked toward her, still feeble, but driven by anger. He grabbed her arm roughly and pulled her violently to him. She winced in pain at his grip. Sheridan looked down into the cleavage of her breasts, held by the corset.

"Maybe I should start teaching you some manners, right now."

Zoé turned her head from him, repulsed by the dark circles under his eyes. He pushed her back from the table and she bumped into the chair behind her.

"You aren't well," she said, looking behind her as she backed away.

"I'm well enough!"

Reaching the cabin wall, she felt trapped, and closed her eyes out of fear and disgust. She could fight; she could probably take him in his weak condition. Then what? Anger him more and have him tire of his game with her? Have him toss her to those animals for sport?

Feeling him press up against her, she inhaled sharply and held her breath. She felt him run a hand along her hips and then shove a hand into her corset to claw at her breast. This was the second time since she'd met him that he'd taken liberties she wished he wouldn't. Sickened, she realized it would not be the last. In this moment, she knew she'd rather die than let him have her. But he saw her defiance rising as she began to struggle against him.

"Fight me if you want, and I'll either have every man on this ship take a turn at you, or wait until we dock and have you hanged for your disobedience!"

"I rather die by the hangman's noose than give in to you!"

"There are things worse than death, proud Zoé. Shall I acquaint you with them?"

She fought to hold back the tears, biting down on her lip so hard that she tasted blood. Refusing to beg or acknowledge his advances, she summoned memories of home: the walks in the garden with Marianne and Marguerite, the evenings singing for her father while he read his paper in the parlor and the nights spent sitting in her sister's room, laughing and whispering about boys. It was just her body, and it didn't belong to her anymore. He could never touch who she was.

"Ah, see… it can be nice," he said in response to her detached compliance. "Just being close to you makes me feel better. Let me show you."

She was amazed that after fever and illness, he had enough strength to think of the lewd things he longed to do to her. She felt him press his erection against her and tensed at the contact.

"Soon, you'll be mine and I'll show you what a real man can do," he said.

He pressed his lips roughly against hers. She remained still and waited until his cold, chapped lips pulled away from hers.

When she felt him remove his hand from the front of her dress, she opened her eyes and stared at him in sadness. He smirked, turning to stumble back to bed.

"Now, fix me something to eat!" he snapped.

"*Oui, monsieur,*" she murmured and went back to the table. She wished the food were laced with arsenic.

❦

Jean-Claude walked over to La Roque. "Monsieur, I am going below for lunch. May I bring you anything?"

"No," La Roque said, looking through a telescope he'd acquired from a deck hand for any sign of the *Aventine*.

"As you wish, *mon seigneur*," said Jean-Claude, walking away.

La Roque walked back to Ferdinand, who was cursing at his second-in-command over bad charting of their course.

"Are we lost? Did we lose them?" asked La Roque.

"I know where Delaflote is and we should be in their tailwind by tomorrow evening. Ye and I shall have a chat."

Ferdinand led La Roque a distance away and spoke to him in a low voice. "Have ye ever killed a man?"

La Roque was insulted. "I can handle myself."

"So you know how to use dat?" Ferdinand pointed at the sword on La Roque's hip. Thankfully he had chosen the appropriate one in his haste. He longed to drive it through his former friend.

"As I said: *I can hold my own*."

Ferdinand smiled and his gold tooth sparkled. La Roque sensed his thoughts. Ferdinand assumed he knew his kind, and wasn't easily convinced. Then La Roque turned and looked him in the eye. Eyes were what men like Ferdinand felt showed a man's soul. In that exchange both men saw a similarity that birth and privilege would choose to discount. Satisfied at the steel in La Roque's gaze, Ferdinand looked away.

"We will have to take the ship at night. A daylight approach will have us spotted and blown out of the water before we get within a thousand metres."

La Roque looked out into the sea. "Isn't a nighttime approach just as risky?"

"For yer pale skin, maybe. Me and my men, we prefer the dark."

"*Bien*. So what is the plan?"

"We have guns and gunpowder, but not much. Ye and that boy choose yer weapon, because the moment we reach the ship it'll be war. We board from the stern, and the fight starts when ye feet tetch their deck. Aye, we clear?"

"A simple, direct plan. It sounds good, but can we speed it up? She doesn't have much time. I feel that."

"I do what I can, but we go after dem at night. If I come upon dem beforehand, I will pull back."

"Understood."

Ferdinand went back to talk to his navigator and La Roque leaned over the edge of the ship. He saw the water bubbling as the *Veuve Noire* cut through the waves. He said another prayer and held his breath. He had to find her fast. He had to save her.

Hours later, in the spectral light of predawn, La Roque came back on deck to see the men rushing about the ship. He looked for Ferdinand, but didn't see him. Walking around the side, he ran into a short, thin man with large keloid welts on the front and back of his chest, remnants of a lashing administered not long ago. The man wore dirty pants that might once have been white, cut off above his knees, and no shoes.

When he tried to push past La Roque, the count dragged his arm and asked what was going on.

"We have spotted the ship," said the man. "And we're pulling back."

Shocked, La Roque tried to comprehend. He glanced out to the sea, but saw nothing, and raced toward the bridge.

They had traveled all night with no sight of Delaflote's ship. Now, finally, at the dawn of the new day, they were approaching it and were about to stop? Damn it! He didn't want to wait another day to get to his beloved. He wanted to advance now!

He could hear the men yelling to lower the sails. Ferdinand was slowing the vessel. La Roque decided he couldn't let that happen.

Zoé lay on the foul-smelling pallet, facing the wall. The evening before, Douglas had arrived with their meals, but Sheridan had refused to let him enter. She had to accept the tray through the cracked door. Douglas winked as he handed it to her and his small gesture comforted her. For the rest of the evening, she sat at the table and listened to Sheridan talk of his plantation, telling her of the people she would meet and the things she'd see. She detested the tale and hated his voice. What sickened her most was that she would soon disappear altogether when he forced her into his life.

At one point, she crept cautiously out to the hallway and hurried to the latrine to empty his bedpan. She returned to find him out of bed and reading her letter to Marianne. A surge of anger took her breath away. Without thinking, she ran over and snatched the letter from his hand, dropping the bedpan, which landed on the floor with a loud clank.

He looked at her, amused. "So you made a friend on the ship?" he said, and made a grab for her. She stepped away from his hand, folded the letter and put it in her trunk. Sheridan laughed and limped back to bed.

Eventually, night came and he was still stiff, but his bruising was fading. He demanded she undress and join him. As she disrobed before him, she couldn't help but let a tear fall. She had to escape. She must find some way to free herself.

In her knickers and chemise, she covered herself with her arms and walked over to his bed. Moving the blanket over, he smiled and let his eyes roam over her exposed skin. Joining him, she hugged herself, putting her back to him.

He kissed her head and moved her hair from her shoulders. "Even now, you smell of honey. How is that possible?"

She closed her eyes, ignoring his comment and cringing as his hand traveled down her shoulder.

"Zoé, you were right. I did come for you as a form of revenge for your rejection and Julien's betrayal of our friendship. I wanted to take what he desired most."

Zoé opened her eyes. She thought La Roque didn't care. Had not he given Sheridan the money for her purchase?

Sheridan kissed her shoulder. "You're the most exotic creature I have ever seen." He buried his face in her silky hair and inhaled. "You have awakened desires in me that I've never felt for a Negress. How is that possible?" He wrapped an arm around her waist and pulled her against him.

She closed her eyes and tears rolled down her cheek. The worst would happen soon. His touch would erase all of her memories of La Roque's tenderness and replace them with nightmares that were ugly and cruel.

Sheridan turned her over so he could look into her face. Leaning over her, he saw her tears and smiled. "Oh, I like it when you cry," he whispered and kissed her eyelids.

She stiffened and clenched her fists. She felt his rough thin lips press against hers and her heart pounded.

The front of her nightshirt had a ribbon laced through it that tied at the bodice, holding the top together over her breasts. Sheridan moved his hand across her neck to the ribbon. Zoé felt the ribbon loosen and the air touch her skin, alerting her that she was more exposed to him. Opening her eyes, she looked into his face. His long sandy hair hung from his head, blocking his face from view as his eyes rested on her breast.

"*Monsieur…*" she said, her voice cracking as she tried to speak.

He looked up at her. "You are so beautiful."

"Please, don't do this. I know that I belong to you and I have no say, but please don't do this. I… I—"

Sheridan put his finger to her lips. "I don't want to force you, but I will."

"You aren't well," she begged. "I just ask that we... that you consider—"

Sheridan grabbed her hand and pulled it under the sheet to touch his stiff manhood. "It's amazing how every bone in my body aches and my stomach is cramped, but my need to have you is still powerfully strong." He lowered his face to the crook of her neck.

"Please, no...." She wept openly, betraying her vow not to beg. Being forced to touch him made her disgusted and desperate.

"Shh." He released her hand and further opened her nightshirt. At the sight of her soft, caramel-colored breasts, he grabbed for her. Cupping one breast, he pulled it free. She winced at his roughness and cried out in pain.

Feeling his chapped lips scrape her skin as his wet, feverish mouth enclosed on her breast made her weep harder. Sheridan clamped his hand over her mouth. Her eyes popped open.

It was happening now, really happening.

In a panic, she tore at his hand and hit at him. She would fight back with every bit of her strength. She just couldn't allow him to have her. She couldn't bring herself to do it.

He became more excited and ripped at her knickers, pulling them down. She squirmed, turning her head back and forth to free her mouth from his hand. Finally, his hand moved. She cried out loudly, screaming for him to stop. Sheridan rolled on top of her, forcing her legs open. As he pinned her down with his weight, her breath escaped her lungs. She slapped him across the head as he grabbed her wrists, capturing both with one hand and holding them over her head.

"NO!! Let me go! *NO!!*" she screamed as she felt grinding her between her legs. She kicked and squirmed beneath him.

He grinned down in her face. "Shut up!" he laughed and ripped open her nightshirt, revealing the rest of her body.

There was a pounding on the door. Sheridan had barely freed himself when he heard the pounding over her cries and screams. Looking up, he frowned.

"Who goes there?" he shouted.

"It is an emergency, sir!"

Grumbling, Sheridan got up. Zoé backed away from him, her hair wild in her face. She grabbed the pieces of her torn shirt and covered herself. Sheridan retrieved his pants from the floor, stepped into them quickly and went to the door. For the first time, he noticed the chair that Zoé kept wedged under the doorknob. He looked at it curiously, then set it aside and opened the door.

It was Douglas, holding a glass.

Sheridan glared at the older man. "What do you want?"

Douglas glanced past him and saw Zoé. A spark of fury leapt in his eyes, but he covered it quickly. Keeping his voice humble, he told Sheridan, "I have bad news, sir."

Sheridan frowned. "What?"

"It's your ailment. It's me who's been helping your slave nurse you back to health."

Sheridan looked suspiciously over his shoulder at Zoé. "Yes, I know. You two have done such a good job. I was just showing her how much better I feel."

Again, the anger flickered in the cook's eyes. He struggled to keep his tone polite. "Well, I gave you the wrong potion and though you feel better now, you're certain to get much worse by the light of tomorrow."

Sheridan was stunned. He glanced down at his chest. Some of the lesions had healed but others remained bruised and raw. "What do you mean worse?"

Douglas raised the glass. "If you don't drink the rest of this, your infection is sure to spread. It could kill you before we reach land."

Sheridan backed up as Douglas gave him the glass and walked in. Zoé had stopped crying and sat with her hand over her mouth. She couldn't believe what Douglas was saying, or that

Sheridan believed him. It couldn't be further from the truth, but because Sheridan was solely concerned with his own self-preservation, he was buying it all.

Sheridan stared at the glass and took a tentative sip. Douglas took the moment to give Zoé a reassuring look.

"Were you planning on having a go at her?" Douglas asked Sheridan casually.

Sheridan lowered the glass and nodded. "What business of that is yours?"

Douglas' eyes grew wide. "Thank God I got here! The exertion would cause your bruising to spread to your wanker. It's the most painful thing in the world. You can't indulge in those activities until the infection is completely gone."

An expression of horror came over Sheridan's face. He rubbed his penis through his pants. At the same time, he looked at Douglas with increasing suspicion. Putting the glass on the table, he said, "You have some fondness for my slave?"

"I admire how loyal she was to you. She braved this ship by herself to seek me for help. If she hadn't, you would have succumbed to your illness and died. She saved your life."

Sheridan looked back at Zoé, who had retreated into the corner of the cot. "She is amazing. I'll give her that."

"Make sure you drink all that," Douglas said, gesturing toward the glass. "Also, I trust that you'll be joining the Captain

in the morning for breakfast. He asked that I extend the offer since he hasn't seen you for two days."

Sheridan nodded and Douglas took his leave. Zoé watched the cook's departure with a sinking heart. He had prevented the rest of the attack, but what would happen now? The very thought tightened her chest.

Sheridan climbed back into bed, grabbed her arm and pressed her down to him. "Very well. I shall be better soon and we shall finish this."

He wrapped his arms around her. Zoé said nothing and lay stiffly in his embrace. She felt him pull himself closer against her as he buried his face against her throat.

"Too bad," he whispered. "But later... later, I'll show you what a... a... what a good, stiff pr..."

His words became slurred and trailed away. Soon, he was snoring and she could push her way out of his arms. Once she was safely alongside the bed, she looked down at him. It was odd how quickly he'd fallen asleep. Had Douglas put something in that drink? A sleeping potion, perhaps?

She stared down at her nemesis and for one long moment of insanity thought about smothering him with a pillow, or smashing his head with a candlestick. But she was incapable of committing murder. Furthermore, he still represented her main protection against the men on the ship. If she killed him, the

Captain would no doubt have her hung, but only after his men had finished with her.

She shivered and hugged herself, then went to her trunk, found some clothes and changed out of her torn undergarments. She went to the door, wedged the chair back under the knob—locking myself in with the monster, she thought, and stretched out on her pallet.

She wanted to disappear.

When the sun rose, Zoé was still looking at the same wall. Fear had kept her awake all night, coming up with schemes to escape, none of which made sense or seemed likely to succeed in the harsh light of dawn. She heard Sheridan moan and her heart skipped a beat. She rose to see him reach for her. When he realized she wasn't there, he opened his eyes, pushed himself up on his elbows and looked around, a flicker of panic in his eyes. Then he saw her, resting on the floor, and his eyes filled with a cruel smugness. He patted the empty place beside him. Her heart thudding, she got up and went to him.

"Lie down," he told her. "Right here, next to me."

She did. He reached for her, shoved his hand down the front of her nightdress and squeezed her one of breasts. She said nothing and waited for him to release her. He finally did and sat up.

"We're having breakfast with the Captain," he said. "I want you to make yourself extra pretty. Put on one of those dresses you pranced around in at Château La Roque."

At the mention of that place, her thoughts went to the man who lived there, of her love for him, the sacrifice she'd made and the cost.

Sheridan slapped her. "Don't ever, ever do that again," he said.

She held her face, her eyes brimming with tears. She looked at him in genuine puzzlement. "Do what, *monsieur?*"

Sheridan looked away. "Let me see you…"

"See me doing what?"

He paused. "*Thinking of him.*"

For a moment, she was quiet, and then she said, "You might own my body, but you will never own my soul."

His lower lip trembled with anger. He struck her again.

"Get dressed, I said. Do it now."

❧

"Why are you stopping?" La Roque yelled, rushing toward Ferdinand.

Ferdinand frowned at him. "Watch your tongue. I am the Captain."

La Roque glared at him. "We have to get to her—now!"

"Well, *now* won't do," Ferdinand said and turned away.

La Roque grabbed Ferdinand's arm and pulled him back. Ferdinand turned on the count, his dark eyes burning through him like smoldering coals. The captain yanked himself free and told La Roque, "We are not in France now. I don't give a shite about how much money ye have or what ye business is with Delaflote. I won't run on a suicide mission at ye command."

La Roque's jaw hardened. "We have a deal. If you try to back out of it, then you and I will have a problem. No one, including you, will keep me from getting to her." He put his hand on the hilt of his sword.

Ferdinand stared at him and two of his men moved in closer, but the captain raised a hand to hold them off.

"Aye, ye want to save her," he told La Roque, "but charging ahead now will kill us all."

After a moment, La Roque dropped his hand. He looked out over the ocean. Delaflote's ship was still no more than a dot on the horizon. What horrors was his love enduring on board that ship? He knew what men were capable of, knew only too well what lust and drink could lead even a decent man to do—and Sheridan, as he could now admit, wasn't even decent.

His sweet Zoé was in grave peril. "If we can see them, can't they see us?"

Ferdinand ran his tongue across his gold tooth. "Aye, but they can't make out me ship yet and since many pass these waters, we are safe. Ye can trust me. Tonight we will have yer Zoé and me revenge."

La Roque sighed and clenched his jaw. He didn't know if she had until tonight. She could very well be lost to him now.

Sheridan, dressed in all his finery, was followed by Zoé, who looked exceptionally beautiful. She wore the lavender gown that she had on the day Marianne discovered her with La Roque. The bodice, beaded with lavender stones, sparkled when the light caught it. No matter how dismal she perceived her future to be, at this moment, to look upon her was a pleasure. It troubled her deeply because the last thing she wanted was to draw attention to herself. She had tried to curl her hair with the iron and candle but Sheridan was impatient so she pinned it up and put curls around the front.

When she neared the corner, she actually saw a woman for the first time on the ship. *Une mûlatresse* like herself, who looked to be no more than Marianne's age, wore a tattered sack for clothing and no shoes. Her hair was raven black and straight. Her lip was cut and Zoé saw bruising around her neck. The woman looked at her with a shocked expression. Zoé assumed that she had never seen another like herself dressed so regally.

"Is she a relative?" snickered Sheridan.

Zoé ignored the comment. The woman dropped her head, realizing she stared too long, and walked quickly ahead of them. Zoé flinched when Sheridan grabbed her wrist and pulled her along. "Come on. We're late!!"

When they stepped on the deck, the ocean breeze greeted her. It was a refreshing relief from the stale sick smell of their cramped quarters. Men busying themselves with their duties stopped and gawked at them. Zoé was aware of Sheridan sticking his chest out as if he had a prize mare at his side.

Revolted by even standing near him she tried to concentrate on the massive sails flapping in the wind. She could feel the sway of the boat as it raced along the ocean, and she became overwhelmed at how vast the blue waters were. Ignoring the evil looks shot her way, she grabbed at Sheridan's arm as he led her to the Captain's cabin that sat up on the deck.

"Gentlemen," greeted Sheridan as they entered the Captain's quarters.

Zoé immediately scanned the faces of the men. She relaxed when she saw Douglas with the slave girl, preparing the meals.

Captain Delaflote rose. "Please join us. Allow me to introduce you."

Zoé held back. Delaflote introduced Sheridan to the men gathered, a New Yorker and two other Southern men from Georgia and Mississippi, all having business ties with the lecherous captain.

She looked up to see the one good eye of the Captain focused on her, and averted her eyes once more.

"Do you wish your nigger to eat?" he asked.

Sheridan took a seat. "If she wishes."

The Captain stared at her a little longer. He then pointed to a chair at the other end of the room. Zoé turned and went to take a seat. Immediately the slave girl hurried to her with a plate. Zoé looked into her expressive brown eyes and smiled, touching her hand affectionately.

"Enjoy missus." The slave girl bowed and backed away.

Zoé looked toward the men, now all speaking at once, to see the Captain staring silently. His serpent-green eye, the one that wasn't covered by a patch, gleamed with malevolent intent, and she really began to fear if she'd survive the voyage. Then Zoé realized what he was doing: Delaflote was toying with Sheridan.

The further they drifted to sea, she knew this game would come to a torturous end. Returning her attention to her plate and eating from her lap, she banished the thought. She could not dwell on what was to come. Her survival depended on her gathering her strength to find ways to endure the moment.

A shipmate came in to announce that there was another ship east of them. The Captain shrugged. "We're in the Atlantic, not surprising in these waters. Keep an eye out for the flag."

Jean-Claude walked over to La Roque, who was leaning on the rail and looking into the ocean, "*Mon seigneur*, if I may, Zoé is very strong."

"*Oui...* she is." La Roque nodded. He looked over at the lad. "How old are you, son?"

"Fourteen, sir," Jean-Claude said, smiling.

La Roque looked back into the cobalt-blue sea. "I shouldn't have brought you with me. When we reach them, I want you to stay here."

"I shall fight at your side," Jean-Claude said with finality.

La Roque cast his eyes upward to the young man's face. "Do you know how to use a sword?"

"I have not had a reason to."

"Stay close. I shall get you a pistol, but you remain close."

Jean-Claude nodded, and turned to look out into the sea. "If I may ask, will you help her, *mon seigneur?*"

La Roque's expression showed his bafflement. Was he not here solely to help his Zoé?

"I mean to say, will you marry her?" stammered Jean-Claude.

La Roque was impressed. Zoé had friends who cherished her health and happiness. He decided to indulge the boy in spite of his untoward question.

"When I get her back I will worship her. She will always be safe with me."

8

La Roque watched the sun set from the deck. He had suffered through a day of waiting and praying that the unspeakable wasn't happening to her. He understood why they had to wait, but with each passing minute he felt more and more like a co-conspirator in the injustices she'd suffered since he'd cornered her that night in his mother's library.

A blazing orange sun simmered in a blood-red sky as it sank below the horizon. The vision was beautiful, but he was barely aware of it. His mind was full of images of her. He recalled how she'd tried to sidestep his advances, how she'd foolishly ventured into his room and stood her ground. Then, he had spoken to her about choices, pretending to give her one, knowing full well that she was young and inexperienced. He fed on her innocence and naiveté without thought. Yet, ironically, it was he who had become entrapped and enslaved.

He had fallen in love with her the moment he felt her soft, silky skin and smelled her sweet breath, the moment she'd given herself innocently, not just because of her virginity, but because of the heat he felt burning inside of her when they connected. The red sky was reminiscent of that fire. Seeing it deepened his worry. He was sickened by all he could lose if Sheridan forced her into his darkness.

She'd been on that boat for forty-eight hours and that was far too long. He'd made voyages on ships like that and he knew the thirst of the men who worked such ships. He knew that Sheridan was weak; those men would toy with him and make a move to possess her, and there was little that he'd be able to do to prevent it.

"Me call that sky *l'heure du diable,*" Ferdinand said, leaning on the edge of the boat and looking toward the setting sun.

"The devil's hour?" La Roque repeated.

"God's plans for man have set and the devil rises for his due."

La Roque looked into Ferdinand's dark, penetrating eyes, and saw a pain that mirrored his own. The loss of family and love, the empty feeling of regret and guilt, the bottomless anger toward those who benefited from their suffering: they'd both known those experiences.

"Will we have our due?" La Roque asked.

"Aye we shall." Ferdinand smiled and his gold tooth glistened.

La Roque's gaze returned to the direction of Delaflote's ship. It was no more than a tiny dot under the sun, which had been all but swallowed by the royal blue sea. "Do you think she has been able to survive?"

Ferdinand shrugged. "She's a Negress on a ship with demons. Be prepared for what we find, that... ye may not find her in the way... No, we may not be able to save her."

A glazed look of despair swept across La Roque's face. A feeling of guilt overwhelmed him and he knew couldn't survive if Zoé became a victim of those unspeakable agonies. His father's madness was real for him now. It was a solid, tangible thing he was able to feel and understand.

Watching Marcela burn, François La Roque had felt the gravity of his obsession, deciding in that moment that if he couldn't have her, no one would. That was the madness. We aren't here to own people, thought La Roque. Or force our desire and will on others to feed our own selfish hearts and needs. Women weren't accessories. They weren't instruments for pleasure, to be used and discarded at a man's whim.

La Roque discovered the truth. When he took Zoé to his bed, he hadn't been looking for a wife. He knew her lot in life would require her to have a husband if she hoped to be happy. He hated to admit that he took her without concern for the price she would pay. He'd forced her to be his in the most selfish and unrelenting way, making her succumb to a passion that engulfed both of them, but left him unable to understand it all.

He'd gotten his wish. In a way she was already Sheridan's mistress, with no man to protect or cherish her, just Sheridan, a devil of a human being who could now be abusing and robbing her of that purity and spirit he loved so much.

"If she is dead or void of hope, then every man on that ship will die."

"Dat is a problem."

The muscles of La Roque's face tightened. "What problem? Dispensing of them?"

"No, me plan is to have Delaflote's head tied right dere." He pointed to the top of a staff, some eighteen feet high, where his ship's flag now whipped in the wind. "We discuss our approach. Now dat the sun has set, we are closer to dem. Dey should know that we are shadowing dem, which may have dem alarmed. We must act as if dey are."

La Roque's hair blew across his face in the night breeze and he stared in the dark at Delaflote with a mixture of determination and fear. "I understand."

"We can't risk getting too close. So, for our approach, we will take three of my smaller boats to approach with all me men. We will leave in an hour when nightfall is complete." He paused. "That leaves but one concern."

"And that is?"

Ferdinand turned and nodded across the beam of the ship. La Roque followed his gaze and saw Jean-Claude, listening intently as two of his men argued about their adventures at sea. The boy was totally enthralled. He laughed when the men charged each other and locked arms to wrestle over their differences.

La Roque looked back at Ferdinand. "We give him a pistol. He will know what to do."

Ferdinand disagreed. "We don't just face men of different positions than us. We face the evil that lives in men. We are outnumbered and gunned. Each man who takes dis voyage tonight understands that he may not return, and he accepts it."

La Roque sighed. "I spoke to him, and he wants it—"

"Then ye convince him otherwise, because I won't be held back by fear of another child becoming a victim of Delaflote's evil ways."

"He's fourteen and not—"

"He is the same age as was me brother! The same age as when we tried to fight back and Delaflote slit his throat right in front of me! The boy shan't join us on this rescue!"

Ferdinand hardened his stance. La Roque understood his point. He didn't want the destruction of the man-child, adventure-seeker or not, on his hands.

⁂

"*Monsieur,* would you like me to go to the galley to get you something more to eat?" Zoé was desperate to get away from Sheridan. Yes, there was danger on the ship but after the near-rape and the constant taunts, she was beginning to realize the danger was just as real inside her close confines with him. Besides, she wanted to thank Douglas for saving her the previous night. However, Sheridan's suspicions held.

"What is this thing with you and the cook?"

Zoé saw what he was implying and understood that his mind could not comprehend the goodness in others without seeing some suspected purpose. "*Monsieur*, he reminds me of papa. It's comforting," she said honestly.

Sheridan leaned back on his cot and smiled without warmth. "So you miss home?"

She nodded, looking down.

"Well, then, I shall allow this request—"

"You will?" She was shocked.

"I want some more ale. Go tell your friend the cook!" His eyes darkened with anger.

"He was kind to me. That's all, I swear it," she offered meekly.

He regarded her with suspicion for a moment longer. Then an evil smirk formed on his lips. "He must like dark meat as well?"

Zoé looked away and remained silent. Sheridan dismissed her. "If your intentions were evil, you could have carried them out as I lay here suffering. It's my reward to you for saving my life."

"Oh, *merci*," she cried and rushed to the door, excited about her freedom.

"No more than twenty minutes. Then you come back and entertain me. There are many ways you can please me, Zoé. When you return I'll show you how."

She didn't want to imagine what her fate would be. Just one look into his eyes made her feel ill. She nodded and left hastily.

∞❦∞

Jean-Claude saw La Roque approach. He rose up from his seat on a small crate and walked over to him, smiling. "Is it time to go?"

"*Non.* We must talk."

"*Oui, mon seigneur.*"

La Roque walked away from the men with his hands clasped behind his back, contemplating his delivery of the news. Turning, he saw Jean-Claude clearly for the first time, saw his youth, his innocence. The boy had removed his wig, revealing his thick blonde curls. He still wore the footman's uniform he had on when he'd fetched the count.

"You cannot join us on this mission," said La Roque.

Jean-Claude frowned. "But why not?"

"It is important that you guard this ship. We are taking smaller boats to access the ship, and we need you here."

La Roque hardened his expression to show the finality of his decision.

"I will stay behind," Jean-Claude said meekly.

La Roque had expected the boy to protest further, so he was surprised and relieved when Jean-Claude acquiesced. He smiled and touched the boy's shoulder.

"Good."

A life saved, thought La Roque. It was a good feeling.

❦

"Captain."

Delaflote stood on the upper deck of his ship, discussing their course with his navigator. Hearing a shipmate call out to him, he turned and glared at him.

"What is it?"

"That ship we discussed earlier..."

Delaflote frowned and narrowed his one good eye on the young man. "What ship?"

Mathieu, a twenty-two-year-old scallywag, was responsible for sitting up in the crow's nest eighteen metres above the deck and keeping an eye out for other ships, both those that they could threaten and those that could threaten them.

"Earlier, sir, I told of a vessel off the eastern bow. It was in our shadow mostly."

Delaflote scowled. "You never said it was shadowing us."

Mathieu swallowed hard. "I didn't think it to be true at the time, but the ship should have moved off by now."

Philippe, the second-in-command, walked up to Delaflote . "We are in the clear, sir. Even if it is following us, it has no hope of getting nearer to us without being spotted. I suggest we investigate in the morning, if it's still there."

Delaflote ran his fingers over his knotted beard and thought it over. "Very well."

Philippe turned to go. Mathieu started after him, but Delaflote grabbed the boy by the arm.

"Stay at the ready all night and watch for any suspicious activities in the water."

Mathieu nodded nervously. Delaflote himself scanned the horizon. He had a feeling, a bad feeling.

It was going to be a long night.

Zoé turned the corner hurriedly, happy at the thought of seeing Douglas, and ran smack into a crewman.

"Pardon," she whispered, putting a hand to her chest and falling back a step.

"Hell's bells! If it ain't the nigger princess!"

He had cold, dark brown eyes. He smelled so bad that she held her breath against the stench. His hair was black and matted. He had a rough, shaggy beard, and his pockmarked face was a leathery nut brown from constant exposure to the sun. He stood at her height, but was muscular beyond belief. He put a filthy finger with dirt caked up under his nail to his lips and smiled, revealing rotten teeth.

Zoé turned to run, but the he immediately grabbed her up and clamped a hand over her mouth, stifling her screams. She kicked and swung at him, but to no avail. He dragged her toward the side ladder, taking her to the dreadful belly of the ship.

She was thrown into a dark, dank room. Landing on the floor, she hurt her hand as she tried to brace her fall. Looking up, she saw the dirty feet of six women. They were huddled together, their expressions terrified, their eyes shifting between Zoé and her kidnapper. He grinned at Zoé and wagged his index finger at her.

"You stay here, sweet peach. I'm going to go get the boys so we can break you in." He glanced at the other women, gave them a wink and then stepped out, bolting the door behind him.

An African broke away from the group and ran to Zoé's side. "Madame?" she asked, helping Zoé up.

"I am fine. *Merci.*"

She saw how abused and emaciated some of the women were. The sight of them broke her heart. They all wore the same potato-sack dresses, and most were peppered with bruises. One of them looked no older than twelve.

"I am so sorry," Zoé said.

The woman she met earlier stepped forward with a deep frown. "Why should you apologize? You did not put us here. We must find a way to protect you."

"Protect me?" They needed to protect themselves.

The woman smiled. "My name is Sheba," she said, bowing.

Zoé realized by the way that they responded to her and her appearance that they thought she was some type of lady. She smiled and extended her hand. "*Je m'appelle* Zoé Bouchard. It's my pleasure to meet you."

Sheba, shook her hand and introduced her to the women. Most of them spoke only their native African language, but smiled at her, anyway.

Sheba glanced at the door. "They will be back, and it will be bad. We must help you."

Zoé shook her head. "No. We must help each other."

La Roque took a moment to roll his shoulders, trying to relax his muscles. He and the other men had been rowing for what seemed like an eternity, and every muscle in his back ached, yet he kept at it, determined to pick up speed. The blackness of the cloudy night made it hard to be sure they were going in the right direction. He said another prayer for her and pulled harder.

Jean-Claude sat in another boat several yards behind, also rowing. He had convinced one of the shipmates to let him to stow away. The man liked the boy, and had given him a pistol, a bandanna to cover his blond hair, and clothes to change into so he wouldn't stand out any more than he already did. The dark night gave him cover from La Roque and Ferdinand. Neither knew he was joining them. He would show them that he could handle himself, and he would help rescue Zoé. Eager for adventure, Jean-Claude rowed faster.

Minutes later, the large outer hull of the ship loomed over them. Ferdinand had them stop rowing as they drifted closer. They shipped their oars and looked for signs that those on board had seen their approach. La Roque examined the sky and saw that a great storm was brewing. Ferdinand made seagull calls, signaling the men on the other two boats to split and take the sides. The *Aventine* was drifting with its sails down. That would make it easier to board her and both Ferdinand and La Roque couldn't be more pleased.

Ferdinand had given La Roque a pistol to carry along with his sword, and a knife to stick in his boot. La Roque hadn't taken a man's life since the war. Driven by his desire to rescue Zoé, he wasn't the least bit repulsed by the thought of killing his former close friend Sheridan with his bare hands. Anyone standing between him and Zoé would die before the night ended.

On board the *Aventine,* Mathieu slept in the crow's nest. He'd tried earlier to watch the blue-black sea for signs of pirates, but with the clouds so dark and the smell of a storm approaching, he concluded nothing would happen tonight. Snoring lightly, he felt the first drops of rain. He slept on as those drops turned into a steady drizzle. He'd slept in rainstorms before; at least in the crow's nest he didn't have to share his bed.

Belowdecks, Sheridan rose from his bed. The twenty minutes he had given Zoé were well past. She defied him by failing to return. In a rage, he stormed down the passageway looking for the galley, determined to drag her back and teach her a lesson for disobeying him. Seeing a group of men laughing and heading to the side stairs, he stopped them.

"Hey! I need a word!"

One of them, a short, muscular man with a shaggy beard and pockmarked face, turned and frowned. The other men glanced at one another and glared at Sheridan.

Sheridan drew himself up. He considered them barbarians, beneath him. "I'm looking for the galley."

The man gave him a smile of blackened stumps for teeth. "Yes, sir. Why the galley is just this way." He pointed to the stairwell down the corridor to their left.

Sheridan nodded and turned in the direction they pointed. A feeling of unease made him glance over his shoulder. The men were staring at him malevolently. They were dangerous, very dangerous, he thought. He would make sure that Zoé was at his side from now on. He should never have allowed her to go out with such animals around.

Downstairs, Sheba and Zoé had armed each woman with a weapon: for the most part they held boards and bricks, but two of the women actually had knives, smuggled from the shelves during their work with Douglas.

"This is insane," Sheba told Zoé. "There are too many of them and they are like rabid dogs. You should let us surround you and protect you. That way, you have more of a chance."

"Absolutely not. Your life and the lives of these girls are worth just as much as mine. We fight together and we fight to our last breath. Understand?"

Sheba nodded, indicating that she understood. Slowly, each captive gave a nod. Some understood; others were just ready to fight back.

Without warning, the bolt on the door lifted. The women exchanged glances. It was time.

Outside, the rain clouds exploded and large droplets fell across the faces of Ferdinand's men, making it hard for them to keep their eyes open. Men on each side of the vessel tossed weighted ropes over the railing that edged the upper deck. Once Ferdinand had secured his rope, he put his long blade between his teeth and started his ascent. La Roque stuck his pistol into his tucked-in blouse, and followed.

Jean-Claude stood in the boat on the opposite end, ready to climb his rope. The rain had soaked his clothes, but he felt energized by what was about to unfold. He viewed it all as an adventure.

Below deck, Sheridan walked in to see Douglas bent over a large pot. Douglas straightened up at the sound of Sheridan's entrance and frowned.

"Yes?"

"Where is she?" demanded Sheridan.

Douglas wiped his fat hands across his apron and looked Sheridan up and down, confused.

"Who?"

"Zoé, dammit! What did you do with her?"

The cook's frown turned into a scowl. "I have no idea what——" His eyes widened, struck by a horrific thought.

Zoé had been warned. Sheba, having grown up on this ship, knew every detail of the demons that tortured her and the others. She'd told Zoé that Alfred Serafu was Satan himself.

Zoé, in their brief conversation, couldn't understand the horrors that Sheba described but when she looked into her captor's eyes it became clear. He reveled in the pain of others, especially women.

Zoé practiced her swing, gauging the weight of the wood. Her eyes cut over to the women.

"How did you manage to survive?" she looked around at the chamber of horrors. "Survive this?"

"Serafu satisfies his thirst for pain through our suffering. The more you suffer, the crueler he can be. Suffering through it is the only way to stay alive."

Zoé decided that Serafu would be hers. Men like him, who worked on slave ships because it gave them access to vulnerable and defenseless girls, should be made to pay. According to Sheba, Serafu had already killed two slave women, incurring the wrath of the Captain for having done so. Each death represented a financial loss to the captain. Delaflote had warned Serafu that his wages would be docked, but that had not curbed the man's sadistic lust.

She looked up just as Serafu and his crew surged inside. He was at the forefront when they stopped in their tracks, stunned to see the women lined up, armed and baring their teeth. And he knew immediately who was responsible.

"What the hell is this?" he yelled at Zoé.

"Your death, *monsieur*, because I will see you dead before I let you touch me!" She held a plank of wood like a bat.

"How dare you threaten me! Who do you think you are, strutting like you some lady or sumthin. I'm going to take my time with you, and when you break, I'm going to start all over again." He licked his lips and advanced upon her.

"Lower the plank," he said. "Lower it and perhaps I won't use it on you before I snap your neck."

The men behind him laughed.

Zoé gripped her plank tighter, she saw his arrogant smugness, and knew he took her silence for fear. She cut a glance at the other women and saw their open terror. It made her aware that these women had apparently tried to fight back, too, but had learned brutal lessons. For a moment, her hand shook, and when she looked back at him she knew he meant every word of his threat. She had nothing left to lose. So she tightened and adjusted her hold on the wood.

"It's time you and I get to know each other," he said, undoing his pants and walking toward her. She raised the plank higher.

She was prepared to swing.

"What the hell is going on?" Sheridan asked as Douglas grabbed a butcher knife.

"When did you last see her?" Douglas asked.

"She was coming here, but that was over half an hour ago."

"Then the men have her! God help her!"

Douglas raced out. In a flash, Sheridan remembered the men he'd encountered, heard their snickers and saw their animosity. Horrified, he ran out after Douglas. Those men could be destroying his Zoé now! The thought sickened him. He had to find her!

Ferdinand threw his leg over the topside rail, still clutching his knife between his teeth. The sound of the pelting rain masked his grunting. He saw three men less than fifty *metres* away, rushing around on deck as they battened down the ship. Taking the knife from his mouth, he ducked to the left to avoid being spotted as La Roque climbed over the railing.

On the other side of the ship, Ferdinand's men were making the same maneuver, coming on board unseen, moving with deadly stealth. La Roque wiped at his face, trying to see through the rain, as he watched Ferdinand run toward the Captain's quarters. Before he could follow, he heard a yell to his right. He turned just in time to see a man charging at him with sword drawn.

He'd been spotted.

Drawing his sword, he engaged the man, defending himself from the deadly blow he was about to receive. They began their dance, their swords connecting in the rain and clanking loudly. La Roque swung with fierce determination as lightning streaked the sky.

La Roque's long steel blade drove his attacker back. The rain pasted the count's hair to his face, making it hard for him to see, but he was such a skilled swordsman that the parries and thrusts were almost instinctive. La Roque knew he couldn't afford to spend much time on this fight. He had to end it quickly. With a quick twist of his wrist, La Roque ripped the sword from his attacker's hand to send it flying across the deck, and then plunged the blade into his opponent's chest.

Jean-Claude came up alongside the ship as the men were being alerted to the invasion. Mathieu was blowing his whistle from the crow's nest, a little too late, but all the *Aventine's* hands were running about armed and ready.

The rain disoriented Jean-Claude a little, so he didn't see the man advancing on him. His attacker struck from the left, knocking the boy off his feet. Landing on his back, he opened his eyes to see the attacker bearing down on him with blade drawn. Quickly, Jean-Claude rolled to the right while aiming his pistol to fire. The man swung his sword to deliver a death blow, but miscalculated within the downpour. His error was a fatal one, because Jean-Claude fired directly into his face.

Ferdinand's men slit the throats of the twelve men on the upper deck and spread out ready for any who ventured into their battle. Ferdinand, however, had another plan.

Armed with a brutal-looking machete, he made his way toward the Captain's quarters. He turned a corner and saw Philippe. Delaflote's Lieutenant fumbled for the sword on his hip, and then drew it out with trembling hands. Ferdinand smiled as Philippe swung at his head. This was child's play for the African pirate. Ducking to the left, he easily avoided the blow, and then brought the machete around in a curved move that slashed Philippe's side.

Philippe blinked twice, his face showing surprise, then made to collapse, but Ferdinand forced him to stand, until every drop of his life bled out. Once done he cleaned his blade on the dead man's shirt, dropped him, then kicked the body out of the way and went in search of the next challenge. He had lived for this taste of revenge.

La Roque drove his sword into another opponent, and then tossed the lifeless body overboard. Lightning continued to flash around him, setting a backdrop clouded with violence. A man jumped on his back, bringing him down to the ground. His sword flew out of his hand. Rolling with the attacker, La Roque felt the blows raining across his body. His opponent pulled out a knife and aimed for La Roque's throat, but the count blocked him with his left arm. The knife slashed his forearm, cutting deeply. His pistol fell free of his shirt. He saw it beyond his reach. He scrambled for it as the other punched him in the face. He almost lost consciousness from the brutal blow and his hand was unable to reach his pistol.

He prepared to fend off another strike, but then saw dark hands grab the man's forehead from behind and yank his head back. There was a guttural cry and then a gush of warm blood as one of Ferdinand's men nearly decapitated La Roque's attacker. Lightning flashed overhead, showing the African standing victorious in the rain.

Before La Roque could smile in thanks, a sword pierced the man's chest. La Roque grabbed his pistol as he watched his rescuer slip into death. As the African fell in a dead heap on top of La Roque, the count swung his gun around the body and fired upward into the chest of his assailant, blowing him backwards.

La Roque pushed the body off him and scrambled to his feet. Despite the rain streaming down his face, he spotted his sword and picked it up. The fighting was all around him and the deck was now strewn with bodies. Ferdinand's men were doing well but could use a hand. Unfortunately, he didn't have time to spare.

It was time to find his love.

Zoé swung her wood plank with enough force to crush Serafu's skull, which it did. Blood splattered on her face and dress. Everyone in the room was stunned as the meanest, vilest rapist on the ship blinked once in shock, then fell over to his side. The women recovered first. Energized by this first victory, they charged their tormentors with their weapons raised. Zoé jumped into the fray, her gown a hindrance, but not enough to keep her from swinging her plank.

The men outnumbered the women, but the men were unarmed. Not expecting to do battle, they had brought neither pistol nor sword, and had only their hands. But they were strong, experienced brawlers and much better fed than their undernourished captives. It was only the women's determination—their bitter, desperate determination—that kept them from being quickly overpowered.

Douglas and Sheridan came in to see the chaos and stopped at the door, gasping in surprise. It was Douglas who reacted first. He saw a woman being beaten across the face and ran to her rescue, stabbing the attacker in the back and killing him.

As Sheridan watched, Zoé brought her plank down on the back of a man's head, splintering the wood. Another man grabbed her from behind, shocking her into dropping the wood. He gripped her throat to choke her, but Sheba ran over and drove her knife into him.

"Zoé!" shouted Sheridan.

Zoé looked back at him, stunned from the pain of her recent blow. He stepped toward her and another woman swung her stick at him, delivering a painful blow to his left arm. Sheridan stepped back in shock. He looked pleadingly at Zoé, but she ran over to help another woman who was being beaten. She jumped on the assailant's back and dug her nails into his eyes. He howled and stopped his attack on the first woman in order to claw at Zoé. Finally, he toppled her and threw her to the floor. Straddling her, he drew back to punch her. She grabbed up a large brick and slammed it against his head. His blood exploded over her.

In one corner, Douglas dispatched the man who was choking the twelve-year-old girl. Meanwhile, Sheridan edged along the wall, seeking a way to advance on Zoé and pull her from the chaos. He was afraid to enter the fray without a weapon. The women were now overtaking the men and he heard them scream as they lost control.

Zoé climbed off the man she and the others had beaten to death, and backed away, realizing—really realizing—that she had human blood on her hands. She looked around her, dazed. Some of the women were crying; others were grinning and hugging each other. Still others were busy with the grim business of finishing off the men who were wounded but not yet dead. Before Zoé could make sense of it all, Sheridan grabbed her arm and pulled her up the ladder, unnoticed by the girls amidst the carnage.

La Roque came down onto the lower deck and saw a man coming toward him. Raising the gun, he fired instinctively and watched the man drop in a dead heap. La Roque tossed the now empty gun and ran down the passageway, holding his left arm, blood from the wound staining his sleeve.

"Zoé! Zoé!" he cried.

Then came a familiar voice.

"Are you mad? We will be forced to walk the plank after what you did!"

Seconds later, Sheridan turned the corner, dragging Zoé, who struggled against him. La Roque came to a halt, his heart beating heavily. For the first time that night, he felt fear.

She wore the lavender dress he'd last seen her in. Beautiful then, it was now covered in blood. Blood, it seemed, was everywhere: on her face, in her hair. Her hands dripped with it. She looked dazed and confused. Her hair hung wildly in her face.

What had Sheridan done to her?

Sheridan froze at the sight of him. He quickly let go of Zoé and stepped back as La Roque raced toward him in a murderous rage. The American turned and fled; Zoé dropped to her knees, hanging her head in exhaustion. La Roque reached for his gun to fire on Sheridan, but then remembered that it was empty and discarded. Reaching Zoé, he knelt down, cupped her chin and lifted her face to his.

"Zoé," he pleaded, fearful of what she might have experienced. "It's me. Tell me, are you hurt?. Are you all right?"

Zoé stared at him without any sign of recognition. At the sight of her paralyzed expression, his heart exploded in his chest. Moving the wild strands of hair from the front of her face, he tried to kiss her.

That revived her, but not in the way he expected.

She pushed him away, shook her head and let out a blood-curdling scream. She screamed so loud and long that La Roque feared for her sanity. Not knowing what else to do, he grabbed her and held her to his chest. She pounded his flesh, but no matter how much she fought him, he held on. Rocking her gently, he tried to ease her pain, and felt helpless that he couldn't.

Up on deck, the battle raged. Jean-Claude saw the man he'd befriended struck down by a ruthless scoundrel. Rain pouring down his face, the boy held and fired on him. The pistol exploded and the man who'd butchered his friend was hit in the neck. Jean-Claude dropped the gun and ran to his fallen friend's side to see him coughing up blood. Tears joined the raindrops wetting the boy's face. He cried. Before that night, he'd never seen someone die. Now he'd not only seen it, but had taken several lives himself. Lightning flashed above his head, illuminating the dying man's face and Jean-Claude closed his eyes and wept. He didn't think he could take much more of this.

"Up, boy!"

Turning around, Jean-Claude saw a man holding a sword to him. The man looked to be someone other than the shipmates they'd been fighting. He wore the garments of a gentleman. For a moment, the boy felt a flicker of hope.

But all hope died when the stranger smiled. There was a cold intelligence in it, a smugness that told Jean-Claude that this man, despite his outer appearance, was just as barbaric and heartless as any of the other killers on this ship.

The stranger put the tip of his sword under Jean-Claude's chin. He spoke only two words, "Get up," but it was enough. The boy caught the stranger's accent.

This must be Sheridan, the man who had taken Zoé.

Jean-Claude wished he had not dropped his pistol.

Ferdinand turned the handle of the door to the Captain's cabin, and jumped aside just as a bullet from inside blew a hole in the door. A less resolute man would have retreated, but not him. He'd suffered too long, dreamed too hard, and killed too many simply give up.

Adrenaline pumping, he kicked the door in and dove inside, gunfire exploding over his head. He rolled to one side, taking a shot in his shoulder, the pain searing him like fire, but not slowing him down. Crouching to avoid being a target, he saw Delaflote by his desk, struggling to load more gunpowder into his pistol. Graceful and strong as a leopard, Ferdinand bounded over the desk. Delaflote was so startled that he dropped the weapon.

Ferdinand grinned and placed the tip of his machete at Delaflote's throat. "Do you remember me, Captain?"

Delaflote's eyes were filled with terror. Still, he tried to sound brave. "Bastard, how dare you charge my ship!"

"Answer me, Captain. Do ye remember me?"

Delaflote squinted at Ferdinand with his one good eye, looking him up and down. "Sure... sure, I remember you."

"Y'are in me dreams. Dis day, dis moment... I've waited a long time," drawled Ferdinand.

Slowly, he drew the tip of his blade along one side of the Captain's throat, leaving a thin line of blood.

"If–if it's mo–money you want," Delaflote stammered.

"I want only one ting from you—your life."

Delaflote's eyes widened. He opened his mouth to speak, but nothing came out. He reeked of fear. Ferdinand could smell it. He could feel it, as palpable as his own hot anger.

"I—I will pay you!" Delaflote squeezed out.

Ferdinand burst out laughing. "You most certainly will. And it will be a payment made in blood." He leaned into Delaflote's face. "But I will be kind to you. Before I kill ye, I will tell ye why I am your executioner." Ferdinand searched Delaflote's eyes for any sign of recognition and saw none. "Dere was once a boy…" he began.

Ferdinand recounted the horrific tale of his brother's death shortly after being plucked from the West African coastline. But even after hearing the story, it was clear to him that Delaflote remembered nothing. It threatened to rob him of this moment he savored.

It seemed to Ferdinand that he misery he and his brother suffered on board Delaflote's ship, the tragedy of his brother's death, were simply mere incidents to the Captain. It was, to him, simply what arose in the routine of running a slave ship and keeping everyone under control.

"Don't you understand?" Delaflote said. "I didn't mean it, not personally. It was just business. I was just doing my job."

"And now," Ferdinand said, "I must do mine."

Raising his machete, Ferdinand went to work, taking his time and savoring every moment.

❦

"It's all right, *ma petite*. It will be all right." La Roque whispered in Zoé's hair, still holding her. Her screams had subsided, but now she was trembling from head to toe. He tried to get her to stand, but she had drawn up into a fetal position and wouldn't uncurl.

A portly man wearing an apron and a ragged African woman came up the stairs and saw him. The woman raised her weapon to charge them, but the man grabbed her.

"I think he's all right," he said.

"Who are you?" shouted Sheba.

La Roque was unsure how to answer. Who were these people? And why were they, like his beloved, covered in blood? He was stunned to see their effect on Zoé. She lifted her head and looked at the woman. Zoé's next words chilled him.

"Are they dead, Sheba?" she asked.

Before Sheba could answer, a group of bloodied women, obviously slaves, emerged from the stairs. Sheba crouched next to Zoé and kissed her hand.

"They are all dead, and it's because of you that we are alive. Thank you so much."

Zoé pulled away from La Roque and hugged Sheba, who hugged her back. La Roque was relieved to see Zoé revived, but remained puzzled. The man in the apron, apparently a cook, La Roque thought, now joined them.

"And who are you, sir?" the man asked La Roque.

"I... well, I came to get Zoé. I—"

Sheba glared at him. "She doesn't belong to you and we will fight you too, if we have to."

Zoé shook her head "No, it's all right. I know him."

"Are you sure?" Sheba asked.

Zoé started to reassure Sheba, but then paused as a blood-curdling scream rent the air. Everyone stilled and glanced around, everyone but La Roque, who could guess the cause of those screams and cries for mercy: Ferdinand at play. The African had found his man and was now exacting his gory revenge.

The thought reminded him of Sheridan. He had to get to him.

"Zoé, can you and the others go up on deck? It's raining, but we will be leaving this boat soon."

His heart nearly broke at the look she gave him. She no longer trusted him. He had to admit that she had every reason not to. He could only pray that she would let him lead her and her friends out of this place. After that, he had no right to expect anything.

"All right," she agreed. "But where are you going?"

"To teach someone a well-deserved lesson."

La Roque stepped through the cabin door onto the upper deck. The rain was coming down with such force that visibility was difficult, if not impossible. He staggered from side to side, trying to gain his balance on the slippery deck of the wave-tossed ship. Before him, the dead and the dying lay everywhere. There was no sign of Sheridan among them.

He headed out into the rain unsure where else to look. He headed for the bow, but came to a halt, shocked at the sight before him: Ferdinand had appeared from the captain's deck, holding Delaflote's decapitated head. The dead man's mouth sagged open, dripping blood.

Ferdinand smiled at La Roque and walked past him. Lightning streaked through the sky, illuminating the entire deck with a flash of white light. Ferdinand appeared unearthly under it.

"We have taken the ship!" he shouted in triumph and raised the head in the air.

"We have to get back to your ship," La Roque said, trying hard not to look at the head, whose one green eye stared back up at him, unblinking.

"Aye. Let me gather me boys."

For the first time, Ferdinand seemed to take note of the dead men around them and that several of his men were among them. His face was stoic, but his eyes showed shock and pain.

La Roque looked around in the rain, wiping his face and trying to determine where Sheridan had gone. He had to find that son-of-a-bitch and make him pay for having taken his beloved Zoé.

Douglas emerged on deck, still carrying his knife, and stopped short at the sight of so many of his shipmates dead under the torrential downpour, and of the tall African that held Delaflote's head.

Ferdinand saw the cook and raised his machete. La Roque saw his intent and put his hand to Ferdinand's chest.

"No, he's not a threat. He saved Zoé's life, I think," he shouted over the thunder clapping above them.

Ferdinand nodded. "If ye say so." The decapitated head swayed in his hand under the stormy and turbulent rocking of the ship.

"There are several slave women who you will need to help back to your ship. I need to find someone. Get him to help you."

La Roque pointed at Douglas, who approached with caution, stepping over dead bodies.

Reaching them, Douglas shouted in the rain. "What is going on? Who are you?"

Ferdinand gave him a grim smile. "We are Justice."

Douglas glanced at Delaflote's head and shook his head. "I'm too old for this shite."

"What's your name?" asked La Roque.

"Douglas, sir."

"Well, Douglas, I need you to get Zoé and the women to our boats. We must get them back to our ship. This storm isn't going to break anytime soon," he yelled and lightning flashed, illuminating them all. Douglas steadied himself as the ship rolled against the crushing blows of the sea.

"Maybe we can steer this ship toward yours. Make it easier on the women. How far off is it?"

"That's the idea," agreed Ferdinand. "The storm is too dangerous now. I suggest we get closer to me ship before leaving."

La Roque nodded. "Get the women in a central location and don't let them out of your sight. I don't know how many men are left on this ship."

Douglas nodded and ran through the rain back onto the lower deck. Ferdinand raced to the bow, still carrying his gruesome trophy. A couple of his men came along and were instructed to hoist the sails.

La Roque braced himself against the deck railing as the boat swayed from side to side. He didn't know which way to go. Sheridan still had to be on the boat. He couldn't have—

He heard shouting. He dropped to a crouch, peered around the wall and felt his breath catch. It was Sheridan and he was holding a sword on Jean-Claude. It was their shouting he'd heard. It looked as though Sheridan wanted Jean-Claude to go overboard. But why was Jean-Claude here? Why wasn't he back on the other ship?

La Roque drew his sword and crept toward them on silent feet, coming up behind his former friend. Sheridan didn't hear La Roque, but he saw Jean-Claude look up. Sheridan spun around, shocked, and his weapon lowered to his side. Jean-Claude charged him. La Roque yelled at the boy and rushed forward to stop him, but was too late.

In one smooth, instinctive motion, Sheridan turned, plunged his sword deep into the young man's chest and then drew it out. Jean-Claude gasped and clutched his wound, falling. Sheridan looked down at the boy with an expression of surprise as La Roque raced at him.

The two men's swords clashed as thunder clapped overhead. The duel moved to the rear deck of the ship, La Roque driving Sheridan back.

"Wait!" Sheridan cried. "Please, wait!"

La Roque's arm was still bleeding, but he felt nothing. All he wanted was to see Sheridan dead and nothing would deter him from his goal. The ship pitched and yawed on the stormy seas, and the deck was slippery with rain, but La Roque pressed forward with his mission of vengeance and retribution.

Sheridan slipped and lost hold of his sword. La Roque put his foot on Sheridan's chest, pinning him to the deck, and placed the tip of the long blade to his throat. He looked down into Sheridan's terrified face and felt a cold rage.

"I trusted you, brother," accused La Roque.

"I can explain. I—"

"Did you touch her?"

Sheridan blinked at him, gagging on the rain as it poured into his nostrils. "What?"

"Did you touch her?"

Sheridan shook his head. "No, I-I was sick. No, we didn't. I swear to you. No harm came to her by my hand!"

Breathing hard, La Roque moved the sword from Sheridan's neck and tossed it aside. He dropped down on to

Sheridan's chest, straddling him, and clamped his hands around the man's throat.

"You're a liar!" La Roque screamed. "You hurt her and now you'll pay for it with your life."

⚜

Zoé had the girls all dressed. She'd removed her bloody clothes and washed the blood from her face and body. As she dressed, she smiled at how alive the girls looked despite of the horrors they had endured. She told them all to grab pieces of her luggage so they could head up to the upper deck. Just as they were about to leave, Douglas burst in to the room, startling them.

"What is it?" Zoé asked, her heart in her throat.

"I need you girls to wait here," Douglas said. "We're going to sail closer and then help you off when the waters calm."

"Where is Comte La Roque?" Zoé asked.

She started past Douglas and he raised a hand to stop her.

"Your Frenchman wanted you here."

"But where is he?" she shouted, fearful that something had happened to him. She had no idea how he'd gotten on board, but that wound on his arm and his bloody sleeve meant that something was going on upstairs. He had come to rescue her, but the danger was not over. He could very well lose his life. A cold sense of dread settled in her stomach and chilled her to the bone.

"He's well," Douglas said.

With a strength borne of desperation, Zoé shoved him out of the way. She grabbed up her long skirt and ran toward the upper deck, ignoring Douglas and the girls as they called after her.

❧

La Roque watched Sheridan's eyes bulge as his mouth gaped open, gasping for air. He couldn't bring himself to take his friend's life, no matter how much he'd believed he wanted to. He stopped himself suddenly and rose to his feet.

Sheridan scooted away and leapt to his feet. He kept stepping back with his hand to his throat, a small smile of satisfaction curled his lips. "You cowar —"

Before he could finish a sword pierced his chest. The silver blade appeared through a growing red circle in the center of his shirt.

Sheridan's face dropped down in horror. Jean-Claude stumbled back and fell to his knees before his victim did, enacting his final revenge. Sheridan heaved a rasping death sigh and fell over on his face.

As the storm raged over their heads, LaRoque was shaken with the gravity of what he'd done in one night and the many lives he'd taken. That's when Jean-Claude's heroism came back into focus. He dashed back to where the lad had fallen.

He was alive, but barely.

La Roque grabbed Jean-Claude and cradled his head in his lap. Jean-Claude was spitting up blood. His lips were covered in it. He looked up at La Roque and smiled. "We did it, didn't we? My Zoé, she is safe, *mon seigneur*?"

La Roque felt the bitter touch of grief. "Why didn't you stay on the ship?"

Jean-Claude reached up and touched La Roque's arm. "It was my destiny, *mon seigneur*." He exhaled and closed his eyes.

La Roque held him and wept. Jean-Claude was just a young boy. He shouldn't have died like this! This was no man's destiny.

A woman screamed behind him.

La Roque looked up to see Zoé running toward them. She fell to her knees, pushed La Roque out of the way, and grabbed Jean-Claude in her arms. She fell across his chest, wailing in grief. La Roque thought of all she'd suffered on board this horrific ship and made a silent, but solemn promise to dedicate the rest of his life to protecting her. He touched her back and Zoé wrenched away. Her cries could be heard over the thunder. Gently but firmly, he pulled her off the boy's body.

Zoé fought him and La Roque held onto her. "Please, no," she wept.

Eventually, she gave up and let him hold her. They remained by Jean-Claude, holding each other in the rain and sobbing.

⚜

Several hours later, La Roque lay naked on the bunk in his cabin on board the *Veuve Noire*, covered only by his blanket. Zoé stitched his wound in silence. She'd barely spoken to him since they'd rescued her and the others. She was in her nightgown now and her hair was pulled away from her face, woven into one long wet braid down her back. Her eyes were heavy with regret, sadness and loss.

"Zoé..."

She ignored him, focusing on stitching and dressing his wound.

"I love you," he said.

At those words, she looked up, her eyes skeptical. "Then why did you give that creature the money to purchase me?"

She yanked on the thread, intentionally hurting him. She was so disillusioned over his betrayal. It was his money and indifference that had sent her on that voyage of death and terror.

"But I didn't," he said. "I gave him money to leave; I had no idea that he would use it to take you."

She wasn't sure if she believed him. "Why was Jean-Claude here? He was a baby. How could you have brought him with you!"

Tears welled in her eyes as she wrapped a bandage around his arm. She chewed on her lip, remembering Jean-Claude's lifeless body in her arms. Ferdinand and his men had put him on their boat so he could be properly buried at home. How would she tell Marianne and Marguerite that he was dead? They all loved him so much.

"My love, I didn't mean for this to happen. He came for me with word that Sheridan was taking you away. We tried to reach the ship, but were too late. He insisted on helping and…"

He reached out to touch her face. She turned away just out of his reach. Ignoring his outstretched hand, she picked up the bowl of bloody water, went to the porthole and tossed it out.

"Come to me," he said.

ZOÉ

She set the bowl down on the table and avoided his eyes. "You didn't want me."

"I did."

"No, you wanted—"

"Zoé, please… come here."

She looked up and saw him reaching for her with his good arm. Jean-Claude was dead, and she had actually killed several men herself. The shock of it all made her want to be in his arms, but she was so afraid.

"I want to tell you things," he said. "Things that will explain my love for you and our future. Don't make me say it like this. Let me hold you when I open my heart to you."

Our future. It was those two words that did it. She went to him, her heart thudding. He moved over to make room for her and she stretched out next to him. She turned her back, afraid to look into his eyes. She felt him kiss her shoulder.

"You're trembling," he said as he lifted the blanket and covered her with it. "I love you, Zoé. I pushed you away because of fear. You were right."

"I was?"

"Yes, but you were also wrong. My fear had nothing to do with the color of your skin. I was afraid of the power of your love and getting lost in it. I thought I would go insane like my father if I gave in to it."

She rolled over looked up at him. His wet hair was tucked behind his ears and his blue eyes were full of love and sadness.

"Insane?"

"Remember the story I told you at the burnt cottage?"

Zoé nodded.

"That was my father and his mistress. It was the ghost of their ill-fated love story that haunted me, and the fear that controlled me."

Zoé reached up and touched his face. "I am so sorry."

"I want you to be my wife. I want you to make babies and take care of me. And I want to do the same for you. I discovered that my insanity wasn't from giving into you. It was from the thought of losing you."

Tears of joy slipped from her eyes. He leaned over and kissed her. The touch of his lips sent currents through her veins. His kiss became more impassioned and she reveled in the feeling of him pressed against her. He began to kiss her neck, and soon she was desperate to have him explore all the intimate parts of her. She couldn't believe she was with him again. She'd thought he didn't want her, and that he'd paid Sheridan to take her away. Instead, he had risked his life to save her. She felt his hard body roll on top of her, but felt him hesitate. She opened her eyes and smiled at him. His strong forehead was furrowed in a worried frown.

ZOÉ

"If you aren't ready," he said, "we can…"

"He didn't," she whispered. "I am… still… yours. Really, I am."

His face relaxed with relief and he began seeking the sweet satisfaction that could only be found in the deep pleasure points of her body. She felt his urgency, his need to possess her. She felt overwhelmed by a sense of safety and comfort as he slid into her.

As he drove himself in and out of her, she cried. Her dreams were about to come true. She imagined that her parents were together in heaven, smiling down on her, that they had sent La Roque to find her and save her. Her life would be so different from now on. She would finally have the family she'd always wanted, the family that her *maman* always wanted.

The tempo of their love reached a climatic crescendo. He exploded inside of her with a cry of surrender and she clawed his back, giving in to the joy of having her lover in her arms again. After he withdrew himself from her, she rolled on top of him. Closing her eyes, she rested her face against his chest, listening to his rapid heartbeat, and allowed it to lull her to the kind of peaceful sleep she hadn't had since before that first day at Château La Roque.

9

La Roque leaned on the ship's railing at the bow, talking to Ferdinand and looking out to sea. After the fight, they'd discovered that the *Aventine* held some passengers headed for the Americas. Ferdinand wanted to leave them adrift. He felt no obligation to anyone left alive aboard that ship. La Roque wouldn't hear of it, and forced an alliance that would allow the survivors to sail back in their tailwind, into France. Douglas had asked to remain onboard with Ferdinand and his band of misfits as their new cook.

"Aye, have you seen me pet?" Ferdinand said, grinning and pointing up to the flagstaff with Delaflote's head stuck on it.

La Roque shook his head. "You can't sail into France with his head posted like that."

Ferdinand shrugged. "We are in the open sea now. I wants it up dere, so up dere it stays."

"Did it help? Killing him I mean?"

Ferdinand shook his head. "No."

La Roque thought about killing Sheridan. It couldn't erase what had happened to Jean-Claude and Zoé. The only satisfaction he had was in knowing that Sheridan could hurt no one else. "I feel the same way."

"Sorry about the boy, didn't know he left the ship."

La Roque stared out to sea. Jean-Claude's death would forever haunt him.

Sheba walked over to them, her long black locks blowing around her face. She wore a pale yellow corseted Victorian gown. La Roque knew that it was a gift from Zoé. Sheba looked refreshed, even though she was barefoot.

"Excuse me, kind sir," she said to Ferdinand.

He smiled appreciatively, his gold tooth sparkling in the morning sun. La Roque saw the instant attraction between these two and smiled as well. Sheba blushed at the blatant attention focused on her by the pirate. She turned to La Roque.

"I would like to see Missus, now."

La Roque studied her face. Apparently, she had bonded with Zoé and was very protective of her. "Your name is Sheba, right?"

"Yes, that's what they call me."

Ferdinand laughed. "Ye seem like a lioness to me."

Her blush deepened.

"Where are you from?" La Roque asked her.

"I was born on land but spent most of my life at sea. So I guess I'm from nowhere."

"You're welcome to come to France with us," La Roque said.

"Or ye can stay aboard the *Veuve Noire* with me," Ferdinand said.

"But I don't know you."

Ferdinand offered her his hand. "We fix that right now, me lady."

Sheba accepted his hand and he slipped it under his arm. As he led her away, she glanced back at La Roque.

"Please tell Missus I want to see her."

La Roque nodded and waved at them as he led her away.

Some minutes earlier, Zoé had opened her eyes to find Gianelli gone. She'd looked around the tiny cabin with a sense of profound relief. It wasn't a dream. He'd made love to her all night and described what their life would be like when they made it home. She was now completely nude and her hair disheveled, with long thick strands in deep curves around her shoulders. She wanted to know where he was. She got up and got dressed quickly. She would go up on deck to find him.

Zoé reached topside just as Ferdinand was leading Sheba away. She saw Gianelli and walked over to him, holding onto the rail as the ship coasted through the open sea. He lifted his un-injured arm to her and she went to him.

"Why didn't you wake me?" she asked.

He kissed the top of her head. "Because you had a rough night and deserved some peace."

"All I deserve is you."

"Such sweetness. I feel unworthy."

"You are worthy, we are worthy. But I do have a question."

"Yes?" He tensed, wondering if she was going to ask him how many men he'd killed.

"The name Gianelli, why am I the only one to call you by it?"

She felt him pull back, so she turned with him to keep him close. He looked past her in an act of avoidance she didn't expect after all they'd shared. The meaning must be closer to his heart than she'd originally thought.

"It was my *maman's* name for me." He paused, clearly affected by his memories of her. "It reminds me of the side of her that wasn't lost to bitterness. I don't know why I shared it with you." His head dropped and his eyes clung to hers, trying to say what his heart stumbled on. Then he spoke with a softness new to them both. "I dare say no woman has affected me as you. So when you shared yourself so fully, part of me wanted to do the same."

Zoé rested her head against the corded muscles of his chest. La Roque held her tightly. He looked out to the ocean.

"I love you."

"I love you, my Zoé."

The lull of the ship caused them to sway in their embrace, and he breeze caressed them gently. He pulled back to look down at her. "We will need to deal with your family when we return."

She slipped her arm around his waist and turned to his side to look out to the sea with him. "I want Marianne to come live with us. We can find her a suitor. She needs to be away from Madame and her poison. I also want Marguerite to come as well."

La Roque nodded. "It is done. By the way, who is this Sheba?"

"Oh, I forgot about the girls!" Letting go of him, she turned and looked across the deck. "Have you seen them?"

"Most of them have paired off with different suitors. The men have taken a liking to them."

"What?" Zoé cried in worry.

"Not like that. The men are just making sure the women are being cared for."

"Finally, they are being shown kindness." Zoé moved her hair from her face as it blew in the wind. "What shall we do with them?"

"It's up to them. They can have new lives in France."

"Will you let me help them?"

"Listen to me. I don't own you. Even as your husband, I will never own you. If helping them makes you happy, then so be it."

She wrapped her arms around his neck and looked into his deep blue eyes. "Let's go back belowdecks. I want to show you how much more I love you today."

La Roque laughed and kissed her forehead. "You have a wonderful way of putting things," he said and allowed her to lead him away.

❧

Marianne walked down the hall, her dress dragging at her feet. Since she'd lost Zoé she barely ate, spending most of her nights in Marguerite's quarters, crying herself to sleep. She couldn't stand the sight of her mother and made every effort to avoid her. The pain of losing her sister and father so close together had left her empty inside.

Now she was being summoned downstairs and she had no idea why. She dressed quickly, pulling on a gray gown with long sleeves. Her hair was pulled away from her face into a bun. She didn't care for beauty or frivolities anymore. Not when her sister was somewhere being destroyed. She left her room without even checking her reflection in the mirror.

Lifting her gown with both hands she took the steps one at a time, barely looking where she stepped.

"Marianne, sweetie?"

Marianne looked up to see her *maman* standing in their foyer next to Claude Chafer. He wore a coffee-colored topcoat with a ruffled shirt the color of cream, and pants tucked into his riding boots. His black hair was tied into a neat queue with distinctive rolled curls above both ears. She looked into his soft blue eyes and, for the first time, noticed how very kind they were.

"Mademoiselle," he said, "it's a pleasure to see you again."

She looked from him to her mother. "What is he doing here?"

Madame laid a firm hand on Marianne's forearm and said in a low voice. "He's come to sit with you."

Marianne recoiled. "Again? Again you do this? I'm no piece of meat to be sold off so you can sit fat and rich in this dungeon. You won't do to me what you did to Zoé!" With that, the girl bolted out of the foyer.

"Marianne! Come back here this instant!"

Ignoring her mother's cries, Marianne dashed down the hallway. Nearly blinded by tears, she turned down the short branch of the corridor to her left and stumbled to one of the large windows overlooking their garden. She leaned against it, pressing her face against the glass, her thin form racked by sobs. To think that *Maman* was so greedy that she'd sold off Zoé and now wanted to sell her off, too. If only Papa were there. If only—

"Marianne."

She spun around, startled to see Chafer approaching her. "Go away!" she cried, edging to one side, ready to bolt again.

"Wait, please. I just want to talk."

"You came to buy me, just like my sister. I won't let you do it! I won't let you!"

"Marianne, it's me, Claude! I would never do that to you. You know me."

She stared at him. She'd always known him to be a kind man. "She's gone, Claude."

"I know."

"*Maman*... she gave her to that cruel man."

"I know and I am so very sorry."

She began to weep again. When he put his arms around her, she let him and cried into his chest.

"I want my sister. I need her."

"Maybe we can look for her."

She looked up at him from her red, puffy eyes. "Do you think so? Can we go to America and look for her?"

Claude touched her face. "We can do whatever is necessary to make you smile again."

She rested her head on his chest. "Thank you," she whispered.

"Of course, sweet Marianne. Of course."

She felt him gently stroking her hair. It surprised her how comforting it was to lean on him. He was strong and sturdy. Not even Marguerite had been able to reassure her as well as he was somehow able to.

After a while, they sat on the window seat together and he took her hand. It crossed Marianne's mind that, normally, young women of her station would not have been allowed unsupervised visits. But nothing was normal anymore, was it? And perhaps her mother understood that her presence would be damaging to any suitor's effort. The events of the past few days had forced Marianne to mature and now she heard herself speaking with the directness that she'd always loved and admired in Zoé.

"If you aren't here to buy me, then why are you here?"

"I've come to ask for your hand," he said. "I've known you and Zoé since you were children, and I've loved you both since forever."

"But it was Zoé you wanted to marry," she said. "Not me. Now, that Zoé is gone, you want me as a close second?"

"I want you because you're you—you're second to no one and nothing."

To her surprise, he slid down on one knee and took her hand.

"Marianne, I don't have much but I'm willing to give up all I have, even my land, in order to keep you safe. It would be my privilege."

Her hand went to her chest. Did she dare believe him? After she had seen how Zoé suffered because of her love for the count, Marianne had sworn to never trust another man. She had known that she must marry—someday. But after the fiasco with La Roque, she'd shoved that day to some point in the far distant future.

She looked down at Claude's clean, handsome face and saw herself reflected in his eyes, warm eyes that were honest and true. Wouldn't it be better to stay with him, safe, protected and loved, than to remain vulnerable to Maman, whom she no longer trusted?

T. A. FORD

Zoé sat down in the galley, smiling at Douglas. "I am so happy to be going home."

He glanced up from his cooking and smiled back. "I knew you were special. The day you came into my galley, I knew."

"Thank you for what you did that night."

He stopped stirring. His expression saddened. "I'm so sorry."

"Don't apologize. You got there in time. And, please, don't tell Comte La Roque about it. He carries a lot of anger over that situation. I've told him nothing happened and I will keep it that way."

"Agreed."

Sheba stepped down off the stair into the galley. "Missus?"

Zoé turned. "Ah, Sheba," she said, rising from the stool "I've been looking for you."

Sheba blushed. "Captain Ferdinand was giving me a tour."

Zoé raised an eyebrow. The boat wasn't big enough for that long of a tour. "Are you all right?"

Sheba grinned and ran to her arms, hugging her. Zoé was shocked by the intensity of the hug. It felt as if she had Marianne in her arms again. As she returned Sheba's hug, Zoé's thoughts dwelled on Marianne. It would be so good to see her again.

Sheba let her go. "The Captain and I, we have fallen in love."

Douglas coughed, half-choking, and Zoé was so stunned that she could utter only one word: "What?"

Sheba was all smiles. "I am staying on the ship with him. Some of the others have chosen men, too."

"Sheba, I…" Zoé's voice trailed away. She didn't know what to say.

Sheba was exuberant. "Isn't it wonderful, Douglas? Isn't it just the best thing ever?"

Douglas winked at her. "Sure an' it is, me lass."

Zoé saw how happy she was and smiled. "Well, I was thinking that maybe you could come to Toulouse with us."

"Thank you," Sheba said, "but the Captain has a place in Narbonne. I will be staying there and also here on the *Veuve Noire*."

Zoé sighed. She wanted the girls to be independent, but was that a real possibility? They could find work in Narbonne, but it would be nothing more than indentured servitude. If they found strong men like these on this ship, why not allow them to follow their hearts?

"What about Marie?" Zoé asked of the little twelve-year-old.

A momentary sadness flickered over Sheba's face, a sadness brought upon by memories. "Marie," she said softly, "is my daughter."

So many thoughts ran through Zoé's mind at the same time. She remembered the screams of the women she'd heard rising through the floorboards that night. It was bad enough to think that a child had been made to suffer such evil. Now, she thought of the horror of being forced to witness your own daughter's defilement. And it hit her that Sheba might have been the victim of such brutality at an early age herself.

"How old are you, Sheba?"

Sheba raised her chin. "Twenty-five, missus. I had Marie when I was thirteen. She is Captain Delaflote's daughter. He first took me when I was nine."

Zoé felt sick to her stomach at the realization that Sheba had endured that kind of life. "*Mon Dieu*," she said. "I hope the very best for you."

Sheba gave her a brave smile. "I know my heart, and I also want to give my Marie a chance. I endured a lot to keep her safe. Captain Ferdinand will give us a home and a life outside of slavery, so I will take him."

Zoé kissed her on both cheeks. "*Bien*, but I want you to come to Toulouse and visit me. Bring as many of the girls as you like."

Sheba gave Zoé another hug and promised. Douglas grinned at the both of them. "Let me fix my girls something to eat, before the rest of these lads raid the galley."

They laughed and let him prepare their food.

As soon as they arrived in Narbonne, La Roque whisked Zoé off to England to marry her. France still had laws against miscegenation.

She would always remember the day of her wedding and its attendant celebrations as one of the happiest of her life, but it was a day of bittersweet sadness, too. When she'd envisioned this day, it had always been with her father and Marianne at her side. Their absence was a painful reminder of what happiness had cost her.

She'd once dreamt of a large wedding, but with her father dead, she didn't see the point. Thoughts of him reminded her of her other loss, Jean-Claude. She had La Roque send the boy's remains to Marguerite for proper burial, but hadn't attended the funeral.

She had given great thought to her return trip to Château Bouchard. She would make that journey only when she was ready, and that meant only after her new husband had given her the wedding gift he'd promised. To make their English marriage legal in France, Gianelli had settled lands and title upon Zoé, solidifying her position as his wife. She would need the strength his gift gave her in order to face Madame and leave with her sweet sister.

Six weeks later, the time to return had come.

As the carriage drew up to the château, Zoé thought how small it looked. It had seemed so big and protective when she was a child. She thought of the last time she'd seen it, when a man who was intent upon destroying her had torn her from it, and how her stepmother had been his willing ally. She'd wondered then whether she would ever see it again.

She sat back in her seat and adjusted the soft, rich folds of her grey cashmere hooded cape. The hood was so large that it covered her face, leaving it completely in shadow. Underneath the cape, she wore a soft blue gown that Gianelli had picked out.

She sensed him sitting next to her. He was dressed in a gentlemen's suit that was the same shade of grey as her cape. Her eyes traced his handsome profile and her heart leapt with love for him. She'd never imagined she could be so happy. Another memory surfaced, this one of the first time she'd seen his home.

How forbidding it had looked and how she'd wondered at the nature of the man who inhabited it. Now, she knew.

Gianelli glanced down at her and smiled.

She asked, "What are you thinking?

"How much I love you." He gave her a kiss, then looked out the window and nodded at the front door. "You're sure you're ready for this?"

"Quite ready." She arched an eyebrow. "The question is, will Madame be surprised?"

"Not at all," he laughed. "I'm sure she won't."

The carriage came to a halt and seconds later, LaRoque's footman opened the door. Zoé and Gianelli gave each other another kiss, and stepped out. As they walked to the house, her mien was thoughtful, her hands clasped within her grey fur muff. Her long, rounded skirt swayed under her graceful cape. Her movements were slow and deliberate. Everything she would do today would be deliberate.

La Roque, unaccustomed to waiting, used the large doorknocker to announce their presence. Zoé kept her head bowed, her face in shadow. Who, she wondered, would open the door? Marguerite or—

It was Madame herself.

Zoé couldn't see, but she could hear her stepmother's surprise. "Mon seigneur?" she heard her ask.

Zoé slowly raised her head, revealing her face. "Good day, Madame."

Madame fell back a step, clutching her chest. Zoé walked inside and pushed back her hood. Her rich black locks bounced into view.

"Aren't you glad to see me?" she asked.

Madame's gaze went to La Roque. "Why did you bring her here?" she gasped.

"Don't speak to my husband that way," Zoé said.

"Your *what?*"

Zoé raised her hand to display the ring La Roque had placed there. Madame put her hand to her throat and uttered an inarticulate cry.

Marguerite came around the corner and down the foyer. She stopped at the sight in the entryway. "Zoé? Is it really you?"

"Oui, mon amie. C'est moi."

Zoé went to her with arms outstretched. Marguerite hugged her tightly.

"I thought I would never see you again." Marguerite patted her on the back, then let her go and held her away. "I have some very distressing news: Jean-Claude is dead."

Zoé held onto her. "I know."

Marguerite's eyes filled with tears of love and relief. She gave the Comte a look of gratitude. "I'm so glad you found her. But where have you been?"

Zoé looked back at La Roque and smiled. "Off getting married," she said, beaming.

Marguerite's mouth formed a perfect O of surprise. She looked at La Roque, who was leaning against the wall, smiling sexily. "Oh, my goodness!"

Zoé took Marguerite by the hand. "It was I who had him send Jean-Claude's body home. I'm so sorry I wasn't here with you to bury him, but I had to attend to some things."

The joy on Marguerite's face faded. "There's something else I have to tell you. It's about Marianne. She's—"

"I know." Zoé squeezed Marguerite's hand.

"You do?" said Madame.

Zoé turned on her stepmother. "Oh, I wasn't surprised that you married her off to Claude Chafer so quickly. I was actually glad that she was out of your clutches. Claude is a good man."

Madame huffed. "Well, actually he's a good *poor* man. He exaggerated his worth."

Zoé walked up to her, peeling off her other glove. "And that bothered you, didn't it, that you weren't able to profit from your daughter's nuptials?"

"Marianne deserves better, but when I tried to stop them, they went off and married without my consent. Now she'll spend the rest of her life living like some commoner!"

"Actually, she won't, but you will."

Zoé's smile was icy. Madame sputtered.

"Wha-what are you talking?"

Zoé looked back over her shoulder at her Gianelli. "If you don't mind."

La Roque reached inside his topcoat and retrieved a yellow crepe envelope. He went to Zoé, kissed her on her forehead and placed the document in her hands.

"What is this about?" Madame asked.

Zoé ran her fingers over the envelope. "It's my wedding gift to Marianne, and it's why I didn't make it here in time for her elopement, although I heard all about it. If you weren't so hateful and full of greed you would have seen the beautiful ceremony that all of Narbonne was talking about."

Madame was livid. "Get out of my house! I won't let you taunt me in my own home! Get out!"

"But that's just it," Zoé laughed. "It's no longer your home."

Madame's jaw dropped open. "What?"

"God bless Papa's soul. He was a good man, but not such a good businessman. He constantly overextended himself, mostly because of us. But you know this already."

Madame watched her with tight, worried eyes. Zoé began to walk in a slow circle around her.

"To keep the business open, and you in your fancy dresses, he mortgaged this house and his family's land to the bank."

"But I have paid off the balance. Monsieur Sheridan's money, it—"

"Ah yes, the blood money. You did pay creditors with that, didn't you?"

"You have no right to criticize. None. And I have no time for this. I—"

"You're right. You don't. Have time, I mean. You only have one hour in fact. Exactly one."

"What are you talking about?"

Zoé stopped. "Imagine how surprised the bank was to know that you and Monsieur Sheridan stole from my husband. You used the money to pay down the mortgage on our family home and gain credit for father's business to remain open."

"Are you mad? I did no such—"

"Be quiet!" Zoé said.

Madame was shocked into silence. She glanced at La Roque and colored to see his expression of amusement. Glancing at Marguerite, she received a withering look of contempt. She turned back to her stepdaughter.

"Zoé," she began. "I want-I demand that—"

"Don't you understand? The bank has signed it all over to *mon cher seigneur le Comte*—" she batted her eyelashes at her husband and he raised his eyebrows merrily to her "—who has signed it all over to me! They couldn't deal with the scandal." She brought her face close to Madame's. "You will get your things and be out of here and you will do so within the hour."

"You can't—"

"I just did. Now, please, please, do me the favor of disobeying me so I can have the pleasure of tossing you out on your ass!"

Madame burst into tears. "What are you doing? Marianne would never agree to this!"

"I believe she will."

Zoé pushed the copy of Madame's eviction notice against the woman's chest, forcing her to take it. Madame unfolded it and read it with shaking hands. She grabbed hold of the banister to steady herself.

"Won't you show me some pity?" Madame asked Zoé. "After all, I raised you. I—"

"You tricked my father into marrying and as much as killed my mother. Once Papa was dead, you sold me to serve as some man's whore. I will show you as much pity as you showed us. That is to say, none."

Madame sagged to her knees, pale with shock.

Zoé put her hood back on. She turned to Marguerite. "Get her things packed and put them out the door. She is to take nothing but her clothes. I will be back within an hour and I don't want her here."

Zoé turned and headed for the door.

"You evil, spiteful girl!" Madame called after her. "May God have mercy on your soul!"

Zoé spun around. "Thank you, and may the devil have his day with yours!"

La Roque tipped his hat to Madame, gave her a charming smile, and then gave Zoé his arm as they both walked out the door.

❦

Marianne got out of bed, her long golden locks all around her head. Claude reached for her.

"Where are you going, *princesse*?" He tried to pull her back to bed to make love to her again.

She giggled. "To make lunch for you!"

He was stunned. "You can cook?"

"*Très drôle*." Marianne grabbed her heavy velvet robe, slipped it over her nakedness and cinched it around her waist. Marguerite had been coming over helping her prepare meals while he was at work.

"I am your wife," she said, "and I shall take care of you. Marguerite has taught me some things."

He sat up and looked into her emerald green eyes. "I'm so proud of you," he said, "of how you have taken to my humble way of life without complaint. You are so remarkably wonderful to me."

Marianne came back to the bed and sat down next to him. For a moment, she was silent. "I didn't think that I could be happy again," she said finally. "Losing my family made me feel so empty inside. In two weeks, you have shown me that I can have a life of my own."

She leaned down and kissed him. "I will take care of you. Our love, although new, is the truest thing that I have now."

He reached up and moved the long curls that hung down into his face over her shoulder. "We shall take care of each other, sweet Marianne."

Pulling her to him, he kissed her deeply. She had spent the past several days discovering her own body's desires. She hadn't known pleasure and pain could intertwine the way it did. Now her virginity was gone and her body responded to him like that of a woman. She was discovering new depths of pleasure and passion by experiencing the power of being loved by a man like him.

He drew her down onto the bed and rolled her over. She arched her back as he opened her robe and kissed her delicate porcelain skin. She watched him gaze at her plump, milky breasts.

"You're so beautiful," he whispered. "I can't believe you're mine."

He closed his mouth over her right breast and swirled his warm, wet tongue over her nipple. She gasped at the sensation. He parted her velvet robe even more so that he could run his hand over her silky skin.

Biting her lip, she moaned, "Take me, take me, *mon amour.*"

It was all he needed to hear. He mounted her and eased his way inside. She closed her eyes and clung to him. Her body trembled under the power of his demands. He held her tightly as he always did when they made love and it made her melt into him.

"I love you," he whispered.

Marianne's eyes opened. She was loved. She had someone and he was all hers. Grasping his head, she kissed the side of his face. "I love you, too. Oh, how I love you!"

Afterward, he held her and whispered of the things they'd do and places they'd see once he had secured their financial future. She listened to him, his deep voice lulling her to sleep.

Having her sister back would be all she needed to make her life perfect.

There was a knock at the door.

They exchanged startled glances. Who could it be? It was Sunday and most of the villagers were at Mass. They shouldn't be having visitors.

Claude got up and retrieved his robe. Marianne sat up, clutching the sheet to her bare chest. She watched him walk over to the window, pull back the thin white lace curtain and look out. She swiped her long hair from her face.

"Who is it?"

"I don't know, but I think you should put something on. It looks like a formal visit."

She jumped up and grabbed the gown she'd thrown across her chair. Slipping it on, she watched him dress as well. They laughed, bumping into each other as they raced around the room, searching for their clothes. As they stumbled into their shoes, the knocks grew more insistent.

Dressed, they raced down the stairs, Claude still buttoning his shirt and Marianne trying to pull up her hair. Laughing, they pushed each other aside to open the door. Claude got the better of her, ran to the door and opened it. His laughter died and his smile faded.

Marianne couldn't see who it was, but she saw his reaction. She walked up, wondering, and then she, too, froze with surprise.

There was La Roque, standing there with a woman wearing a hooded cape and her head down. Something about her seemed so familiar...

She lifted her head and Marianne gasped. "*Mon Dieu!*"

Zoé opened her arms as her sister rushed into them.

"Zoé! Zoé!" Marianne cried, hugging Zoé tightly.

"Marianne! Let go. I can't breathe," Zoé choked.

Marianne released Zoé, held her away for a moment, and then hugged her again. "*Mon Dieu! Mon Dieu!*" she kept whispering through tears of joy.

Claude was speechless. When La Roque extended his hand and said, "I guess we're family," Claude shook it, but blinked, confused. "Family?"

Marianne let go of Zoé and also repeated in bewilderment, "Family?"

"*Oui,*" said Zoé. "We're married, just like you."

"You are?"

Zoé nodded.

Claude stepped aside. "Come inside, everybody."

"Yes, do," Marianne said, pulling Zoé along.

Marianne cleared off a place for them to sit in their modest living area. She saw the smiles and glances of love shared between her sister and La Roque and felt happy for them. She had castigated herself many times over for not having given Zoé a chance to explain, for having run to Papa, weeping and wailing, so that he too was so outraged he would not listen. She was happy to realize that she felt no jealousy either. She was simply happy–happy to have Zoé back again, happy to see her with the count, and happy herself to have someone as wonderful as Claude.

Marianne asked Zoé a million questions and listened with widening eyes to Zoé's tale. Although Zoé told her a great deal, Marianne sensed that her sister held back. There were details that perhaps they would only discuss in private. She was sure that nothing was left out about Zoé's wedding, however. It was wonderful to hear all the details. If only she could've been there.

"Why didn't you tell me that you were back? I could have stood up for you at your wedding? Zoé, you weren't even present at mine!"

"I'm sorry, but I wanted to wait until my wedding present for you had been finalized."

"Wedding present?" Marianne perked up.

It was then that Zoé told them of her visit to Madame. When she was done, she reached into her muff, pulled out a folded envelope and passed it to Claude. He opened it and leaned toward Marianne, so they could read it together.

"The château and Papa's fishing company are now part of your dowry and go to your husband. You can move into the house as soon as you like."

"Oh, my!" Marianne gasped.

"What about Madame?" Claude asked.

Zoé's expression hardened. "My only stipulation is that she never set foot on the property."

"But Zoé, she's my mother!"

Zoé gave an elegant shrug. "I know, and if you two choose to show her kindness, I can do nothing about it. However, I forbid her to step foot on Bouchard land or business properties. It's what she deserves and it's non-negotiable."

Claude looked at Marianne, who blinked away tears. She couldn't blame Zoé, and she had to admit that she, too, hated her mother for what she'd done and wanted some degree of revenge. She felt ashamed of those thoughts. Then, she looked up into her husband's face and saw how happy this would make him.

"Agreed," she said.

Claude pulled her to him and kissed her as Zoé laid her head on La Roque's chest. Marianne said a silent prayer of gratitude. She had her Zoé back and that was a miracle.

Toulouse, France – April, 1829

She moaned softly and turned her face toward his. She felt him lean over and kiss her lips softly. Still tired, she opened her eyes sleepily and looked up at him. He was propped up on one elbow, studying her.

"What is it?" she asked, caressing his face.

"I couldn't sleep."

She touched his forehead. "Are you feeling well?"

He smiled. "You've changed my life in so many ways."

"We are connected. We belong together. I know that sometimes frightens you, but I know that our love will always sustain us both."

He lowered himself to her, rolling her onto her back. She closed her eyes as she felt his tongue slip into her mouth. The taste of him was always the best part, next to actually having him inside of her. Feeling his strong hands travel down her body, she sighed under his kisses and waited for him to take her in the now familiar way.

"I love you," he whispered.

"And I you," she said as he parted her legs and entered her. She didn't understand why God had shown her such favor, but she was eternally grateful that He had. Being in her husband's arms was the safest place in the world.

La Roque pushed his way deeper into her and kissed her again hungrily. Feeling the blood rush to her head as their bodies rocked in a passionate embrace, she gave into her urge to climax, crying out from the rush of pleasure that overtook her senses. Zoé clung to him, humbled by the overwhelming sense of being loved and loving in return.

He slid out, but remained between her legs and rested his head on her chest. She stared at the ceiling as she stroked his head. Lying in their bed, basking in the afterglow of their love with his seed inside her, she said a silent prayer, asking God to bless them with an addition to their family and make their joy complete.

Smiling, she thought of her sister. Marianne was happy and expecting a baby. She and her husband had turned *Bouchard Pêche* around and even employed Ferdinand and his men to lead most of their fishing expeditions. She was glad that Ferdinand had given up his pirating ways to provide a stable home for Sheba and Marie. The other women were working in Narbonne with their husbands and also seemed happy.

Douglas now owned a restaurant in Toulouse that La Roque had helped him acquire. He was able to send for his family and Zoé finally met his daughter. She wanted him to be happy. She was grateful to him for saving her life. He reminded her in so many ways of her father.

Madame had moved to England to live with her sister. Marianne wrote to her and told Zoé that Madame wanted to return after the birth of her baby. Zoé refused, of course. The one thing that she would never abide was Madame's presence on their father's land. Marianne understood, and mentioned that she might travel to England after the child was born.

Zoé had asked her husband if she were being too cruel. He just smiled at her.

"You are doing exactly what Madame would do were she in your position."

Zoé loved that response and loved him. Closing her eyes, she smiled.

The story of her parentage was one she'd never really understood. Her mother had given up everything for a love that was forbidden. Now Zoé had found the same forbidden love and it was intoxicatingly splendid. Everything had come full circle.

It was, thought Zoé, as though destiny were a woman, and when she failed with one heart she made it up with another.

The End

ZOÉ

If you wish to contact the author, comment about this book or be on the mailing list for future books, you may visit the website dedicated to Zoé at:

http://www.thedivaspen.com